THE ARCADIAN MATCH

THE ARCADIAN MATCH

RISING WORLD
BOOK 2

ANNE MORTENSEN

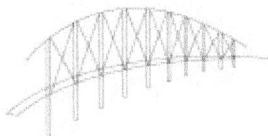

Puente Press

United Kingdom
First published
2023 © Anne Mortensen
Written by Anne Mortensen
All rights reserved.

Cover Design by Nick Castle

British Library Cataloguing in Publication Data.
A CIP catalogue record of this book is available from the
British Library

ISBN 978-1-907688-06-5 (ebook)
ISBN 978-1-907688-07-2 (trade paperback)

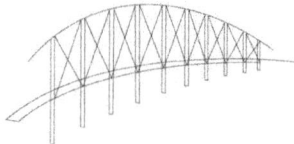

Puente Press

Dedicated to my sister, Andrea.

Q-Score Leaderboard

POINTS

RANK 1-10

TIER 1	TIER 2	TIER 3	TIER 4	THE UNTIERED
(4,000,000)+	(3,000,000 - 4,000,000)	(2,000,000 - 3,000,000)	(0 - 2,000,000)	(less than 0)
Ulrich Tokvej	Jacob Rasmussen	Judomaster	Gingeraroma	Alexander Jonsson
Alice	Stine Poulsen	Agnes Sundstrom	Vincent Larsson	Janna Magnusson
Christian Karlsson	Schroeder	Daniel Bengtsson	Robin Jansson	Elisabet Finn
Dan	Agnetha Oliver	Peter Gustafsson	Salomon Johansson	Natanael Hedlund
Max Bekken	Ulla Jakobsson	Thomas Olsson	Bella Berglund	Berfin Nyman
Lorelei Lindbergh	Asa Felix	Vincent Larsson	Thomas Simon	Oscar Mattsson
Torn Vester	Philip Abraham	Robin Jansson	Benjamin Pettersson	Maia Engstrom
Gamemaster	Adam Olofsson	Salomon Johansson	Daniel Nilsson	Ester Svensson
Viktor Hansson	Paul Andersson	Bella Berglund	Matthias Werner	Amadeus Pettersson
Harald Seversson	Tobias Love	Thomas Simon	Gabrial Martin	Matilda Holmgren

PROLOGUE

June 2031, London

KELLY BLACKWELL HAD THE FEELING THE BUILDING COULD STILL read her mind. What would it think about the dream she had last night? Where she was back inside the lab, lights bearing down on her, Omar holding the syringe filled with kill-serum.

She shook her head as if to dislodge the memory from her system, and then she stopped and let it be, reminding herself that Omar had made his own choice, and that she survived. She reminded herself that her dreams were changing, aided in part by a daytime routine that kept her late nights to a minimum, her stress levels in check, resting when she needed, and a healthy diet. She crossed the candy-cane barrier at 8:30 a.m. and stepped into the Zone.

Footsteps away from the building's entrance, she could feel the humdrum of online transmissions happening on the other side of the door. In this very building, she had fought and clawed her way out of Lydia's grip of control, but this stayed—the nano-bot in her head.

A year ago, it connected to every Wi-Fi device willy-nilly. She got dragged along with it, and it nearly blasted her head off. But her bot was different now; she was different now. After months of rigorous attention-focusing exercises, she wielded greater command of the bot in her brain, and the building read only what she allowed. The truth was, she knew more about the building than it knew of her. She climbed its steps.

At the front door, she paused. Though yellow and gray paint brightened the building, she could still discern the elite squad's old matte black logo. She was never one for masks and that would never change, she thought, but today, something felt different. Not sure what, she brushed it aside. "Open the door."

A bell dinged. The dome-capped communications center hummed even though Harry was, as usual, the only one in.

He pulled off his headphones. "Morning, Boss."

Harry's lustrous smile and large screen lit the room. Seeing his unwieldy red hair jut out from behind his monitor was one of her routine comforts. She nodded her good morning.

"No attempted cyberattacks today," he said, "but I'm sure our guy will come sniffing around soon."

He was the best watchdog she had because to him the job wasn't work. He enjoyed monitoring online chatter, logging visitors, constructing firewalls—whatever was needed to keep out the cyber criminals. "Another predictable day is another comfortable day," she said. "You're doing a great job, Harry."

She made her way to the espresso machine. Since taking over the building, they had opened their digital doors to UK-based IPs. People logged on whenever they pleased. Everyone. And she was beginning to regret it. She pulled open a bag of coffee beans.

A bright aroma tingled her nose, and a deep tone mellowed her mind. She poured the silky beans into the grinder and pressed the button for a double espresso.

A high-pitched sound echoed through the panopticon's halls, so piercing it cut through the concrete walls.

She winced. "Harry, you poking around in the Prime Minister's emails again?"

"Very funny," he said.

Another high pitch whipped through the hall.

"It's a transmission." Harry's hand rested on a dial. "It's coming in from a primary server."

Kelly lifted the warm cup to her mouth, and the coffee's mist heated her lips. As long as it wasn't coming from her own private servers—the ones she used daily to download and decompress—was all that mattered. "Do we know the source of this transmission?"

"I won't know until—oh my God." He sat up. "It's our guy."

She put her cup down on the desk. "Are you sure?"

"Yes. Looks like he tried to mask his digital footprint, but it's him. And he sent a video this time."

"Who sends video files these days?"

"Let's just crush the whole thing," Harry said. "He could be a pirate."

"He's so persistent we should have a look," she said. "Can you trace his footprint without opening the message?"

"His IP is bouncing around. I don't think he's in the UK."

The face of a thirty-year-old man flashed on the screen, his eyes a deep blue, his thin lips steady. He reminded Kelly of a more intense version of Troy.

Harry took off his glasses and laughed. "This is the dude who's been trying to send messages for the last three months?"

Kelly leaned into the screen. This guy had no greasy hair, no dark under-eye circles from pulling all-nighters. This one looked bright and fresh. And corporate. "He doesn't look like your average hacker." She stepped back. "He got this far. Let's see what he has to say."

"I'm doing a reverse image search now," Harry said.

The search result came up empty; Harry looked up at Kelly.

"If you can chain down one of his IP addresses," Kelly said, "I might be able to get some info on him."

"Using your brain-bot? I strongly advise against that. We don't know who he is. The pipeline could be loaded with viruses."

The new connection ignited her curiosity, and before she realized it, her attention was drifting along an unfamiliar tunnel. "No, no, stop," she said to her bot.

Her heart sped up, and her mind revved up. Our guy's photo metadata zoomed past her, faster than a bullet train, and suddenly she found herself plunged into soundless deep space. "Return!" she commanded her bot.

But she found herself on slick foreign glass. Unlike the coal-fired British fiber-optic cables, this crystalline cable—powered by rocket fuel—pulsed. Where had her brain-bot taken her? She grasped for one of her own real-world memories, where she was in Hyde Park under the soothing watermelon sunset, but her brain-bot shoved past the mirage, undaunted, and ported the guy's encrypted video.

"Hey, Kelly. It's Christian Karlsson, in case you've forgotten me."

Only the audio was coming through. How did he know her? "This is a video file right?" Kelly said.

"Yeah," Harry said.

"I'm not seeing anything. I only hear him."

"It's playing? I don't hear anything. It should be on the screen," Harry said, tapping his keyboard.

Stockholm is under attack. Repeat. Stockholm is under attack. Just thought I'd let you know. Hope London is treating you well. Look forward to catching up at a better time when life isn't so crazy. Over and out.

The audio went silent.

"I don't know him," Kelly said, pulling back.

"Who was it?"

"Our guy."

A text box popped up on Harry's screen.

THIS MESSAGE WILL SELF-DELETE IN FIVE
MINUTES.

Kelly stared at Harry, stalled somewhere between confusion and disbelief. As soon as the message self-deleted, she'd have no proof of what she'd heard. Quickly, she flipped on twenty-four-hour news.

A weather map of England colored the screen.

"What are you doing?" Harry said.

"My brain-bot connected, and I heard our guy say Sweden was under attack. It should be all over the news."

"You went in without protection?" Harry shook his head. "Are you nuts?"

"Is there any way to stop the file's self-delete?"

"It's preprogrammed. You could play it again, record it with a digital recorder, and then we have a copy." Harry breathed out. "But, Stockholm isn't under attack. If it were, there'd be chatter all over social media." He gestured toward the screen. "Clearly, it's a prank."

Kelly scratched her jaw. This didn't feel like a prank call. The feeling was similar to the one from the anonymous whistleblower many, many months ago. "Don't touch that switch."

Harry withdrew his hand from the off switch. "Maybe we should call the PM."

"And tell him what? That Stockholm is under attack?" She shook her head. "Let's not give him a reason to shut us down."

Her bot zapped her brain.

Stunned, she saw a giant deck of flash cards in her mind's eye.

One card displayed an enlarged image of a stereotypical Swedish man, the next card had the name Christian Karlsson, the next one, his online profile data, then his avatar, followed by hundreds of cards containing tables of numbers.

The information poured into her mind so fast that she could barely process it.

Adrenaline pumped through her arms, tightening her muscles until her fingertips grew cold. The only way through fear was to face it, she thought. She sucked in a deep breath, easing the tension, and she zoomed ever forward.

The rhythm of a steady beat barreled out, du-dung, du-dung, du-dung, and its reverberation pervaded her mind. Not a bass drum. This was the sound of a calm, confident heart. She felt it.

"I've entered some kind of…," she said.

"Get out of there."

She stumbled, but at last, she was standing, however unsteady, on the pulse of his flow and all she could do was roll with its beat. She focused on a card displaying a table of numbers. Biomarkers. "This is a biochip," she said. "I'm inside his biochip."

"Oh wow." Harry said. "How is that even possible?"

"I don't know." She scratched her nose. "He has a biochip tracker embedded under his skin. I'm inside it. I can feel his heart beat."

"You're in his biochip, under his skin? Cool. I've been meaning to get one."

"That would make me nauseous."

"Funny," he said. "Biotrackers are a thing in Sweden. A chip the size of an uncooked grain of rice, and you pay for stuff with it. It holds all your ID, your medical records, travel documents. Everything. People are doing it here too. For health, mainly."

She shook her head. She had worked hard to master the chip inside her brain, and here were people deliberately stuffing themselves with metal junk. Why would they do that to themselves?

She blew a stream of air through her lips. "Forget it, Harry. Not in my comms room. One of us is enough. Just save the passcode, Stockholm."

Harry's fingertips tapped the keyboard. "Saved. Now what?"

Her chest lifted on a deep inhale. "Get me background intel on Christian Karlsson. I want to see what this guy is all about."

"Can your brain-bot do a preliminary search?"

Her eyes watered at the stress. She'd have to travel through underwater ocean cables, bounce between satellites in outer space, and jump between IP addresses scattered around the globe. The thought was dizzying. She cupped her face. Her training exercises were designed for in-country bandwidth surfing, not globetrotting. And even if she did get to Sweden, what then? "I don't know if I can, Harry."

"Things are different now," he said. "You've been doing so much work."

Her throat tightened. Her fears of not being in control of her life had left their skid marks on her, but she reminded herself that she knew how it had happened, and why. That was then and this is now. And now, Harry was right. She dabbed a tear attempting its escape from the corner of her eye and rolled her shoulders.

Stockholm wasn't under attack, clearly. Even though she had only his voice to go on—no denying it was real—she had connected to Christian Karlsson for a reason. And she was going to find out why. She flicked her hair back. "Code up my avatar, Stormykitten, with some eye-catching outfits. Make one that will make me seem Swedish. Jeans and a white T-shirt kind of thing. Just keep my hair color the same."

"Brown. You got it. It'll take a bit of time to code up all the outfits."

"Good. I need the time to practice more. But as soon as his next transmission comes in be sure to tell me."

Harry nodded.

She felt inexplicably drawn to this Christian Karlsson, and she wasn't sure which of them was the magnet. Maybe, just maybe, something was expanding inside her, or her brain-bot was morphing and changing, and she feared, not her brain-bot this time, but she feared losing control of herself. She sniffed. "Yes, I want to meet him."

CHAPTER 1

June 1, 2032, Stockholm

STANDING IN FRONT OF THE RIVER IN HIS EVERY-OCCASION SUIT, Christian Karlsson held his finger over the Q-score button on his augmented reality glasses. The last time he checked the Q-score leaderboard, Jacob's position held steady in Tier 2. But that was twenty-four hours ago, and the trial was days away.

What was the old saying? It takes twenty years to build a reputation and five minutes to destroy it. In a world where rumors were more powerful than the truth, and malicious gossip could destroy everything, Christian had to know Jacob's social status. He sighed and pushed the button.

A screen expanded across his field of vision, the sky above him, the river before him, the pavement beneath him, until everything and everyone, near and far, became a midtone shade of gray. Only one bright light shined in his eyes: a heads-up display of the Q-scores leaderboard.

The HUD showed real-time information about players, their tiers, and their scores. Page one listed Sweden's top players in their rightful tier, and it was a page Jacob would never inhabit, certainly not today.

Into his glasses mic, he said, "Find Jacob Rasmussen."

His query churned through the population of Sweden while names and avatars slid from tier to tier in real-time, their livewire scores updating, their ranks adjusting. Eventually, his query threw up hundreds of rows, each containing the name Jacob Rasmussen.

Christian groaned. "Too many. Find Avatar ID Jonah Whale."

One row surfaced like a bright yellow submarine. He scanned it.

Username: Jonah Whale | ID | Jacob Rasmusson | Rank: Tier 2

Jacob's position held steady.

Bullish pride glowed inside Christian. "Good for you, buddy."

Two months earlier, the online vultures plucked at Jacob's virtual flesh, and not for the first time. All because Jacob walked —well, stumbled—onto a cat trapped in a tree and hadn't rescued it. Jacob's walk-by was blasted all over Sweden, and the public deducted so many points from him that he dropped into Tier 3 status overnight. They didn't care that he was drunk. Vulture food, being scarce these days, turned Jacob into a feast.

Christian had looked out for the mathematics genius who'd been bullied since they were in school together, and he wasn't going to stop now. He double-tapped the glasses sidearm.

The digital screen disappeared, and the salty breeze restored his attention to the here and now, his body. He rested his glasses on his head.

Right on time, Jacob rounded the corner of Erstagatan, his skin radiating, his hand clutching Karen's. The hem of her figure-hugging dress swooshed at her knee.

"Hey, Jacob."

A grin broke out across Jacob's face—the kind of grin worn by all of Christian's clients after he rescued them from the online vultures. Look at him now, walking strong in shiny black shoes, smelling all citrus, vetiver, and musk. That light scuff on his toe tip—a brilliant touch.

With his pride rekindled, Christian hugged his friend. "Shiny new reputation does a man wonders."

Jacob chuckled. "I owe it to you."

Christian buffed his nails on his sleeve and smirked.

Karen patted Jacob's shoulder, as if to tame his ego. She flashed a bashful smile.

"The credit is all your husband's." Christian stopped himself from descending toward the same closing comments he gave to all his clients. His friend deserved better. "I couldn't let you languish in Tier 3. True friends are hard to come by." He back-handed the air, and his too-soft-a-sentiment floated away. "You wouldn't believe the number of clients who don't follow basic instructions."

Karen's smile creased, her eyes glowing with admiration.

Christian stepped back and rubbed his hands. "So! Where are we off to?"

"Where we're going, you won't need these." Jacob plucked Christian's AR glasses from his head and slid them into his pocket. "You're going to love White's."

"Intriguing." Christian tucked in his chin and folded his arms. "I hope it won't get me in trouble. I have to be at work tomorrow."

"What work? Everyone's on their best behavior."

"Everyone except you," Christian chided, poking Jacob's shoulder. "My other clients aspire to be Tier 1. Keep your nose clean, and you might just get there too."

Jacob squeezed Christian's arm. "You deserve a promotion. You're the best Quant PR man alive."

Christian shrugged. Quant PR man sounded so dramatic. "I just fix people's online reputations and the results are measurable, not like in the old days. Now we have the Q-scores and algorithms so anyone can do it."

"You mean VIPs' reputations," Jacob corrected. "And not anyone could do what you can. You're like a Q-score manipulator."

"It's really you who does the work," Christian said, trying to deflect the compliment. "I just make sure you know what work you need to do."

Karen bounced on her heels. "Okay, okay! All this love is making me sick. Let's get moving."

They walked along the pavement above the river, and a salty breeze whipped around them. Jacob's dark brown curls mobbed his forehead.

He swept them back. "But you've built algorithms that always fix your clients' problems. I bet the Q-score designers didn't expect you to come along and game it."

Christian had decided long ago that everyone deserved a shot at the top tier, be they gangster or priest, man or woman, because so much depended on the Q-scores. Who was he to judge? He lifted his hands in mea culpa, admitting defeat. "If they didn't want it gamed, they shouldn't have created it. My algos happen to give my clients advantages." He lowered his hands. "I don't even have to use my algos that much anymore. As you say, everyone's on their best behavior. No crime. It's just rep enhancement now." He smacked his teeth. "Kind of boring, really."

Karen led them onto a side road off Erstagatan. "Have you heard? They're talking about making the Q-scores our primary currency." She laughed, sarcastically. "Imagine that! The gall! Replacing our beloved krone?"

Her comment landed on Christian like a bump. She had known, and indeed, seen, the work he put into securing the upcoming hearing at Nationalbanken and into protecting Jacob, the star witness. The Q-score system wasn't an innocent government project; the Landström Society had developed the whole thing, and the public had the right to know.

With her comment, he wondered if Karen still doubted that they could expose the most powerful social club in the nation and stop the scores from becoming the national currency. As long as Jacob presented his evidence, all was good. But to some people, to Karen, hearings were unpredictable.

"Not gonna happen," Christian said, almost in a reassurance.

They stepped into a dark entrance and followed a woman down a halogen-lit corridor, walls adorned with black and white moving images of Stockholm's skyline. Her bare shoulders shimmered to the beat of Mozart remixed. At the end of the passage, she opened a door and out blasted the scent of sweet gardenias.

His heart beating, Christian caressed his tie. The silky fabric absorbed the sweat on his fingertips.

A second platinum-blonde-haired woman guided them to their table. They settled into upholstered armchairs.

"Whatever you need is on the menu." She pointed at the digital tablets on the table. "And if it isn't." She double-tapped the tablet screen and pointed to the white space at the bottom of the menu. "White space for special requests." She and handed out electronic pens. "Enjoy."

Another server approached the table.

Jacob leaned toward Christian. "What did I tell you?"

"You're going to get me in trouble."

Jacob's cheeky smile returned. "No one gets in trouble in fantasyland."

Christian tapped on a menu. Bubbly featured at the top, boutique beers at the bottom, and every known spirit in between. "Do they even serve food?" he said.

Jacob shrugged. "Who cares when it's all on the house. Every-thing." Jacob turned to the server. "Let's start with champagne."

Christian set the tablet aside and rested his hands, fingers loosely knitted, on the table. "I know most places in town, but this place..." He tapped the table. "Didn't think these places existed anymore."

"This is my way of saying thank you."

The expression in Jacob's eyes wasn't gratitude, and that was fine. Christian didn't need more praise. He needed to know who gave Jacob access to this place. He didn't do all that work fixing Jacob's reputation, shielding him from the vultures, just so that he could squander his points, his rank, his status, and drop back to his old ways. "The person who really deserves the praise is Torn, my boss. He let me bring you in."

Jacob raised his hand, pretending to hold a glass. "Let's drink to Torn."

Karen laughed. "Skål, Torn!"

The server returned to their table, holding a tray with a bottle of champagne and three crystal flutes. She popped the cork and poured the effervescent liquid.

Christian grabbed a glass and waited for the bubbles to finish popping inside the glass. "Just one more week, Jacob. Sit tight. One more week, and we'll be cheering to your new life. May it last forever."

"Skål!"

He took a sip and scooted closer to Jacob. "Who runs this place?"

Jacob picked at a fresh scab on his wrist, and a dull smile shone in his eyes. "My potential new club."

The scab, next to a year-old scar, made Christian's heart sink deeper this second time. Jacob wasn't just a client, he was a friend he'd known all his life, the kind of friend Christian looked out for because, without the Jacobs of this world, people would be ruthless. Christian cradled his crystal flute. "And who are they?"

"They have access to places like this. And other things you didn't know were possible."

Christian held up his hand. "Don't tell me more."

"Why not?"

He slapped the table. "Because I might want to join."

Jacob smirked. "I haven't even told you the best part about this place. No points. No cameras. No judgment."

Christian paused midsip. Points were everything. Points gave bargaining power and leverage and a reputation. People spent days, weeks, discussing point management strategies. Give too many, you'd have less for yourself. Hoard them, you'd look bad. He didn't have to do that kind of work. His own algorithm, personally developed, lit up everything for him. He knew who was going on holiday, buying toys, frequenting restaurants. Points were everything. Unless they weren't.

He gulped down the bubbles. "Okay, tell me the name of this club. No. Don't tell me. I don't need the temptation." He downed the rest of his champagne. "Okay, tell me."

"Landström Society."

Christian's ribcage tightened. The oldest social club in the country, the one with the worst reputation, the one rumored to be a secret society, the one his late father belonged to, the one Christian worked to expose at the Nationalbanken hearing next week. If the points turned into the national currency, Landström would be in charge of the country, and the country would be doomed.

He lowered his champagne flute. "You know better than that, Jacob. Stay away from them."

Jacob's sly smile faded. "Calm down. They're on a recruitment drive. I haven't joined. Thought it would be best to play along with them. Throw them off the scent."

Sweat burst from his palms. He didn't like it. His friend was too fragile to be playing with those dragons, and he didn't know how to say no. But what choice did he have? "It's good you're attracting clubs, but let me introduce you to other clubs. Smaller ones—"

Jacob slid his hands under the table. "Who look after guys like me?"

"That's not what I meant." Christian pinched the tension stuck between his eyebrows. "I wish you wouldn't—"

Karen touched Christian's arm. "Let's stop talking business and enjoy the evening."

Christian gripped the edge of the table, preparing to propel for the exit. "I have a meeting in the morning. I should go."

Jacob grabbed Christian's arm. "Don't go. I haven't accepted. All right?"

"Promise me you'll never say yes."

"I promise. Done. Now, drink up."

Christian released his grip from the table's hard edge and scooted in.

Several drinks later, awash in alcohol-loose minds and looser morals, a woman came out of nowhere and brushed Christian's hand.

His legs tingled.

"You're free to do whatever you want, buddy. No points here." Jacob pulled out Christian's AR glasses from his inside pocket. "But you might want these back."

Christian took in the woman's sun-kissed face. "Yeah, I need them for work."

Jacob patted him on the shoulder. "I'm glad you have your priorities straight."

Too weak to resist, he rose from his chair and met this stranger, a real woman, not a virtual reality doll or avatar. Her hand's soft skin dissolved the last cinder brick within him, and they left in a taxi, headed for her place.

CHAPTER 2

A SHRILL BEEP HACKED INTO CHRISTIAN'S DEEP SLEEP.

His eyes flickered. Sunlight seeped through the broken shades. Stale booze and stranger-sex perfumed his skin. He winced and scraped back his hair.

Beep!

The woman he had gone home with last night stirred on the bed beside him. He couldn't remember her name. Groaning, he raked through the wad of clothes on the wooden floorboards and rooted out his glasses.

7:15 a.m. | 1 Message from Yolanda (!)

Alert: Get Ready for Work.

He groaned louder. "What could be urgent on a Tuesday?" he mumbled. "Open message from Yolanda."

The woman sat up. "What time is it?"

"Too early."

She laid down and tucked her head under the duvet.

Silently, he read the message from Yolanda:

> There's a situation. Torn and Max need you at the office. Now.

He launched off the bed, shoved his foot into a twisted pant leg, and scooped up the rest of his clothes.

The woman shot up, her hair a tangle. "Why are you leaving?"

"It's work. I have to go."

A frown cursed her beautiful face, and he knew he shouldn't leave so abruptly. The last one, a couple of weeks back, stalked him on the feeds until he responded. Cost him a few points. He splashed water on his face from the kitchenette faucet, washing his sweat and guilt away. "What's your name?"

"Lisandra, username gingeraroma. Call me."

She dropped back into the bed, and he closed the door gently behind him.

OUTSIDE NOW, the sun seared the remnants of Christian's grogginess. Surrounded by red and white stone buildings, facades positively nineteenth century, he stood square in the eastern district of Östermalm. He needed to be in the West. Now.

He hailed the first taxi coming down the tree-lined boulevard and scooted onto the back seat. "Take me to Sveavägen, near the Observatory."

He fastened his tie around his neck. What was he thinking? Going home with a total stranger, if that was a home at all. That bare room, the stranger—Lisandra—was that where she lived? He must've been more drunk than he realized. He bent down and tied his shoelace.

Nausea swam through him. He opened the window and let the fresh air clear his queasiness. "Send Lisandra, username gingeraroma, a bouquet of flowers," he said into his AR glasses mic. "Add a note that says 'I'll call you.'"

The taxi halted in front of a blocky high-rise, and the driver shifted into park.

The cabin's static silence bolted through Christian. They were nowhere near the Observatory. "What's going on?"

The driver lowered his white-rimmed glasses—the kind a wife buys a domesticated husband. "Helper101's crossing the road."

Christian peered through the windscreen.

A twenty-something woman trundled beside an elderly lady, her hand clasped to the old woman's elbow.

He dug deep for a wisp of calm and slipped on his glasses. 7:46 a.m. He double-tapped the sidearm. "Message Max," he said into the mic. "If Torn asks where I am, tell him I'll be there in ten minutes. Send."

The driver's thumb drummed the steering wheel. "I'll do my best to get you to your destination, as soon as these two get to the other side."

The urge to dash out of the taxi surged through Christian, and he gripped the door handle. The driver's voice was flat, but his thumb drummed the wheel impatiently—a telling sign. He would bet the driver was a climber with a craving. He slipped on his glasses.

A purple text box hovered beside the driver's head. His avatar name was Judomaster, his Q-score 2.656m. That number made him a Tier 3 player, the Tier most law-abiding citizens resided.

"How about extra points if you take the side roads?" Christian said.

The driver gave a quick nod. "I'll do what I can."

A brusque back up and U-turn later, they were driving down a residential road.

Christian tapped the arm on his glasses. "Give Judomaster three hundred and fifty points."

"Very generous, tak." Judomaster tapped his white rims. "I shall reward you too."

"No need. Just get me there as soon as possible."

The driver's knuckles whitened as he gripped the wheel. "Thank you, uh, Christian Karlsson." He turned left. "Is that your real name?"

Christian half smiled. Some of the other Tiers knew about Tier 1 benefits, like getting extra code that changed their public avatars. But some weren't aware, and time was too short for a lengthy explanation. "I made the mistake of using my real name when I first opened my Q-score points account. Never got around to changing it."

Olof Palmes Gravplats sprawled out in front of them.

"Anywhere here will do," he said in a tone both agitated and grateful. He slipped out of the cab and backtracked up to the quieter Tegnérgatan.

Breathing heavily, he shot through the doors of Nyström Image Architects.

IN THE CORNER of Christian's lens, the red owl icon flashed. Panic lit up his senses.

Owl was his self-made algorithm that ingested and monitored data from his clients' charts, vital feeds, and Q-score points. When two of their data points dropped below acceptable levels, owl went red and flew into action. Bottom lining it, a vulture was on the prowl, pouring poison on one of his clients. Not. Gonna. Happen. He shoved his panic aside, jumped the last step, and skidded to a halt in front of his desk.

Max, Christian's number two, whipped around. He looked like distress had worn him down. "Where the hell've you been? I was calling you all morning."

Christian grabbed the controller. "Things got crazy last night."

Feet firm on the tiled floor, he pushed his glasses so close to his face, his eyelashes brushed the lenses. He twirled the controller in his palm as though gathering cotton candy threads. Appetite primed, he clicked the red owl.

His glasses dimmed, and the HUD screen superimposed its midtone gray over Max, the desks, and Nyström Image Architects' gold logo across the floor.

A black graph popped up on the HUD, and a jagged red line was sawing right through it, point by point, second by second. His client's rep was falling faster than an earthbound meteor. Bold letters at the top of the graph identified the client: Jacob Rasmusson.

Christian fought his jumped-up nerves. If the red line dropped to the bottom of the graph, the zero line, it would form a cliff of doom. The rate and trajectory forecasted that Jacob would be a Tier Zero by the end of the day—a status lower than a homeless man living in the outskirts of Stockholm, smack in the center of social pariah territory. He squeezed his tight neck.

"How many times are we going to rescue this guy?" Max said in a tone of imminent defeat and all that came with it. "He's been with us, what, two months?"

Christian's belly tightened. The speed of the attacks was fierce and time was of the essence. Letting his own emotions cloud him wouldn't help anyone. Calm pearled inside him. "What time did the first rumors appear?"

"Right before I called you," Max said.

Christian braced himself. "Around 7 this morning, then. Let's go back and see what they started with."

The earliest, related post on the vitals feed read:

First Crime Since Q-Scores Began.
7:05 a.m.

The bold text dressed up the accusation like a headline. He stripped it down to but a rumor. With the discipline of a soldier on a mission, he pointed the controller at the expand button.

Jacob Rasmussen avatar Jonah Whale
assaulted his wife.
7:06 a.m.

White hot shock minted his breath. His first duty was to the upcoming hearing, but Jacob's credibility was central to exposing Landström. These online vultures had no idea. No idea! Christian gripped the controller. "Jacob's the target."

Max shook his head as he pulled up the search bar. "What happened?"

Christian drew in a deep breath, vacuuming up particles of shock in the whole room. "Their claims are shit," he declared. "Has the data fed through to the leaderboard yet?"

Max tapped on the shared display. Points data for every adult in Sweden, all ten million, colonized the screen. He typed Jacob Rasmusson, avatar Jonah Whale, into the advanced search bar and hit return.

"Jesus Christ," Max said. "He's on the social pariah page. Less than zero."

Heat surged through Christian, and the controller slipped from his hand. "What the hell happened, Jacob?"

"Just yesterday, he was a T3." The white of Max's eyes flashed in the monotone world. "How did he drop so fast?"

Christian rubbed his hands. "Looking at the time span, the repetitive headlines, the matching words used in the posts, it all points to a coordinated attack."

"Who do you think ordered the hit?"

Christian shrugged outwardly, but inwardly he knew who was behind the attack; he just needed to prove it. He double-tapped the side of his glasses. "I'm going into the Wreck Room. See if anyone let it slip."

The cliff of doom graph folded down to a black point.

He pushed an earpiece in and pressed a button at the bottom of his AR glasses. The floor blacked out. The in-built hood jutted over the frame's top, bottom, and sides, while the rubber seal suctioned his cheeks and forehead. Other-worldly chirps and chatter pricked his eardrums.

"Open up my avatars," he said into the mic.

An array of AI-generated substitutes lined up. Christian clicked the bright-eyed, dark-haired twenty-year-old human—his most disarming-looking avatar—and it slipped over his real-world face.

"Go to the Wreck Room."

A bamboo forest encircled a chat area. On a sofa sat a cat, a blue-nosed whale, and a gladiator huddled around a table—the paid gossipmongers, usually directly hired by the hitman. Not one of the gossipmongers' heads turned toward his bright-eyed avatar.

If he could identify one of them, he could track down the hitman who placed the order. Christian switched on the text boxes for the hard of hearing. It was the only way to capture their whispers in real-time:

> "I heard the wife's eye is all swollen and black."

Trapped heat built around Christian's face.

> "And bruises up and down her arms."

> "Probably covering up old ones, too."

> "Saw her neck and face all scratched and red. Poor woman."

"He needs to pay."

Christian scratched the back of his head. Listening to their poisonous words wouldn't give him the identifiers he needed. "Waste of time."

Christian exited the Wreck Room, and his avatar landed in a lobby.

Brilliant white dazzled his eyes, his body so light he felt airsick. He pulled off his glasses and yanked out his earpiece.

The architects were urgently tapping on air screens and rattling into their mics—probably reassuring fearful clients who'd seen the news about Jacob that his reputation would not sully their own.

His boss, Torn, rushed onto the floor, his face the color of a popped vein. "What is going on?" Torn demanded. "How did this happen?"

Christian gulped a boatload of air. "The rumors are malicious. I was with Jacob last night. Both he and his wife. Nothing of the sort happened."

Torn's blue eyes froze over. "Were you with them all night?"

"We went our separate ways after dinner. But I know Jacob. No way is any of this true."

Christian leaned against his desk. He knew how this worked. Someone puts out a smear. Avatars enter the gossip rooms, magnify the original rumor, and plant seeds for more rumors. Then, the vultures multiply the posts until their victim drops a Tier. Usually, that's all the perpetrator wants. Jealousy, anger, or fun usually fueled them, and plenty of innocent men and women had been tarnished by false accusations this way, but these emo-led attacks never resulted in a relentless drop to the pariah Tier, Tier Zero.

This was a different feeding frenzy. Chiefly, it was organizations who aimed for total destruction of a competitor's reputation, and Christian would bet any number of points Landström put out the hit. Jacob hadn't joined them, so they attacked him. This was a vendetta.

He rested his glasses on top of his head. "I've done my assessment. I know how to fix this."

Crossing his arms, Torn gave a jerky nod. "Debrief me when you're done," he said and walked away.

It wasn't an *if*, but a *when* Christian confirmed Landström was behind the order, he'd get his most lethal algorithm—Octopus—to rip off their limbs with its beak. But so far, only online rumors encircled Jacob, and the punishment had to fit the crime.

In the meantime, they needed to fend off the vultures, efficiently. He blinked hard. "Max, get Lorelei Lindbergh on the line."

Max pointed at the TV screen on the wall. "She's already working the story."

Lorelei Lindbergh stood outside Jacob's apartment block, clutching a furry mic.

The scene was like an arrow striking Christian's armor. "She's outside a client's home, already?" He puffed out hot air. "Try the other one. The one who covered the Dan story for us last month."

"Karen Lindqvist?"

Christian pointed at Max. "That's the one. Get her to poke holes in Lindberg's story."

He twirled around to the vitals desk. Serena stared at Lorelei Lindberg as if struck by a fairy wielding a golden chalice.

Christian snapped his fingers. "Earth to Serena!"

She jumped.

"We need to get a backup scenario online. A regretful ex-girlfriend story. Upload it to every vital feed. Then, go in as Jacob's ex-girlfriend. Wait. Scratch that." He held up three fingers. "Go in under three different accounts, three different exes. The story is…" He stretched his arms up and gestured blinking lights.

"Jacob, the one that got away, yada, yada." He lowered his arms. "You know the drill."

"You got it," she said.

His fingertips iced his hot neck. "Max. What backup solutions do we have?"

"We can try out the Octopus program."

Christian scratched his forehead. Octopus needed just one gossipmonger's real-world ID, and he didn't have it. "I was the only one with a human face in the Wreck Room. It'll take days to identify just one of the gladiators."

"I could start a hunt for an ID."

"Takes too much time."

There was one algorithm he had developed called the Croupier. It gathered all the Q-scores, calculated the average, and distributed the points across all players on a section of the leaderboard. It could prove the Q-system was compromised, but it would also reveal he knew the weakness in the system. Landström would hunt him down no matter where in the world he hid. He could only use it once; ideally, never.

The shared display dinged. Jacob's row moved up one slot on the Q-score leaderboard.

A ripple of hope weaved around Christian. "Let's go with the fire blanket template."

"IT hasn't updated it in ages," Max said.

Christian scanned the floor for a solution.

From the balcony, high above the heat, Torn watched them rescue a client, holding what looked like a paper card. It couldn't be paper, though. Ever since Sweden went paper-free, the first country in the world with such a status, paper had become nigh-on impossible to find. Maybe it was fake paper.

"Christian, you still with us?" Max said.

"Yeah."

"The blanket template hasn't been updated," Max repeated.

"What do you want to do?"

Christian narrowed his gaze on Jacob's Q-score. An untested template over the vital feeds would hush the rumors, but it could also cause a malfunction. The worst case was that it would block the whole country from access. The cyber police would track down the culprits—him and Max—and the tech companies would mount endless legal suits, possibly even shut down Nyström Image Architects. On the other hand, the best case was that no one would know. The gossipmongers would disappear, and Jacob's status would be restored. But if it landed in court, the prosecution's legal grounds would be unshakeable. The risk was too high. He squeezed his sweaty hands. "Apply the old blanket version."

Max typed into the instant message system. "IT will have it in place, but they say it's risky."

Christian pinched the bridge of his nose. Old code could trip things up, but the giants can't move as quickly as the architects. "Even if we just blanket half of what's being said, it'll work. Any interruption is disruption."

"I'll let them know."

Seconds later, a message dinged on Max's screen. "IT managed to apply the old code to everything Jacob-related that's been online for the last twenty-four hours."

Calm bloomed inside Christian. Within minutes, all Jacob-related rumors would be whited out, hidden under a blanket of code. Some might call the blanket a server attack, but legally and practically, it wasn't; it blanked Jacob's presence from the feeds and there was nothing illegal about that.

Max turned to Christian. "Do you think he's capable of assaulting his wife?"

The words doused Christian like gasoline on an open wound. He wiped his face. "No way could he have done that."

As the minutes drove on, they watched in silence as Jacob's

row climbed up the leaderboard. And then five more rows.

"You said you saw him last night. Was there any indication something like this would happen?"

Christian resisted the urge to collapse. "He was doing fine. Karen was there too. Both were in good spirits." He tossed his glasses onto his desk. "But yeah, something must've happened between last night and this morning."

"Looks like he made a swift enemy."

Empty of adrenaline, Christian's neck slackened, and his head dropped back. Landström must have heard about the National-banken hearing. It was in their interests to see Jacob never reach that hearing because his evidence would prove, beyond any doubt, that Landström Society developed code that was manipulating the Q-scores.

His finger's numb, Christian unbuttoned his sweat-soaked shirt. That hearing was going to happen whether they wanted it or not. His efforts to get the bank members gathered, the preliminary evidence organized, the backup witnesses to agree to attend—as scared as they were—and then, of course, protecting Jacob was all too momentous to stop now. People needed to know that the Q-scores, their future currency, was under Landström Society's control.

No one ever said no to that Society, but there was always a first time. The sad fact was that Jacob was too weak to fend off their frenzy, and it wasn't going to be him to do the job. Christian had to push them back himself. "Tell Torn I'll debrief him when I get back."

"You going to see Jacob?" Max said.

From his desk drawer, Christian pulled a fresh shirt from a stack. The fabric weighed head-heavy in his palm. "I think I know who's behind this. Keep an eye on the feeds and update me every hour until midnight." He struggled to button up the stiff collar. "I'm going to put a stop to this."

CHAPTER 3

THE LANDSTRÖM SOCIETY'S TWO HIGHEST-RANKING GENTLEMEN played chess in the mahogany library of their meeting house in central Stockholm. No judges, no spectators, and no pressure, just man to man, Harald on the black side, Viktor on the white side, a marble chessboard between them.

Harald contemplated how to take down Viktor's king and how soon, too soon, he'd have to pass his position to a worthy man. He had heard what the members of the Landström Society wanted, and he was at a point in his own life when it was time to rest. Viktor's face bore fewer wrinkles, brighter eyes, whiter teeth, and his brick-red scarf underlined his younger years, but Harald's doubts about Viktor leading the Society crept around him like heat rising out of broken ground.

"You sent the invite to the boy, right?"

"First thing this morning."

Harald eyed Viktor's bishop. He stretched out his thin-skinned hand, graced with fat blue veins, and wiggled his finger-tips above a pawn. If Viktor leaped at the opportunity Harald's next move offered, Viktor's king would be vulnerable. He paddled the pawn until it roosted in a square across his opponent's rook—a taunting sacrifice, he hoped. He released the pawn's neck and clicked the timer. "The boy could bring new ideas to the Society."

Viktor's dark blue eyes flicked from pawn to bishop. "He should've been here by now," he said, a bitter ease in his voice.

Harald leaned back. "He can learn."

"There's no time for that," Viktor said. "You're about to retire."

From the hallway, the grandfather clock chimed its familiar warm notes. It had been a gift from a dearly departed member of the Society. His name was etched on acid-free parchment, protected by glass, framed in glossy hardwood, and hung on the library wall. The clock's knell ended on the eleventh chime.

Harald shifted, and his summer suit swished against the chair's silk seat. "What's it going to be, Viktor?"

Viktor moved his white pawn forward, and it clinked against his opponent's.

The two high-shine pawns huddled uncomfortably on the front line.

Harald sucked air through his nostrils. The move took the game in an unexpected direction. "We're both a bit tired."

"It has been a long month," Viktor said.

Harald shuttled his rook to Viktor's side of the board. "In all my years, I've never seen change be a comfortable affair." Harald released his chess piece on a black square. "But it looks like the position is yours."

The cogs behind Viktor's eyes hissed into motion. "You sure you want to play that move?"

"Ever the courteous." Harald adjusted himself in his chair. "One suggestion, if I may."

Viktor jutted his chin out like a silver platter in waiting.

"Let me hand over the keys to the Hall in a month or so."

Viktor arched his brow.

"That's when I publicly retire," Harald added. "Best we keep continuity. Wouldn't you agree?"

Viktor scanned the board. Every single move would hand him victory. "Agreed." He pushed his queen into the game. "Check."

Harald rested his forearms on the chair's padded armrests and resigned himself to the game. "You'll make a great leader, Viktor."

Viktor scooted his chair away from the table. "Just as well the boy didn't show. He's a little too charming for his own good. And I'm not the only one who thinks so."

"Yes, that is a problem."

Viktor glided his hand over the game table's smooth wood. "It can get a man in trouble."

CHRISTIAN FACED the red door of Landström Society's lair—their meeting house in central Stockholm. The sound of cars, pedestrians, and bikes bustled behind him; two ravens perched on a window above him. Their black coats glistened gold in the afternoon sun, and their black eyes peered at him as though he didn't belong.

He agreed.

But he was here to keep the Society off Jacob's back. In one week, the hearing would begin, and it would expose their connection to the Q-scores. Just one more week. He rang the doorbell.

The door opened, revealing the house's butler. "Mr. Karlsson. Good to see you."

A chill went through Christian. "Is Harald in?"

"He's expecting you."

This was the last place he expected to be expected, unless they were behind Jacob's cliff of doom and they knew he'd come knocking. "Somehow, I'm not surprised."

The butler opened the door wider.

Christian steeled himself and followed the butler down the narrow hallway. They passed a parlor, where a black and white cube encased in glass sat on the fireplace mantel. His watch vibrated, sending a quiver up his arm.

A message popped onto the screen: it was his own club.

Their timing was odd. If they knew he was inside the most reviled club in the country, his points would drop instantly. He dialed off, and the screen went dark.

The butler came to a halt in front of a solid oak door. Christian stepped back, and the floorboards creaked underfoot.

The butler knocked three times.

Christian rolled his eyes. The Landström Society and their cryptic riddles. Nothing was ever straightforward with these guys —one of the many reasons he wanted nothing to do with them. Maybe there was something to those secret society rumors.

"Come in," a voice called out from the room behind the door. It sounded like Harald, the decades-long leader.

The butler unlocked the door. Christian tugged on the cuff of his sleeve and stepped through.

Harald Seversson sat on one side of a round table. Across from him sat Viktor Hansson, twenty years younger but still old. A chessboard sat between them like an angel holding two beasts apart.

Christian hadn't seen either since his father's funeral a year ago. With all that was going on with the hearing, the anniversary of his father's passing had slipped his mind, but to them such disregard for protocol and tradition was almost a crime.

Tentatively, he stepped onto the oriental rug. "Gentlemen."

Harald peered at Christian over the rim of his reading glasses and turned back to Viktor. "This is our new Sweden. Up is down, and eight a.m. is five in the afternoon."

"Don't mind him," Viktor said. "It's good to see you, Christian. How is your mother?"

"She's well, thank you for asking." Christian came to a halt in front of them. "I hope I didn't interrupt your game."

The black queen lay sideways on the chessboard.

He clasped his hands in front of him. "Sorry for your loss."

Harald's lips pursed, and he pushed himself away from the game table. "What a way to speak about your father. And on the anniversary of his passing."

"My apologies." Christian bowed, giving himself time to refocus on why he was really here. "Busy day in the office. Saving a client from reputation damage is consuming."

"Oh, that," Viktor said.

"Tell me, Christian," Harald said. "What do you know about the Society?"

"Landström is the oldest gentleman's club in the country—"

Harald batted the air. "Don't give me the stock answer." He leaned toward Christian. "You do know your father was a member, don't you?"

Christian nodded. "But other than my father, I don't know any others in your vast network."

Harald tapped his finger on the armrest and shrugged his shoulder. "Yes. It's best you don't know."

That was a problematic attitude, Christian thought. He needed to know how vast their network stretched, one of many reasons he was inside their lair.

"How about the initiates?" Christian asked. "Are they considered members?"

"Initiates are different," Viktor said. "They aren't members."

Christian couldn't prevent the corner of his mouth from flinching. The initiate was in an impossible position: bound to their rules without any protection. Initiates didn't live their own lives, their backgrounds got scrutinized, with the help of the vast network, and the mental pressure was intense. It could break someone like Jacob. Whether Jacob wanted to or not, he would end up telling them about the hearing. "At least members get protection."

"Rumors are... useful," Viktor said. "Everyone should be acclimated to the social atmosphere by now, so it's an easy hurdle to jump."

Anger mounted in Christian. Just as he had suspected, the Landström Society was behind the rumors already plaguing Jacob. "Useful?"

Viktor plodded to the sofa. "Useful for someone or something. Who could also be a what."

Harald ran a quick eye over Viktor. "For whom, to whom, for what. Who cares?" He flicked his hand in the air. "Reputations are the least of our concerns."

Christian dropped his hands to his side and held himself back. "That's good to hear because Landström's reputation is dismal. People don't know what to make of you and your ancient traditions and symbolism. They all think you should sink to the bottom of the North Sea."

"People aren't pouring their true feelings online. They're posing. We don't pose." Harald stood up from his chair. "You young people don't know what's real anymore." He pointed at Christian's breast pocket, in which his AR glasses resided. "Those things have turned your brains to gruel."

This new reality was too complicated to explain, so Christian pushed past the old man's jab. "Everyone thinks this place is a secret society."

"I've never heard that rumor," Viktor said.

The claim landed like a dead tree on an open country road that Christian was driving down. It paralyzed him, but only for a moment. "The only reason the rumor isn't online is because people are terrified you'd come after them."

"Rumors," one of them growled.

"I didn't make the Q-scores," Christian shot back. "I just make sure they work for my clients. Jacob Rasmussen is a client."

"And that's why you're here?" Harald's eyes narrowed. "Not for us, not for your father. But for some client? Or are you here to add us to your list of clients so you can fix our dismal reputation?" A look of disgust shadowed his face. "If so, save your breath because we only work within our network." Harald let his gaze fall to Christian's shoes. "But since I'm no longer the leader of this Society, all business must now go through Viktor."

Viktor crossed his legs, and the taut sofa leather squeaked.

Tangy wax scented the room.

Christian's senses cleared, and he widened his stance. "You were behind Jacob's Q-score downfall."

Harald snarled. "We invited you to our sacred meeting house, and you accuse us of coercion. How preposterous!"

"So, you're saying you had nothing to do with Jacob's score, the vultures, the rumors?"

Harald stared at Christian. "Out of respect for your father, we did our duty by offering you a position in the Society. Now your invitation has expired, as has the mourning period of your father's passing."

"Indeed," Viktor said.

Their nonchalant manner told Christian everything. They were behind Jacob's rumors, probably to coerce him into becoming an initiate, and they wanted Christian to join too. No way would any of that happen, but the two old men were closing the drawbridge, and Christian still needed to know just how vast their network spread. "I received no such invitation."

Harald glanced at Viktor.

"I sent it to your workplace," Viktor piped in.

"My workplace?" Christian cupped his face. That's what Torn was holding on the upper deck. He was holding their invitation. Torn knew he was here. "Are you insane? People will talk."

"We had no choice. You're never at home. We had to invite you somehow," Viktor said. "We must honor the rules of the Society."

The menace in Viktor's tone sent heat down Christian's collar.

"Seeing as you've decided against joining Landström," Viktor said, pulling out a ledger book from under the sofa, "we'll need all your father's files concerning the Society." He opened the book and scanned the pages. "Papers, drives, disks, books, notes."

Christian's neck tensed. Junk. That's all it was. Pure junk. But one missing drive and they'd be on his back. The fact he was still in front of them, still in talks, meant they wanted something more. Maybe they were setting it up so that he had no choice but to join them. Not gonna happen.

His father had left him all the leverage he needed: the Q-scores source code, secretly developed by members of Landström Society. The source code enabled him to build his own propriety algorithms while he worked through official channels to secure the trial. He exhaled quietly through softly parted lips.

The Society didn't know he had their source code—now tucked away in safe keeping. It would come out during the trial. In the meantime, he'd courier over their junk papers, drives, books, notes—everything but the source code—and one or two courier mishaps could buy Jacob and himself time. He gestured at the ledger book.

"If you give me an inventory of what belonged to you, I can arrange for it to be sent."

Viktor's brow bunched, and he glanced over his reading glasses.

"As long as you leave Jacob Rasmussen alone," Christian added.

Viktor snapped the book shut and removed his glasses. "The list is long. I'll send you a copy."

"Viktor needs time to learn the ropes," Harald said. "He's in charge of inviting new members. At this point, according to Society rules, if you ever decide to join, you'll be considered an initiate and go through an initiation process like everyone else." Harald bowed toward Viktor. "Should you be re-invited, of course."

"That won't be necessary," Christian said. "I already belong to a club."

"Those temporary pop-ups are vulgar," Harald said.

"The way you treat your initiates, the vulgar pop-ups appeal to me more."

Harald lifted his chin. "We treat our initiates with the respect they deserve."

"And that includes Jacob Rasmussen." A perceptible curl cracked through Viktor's lips. "Of course."

A spike of defiance rushed up Christian's spine.

Harald jutted his chin. "We didn't plant any rumors about this Jacob person online if that's what you're implying."

The room fell silent.

"Rest assured, Christian, all your... history, will remain behind these walls, sealed and secure."

Christian tensed. Typical of him to slip in a sleek little counter-threat, one that could come from any of the faceless members. "Everyone in this room has done something they'd prefer to remain inside these walls."

"What Harald is trying to say," Viktor said, "is that, unlike most other clubs, we keep our word."

The grandfather clock chimed from the hallway.

"Right then." Viktor slapped his thigh. "Please send our regards to your mother."

The butler entered as though he'd been listening the whole time. His white-gloved hand held the door ajar.

"It was good seeing you, Christian," Viktor said.

The door closed before Christian could even think of a reply.

OUTSIDE, he stretched, and a slab of tension that had settled
between his shoulder blades dislodged. Now they knew he knew
that they had manufactured Jacob's cliff of doom. Christian could
repair the damage the rumors caused Jacob—that wasn't an issue.
The issue was Jacob. As long as Jacob never became an initiate,
he'd be okay, and the hearing would be on track. He switched on
his AR glasses.

Multiple messages popped up. Ulrich, from his club, Torn, for
the debrief.

He tapped his club's icon.

Ulrich picked up.

"I was—"

"At the Landström Society?" Ulrich said. "We heard."

Christian squeezed the corner of his eyes. "Who told you?"

"Word gets around. Your points are dropping."

Christian's stomach fluttered. He logged onto the leaderboard.
"A one seven five-point drop but still a Tier 1."

"Our policy allows a two hundred points drop a day, max,"
Ulrich said.

"Maybe I should change clubs." Christian sighed out regret
for his biting tone. "I was called to meet them. It was required."

"Just had to alert you," Ulrich said and closed the call.

And Christian had to be sure he'd never return to this meeting
house. Maybe his father had something in his old files on them.
He recalled his dad's old junk box, the one Christian put in storage. He'd locked the safe and never looked back. It might contain
leverage against them, but then again it might just be junk. He
couldn't count on anything his father did, or didn't do, but it was
worth checking it out. He spoke into his mic: "Connect to Westland Storage Company."

CHAPTER 4

TORN ENTERED THE BOARDROOM WEARING A WHITE SHIRT TUCKED into straight-legged trousers, finished with brown suede shoes. "Glad to see that Jacob's points have recovered. Somewhat."

"Tier 2 and climbing," Christian said, noting the unease in Torn's tone. Having had clients call from a jail cell over a hit-and-run or drug charges desensitized him to these debriefings. "Credit goes to the entire team."

Torn's face flickered caution while he unlocked the chill cabinet. He pulled out a bottle of aquavit, almost full, and poured the syrupy liquid into two tulip glasses. "I got a call from a journalist yesterday. Said you were out with Jacob on Monday night."

He held out a glass of aquavit.

Christian smoothened his pant trouser underneath the table. Life was messy enough, but he took the glass. "A journalist isn't worth a skål."

"This isn't a skål. We need this." Torn swigged down alcohol. "What happened with Jacob Rasmussen?"

Christian set down his tulip glass. "Dinner, so what? Why would a journalist care about that?"

"That's what I'd like to know." Torn rubbed the back of his neck. "It was Lorelei Lindbergh."

Christian could feel his blood pressure drop. "That woman is a viper, stirring up trouble where there is none. I'll handle it."

"I swear she has a vendetta against us," Torn said. "Have you spoken to Jacob?"

"Better. I found the source of the problem."

"The hitman?"

"Something like that."

"One last thing." Torn bent down, pulled out a wooden box from his canvas bag, and laid it on the table. He snapped open the lid. "This came for you, but you were busy."

Inside of the box was a white envelope adorned with Christian's name, handwritten in black ink. The paper was cradled like an easter egg on a bed of spongy coils.

A chill ran down his spine— a feeling that was all too familiar. Without even opening it, he knew it was the invitation that Viktor had sent. "When did it arrive?"

"Yesterday." Torn's eyebrows twitched. "This is why I wanted to meet in this room."

"They could've sent it to my home," Christian said.

"How often are you at home?"

Christian recalled Viktor saying the same. "Am I that predictable?"

The top button on Torn's Oxford shirt brushed against his jaw. "You have a strong work ethic, and everyone knows it."

Christian's gut tightened as he picked up the envelope, the paper's weave numbed his fingertips. On the back was the Landström Society's waxy red seal. "Landström, obviously."

He placed it back on the coils.

"Aren't you going to open it?"

Jacob's promise not to join them echoed in Christian's mind. "They're looking for recruits, and I already have a club."

"Despite their less than stellar reputation," Torn said, "they're still the country's oldest and most powerful club. We don't want to upset them."

"You'll probably get an invite to join too."

Torn's lips pursed. "Whatever you tell them, be polite about it. Reputation is everything."

The pit of Christian's stomach hollowed at the thought of yesterday's visit to their meeting house. He took a sip of aquavit, and the ice-cold liquid filled the hole in his belly. "I'll let it expire. It probably already has." He swigged down the rest of the aquavit and glanced at Torn. "Just to confirm, my answer would've been no."

"Good to know," Torn said.

CHRISTIAN CLICKED OPEN A NEW LINE. Lorelei Lindbergh knew about his dinner with Jacob and Karen? How? He tapped on Jacob's number.

"Jacob!"

"It's not Jacob. It's Karen."

"Is everything all right? Where's Jacob?"

"I have his phone."

A chill rattled down his spine. "Take me out of my misery and tell me one thing. Is Jacob okay?"

"Yes," she said, her breath so light he could barely hear her. "Can you meet me at Humlegården? Around nine p.m.?"

"What's this about? Where's Jacob?"

She hesitated. "I'm worried about Jacob, but please don't tell him."

His instinct was not to believe her, but everything rested on this trial. "I'll see you tonight."

CHRISTIAN DROVE SOUTH TO KUNGSHOLMEN, the exhaustion of the last few days catching up with him. Twenty minutes later, his building fanned out in front of him, high-rises side by side, close but not so close that he bumped into neighbors on one of his eleventh-hour treks to the corner shop. He parked in front of Building 55.

The clock displayed 5:45 p.m., enough time to put on fresh armor in preparation for his meeting with Karen. The elevator bell dinged, and he pressed the button for floor three.

"Hold the door!"

Christian straightened as his neighbor Schroeder appeared. Though he was a nice guy and a lawyer, Schroeder seemed to know the schedule of every person in the building and was known to be a brown-noser. Christian gripped the elevator door, but it kicked back like a wild buck when Schroeder poked his knee through the gap.

He squeezed through, his khaki slacks hollering ease. "Tak!" he exclaimed. "Ah, Christian, good to see you. Did someone have a good time last night? Or was it Monday?"

Christian ran his fingers through his hair. "Client work."

His AR glasses buzzed, and he lowered them over his eyes. Karen was calling. "It's my boss. Got to take this."

Schroeder's fake examination of the elevator's aluminum panels smogged up the space.

Karen changed their meeting time to an hour later. Christian lowered his glasses.

"A box came for you today," Schroeder said. "I took it in. I'll bring it right over."

"Thanks, I appreciate it."

Schroeder bounced on his heels.

"I'll send you points," Christian said.

On the third floor, they parted ways, Schroeder to the left, Christian to the right.

"BRB," Schroeder said.

Christian entered his flat, leaving the door unlocked for Schroeder, and shrugged off his suit jacket. Schroeder stood at the door holding a large metal box. Christian's stomach tightened— his oh, so friendly neighbor was holding the box of junk. He attempted a smile. "Come in."

Schroeder ambled in and placed the box on the table like a waiter offering a glass of champagne.

"Thanks for taking it in."

Schroeder swiped the air. "It was the least I could do. There's a paintball game coming up in a couple of days, and Stormykitten is proving to be quite a fighter. You gonna be there?"

Christian thought about it. He could use the downtime. "With any luck."

Schroeder cocked his head. "Christian doesn't need luck."

Christian glanced at Schroeder. "We all need luck."

"We'll catch up in a couple of days," Schroeder said and left.

Christian was alone with the junk box on his kitchen counter and looked at it for a long time. There were more important things to attend to right now, like the upcoming meeting with Karen.

CHAPTER 5

AT 8:30 P.M., CHRISTIAN ENTERED HUMLEGÅRDEN FROM THE south and stepped onto the earthy path. Walking along the tree-lined track, he welcomed the silence. His need to know what Karen had to say pulled him deeper into the park.

He sat on a bench opposite a smiling statue of Carl Von Linne. The stone statue's blank eyes stared down at him.

Behind him, footsteps pattered across the path, and within seconds, the wooden bench flexed.

He could almost smell anxiety underlying a whiff of perfume.

"Thanks for meeting me here," Karen's voice rang out, laced with a touch of nervousness.

For a moment, he feared the rumors about Karen's assault were true. Turning to face her, he braced himself.

Not a broken capillary in any of her eyes, not a bruise on her face, not a scratch on her arm. Nothing, but her eyelids weighed heavy.

He should've felt relief, but all he felt was tension twisting up his spine. He eased, but only slightly. "Why are we meeting here?"

Her breath wavered. "Someone's been following me."

His skin went taut, and he turned around. A couple walked through the park, holding hands. He folded his arms. "There's no one here."

"I must've thrown them off."

Or she was imagining things. "Did you call the police?"

She seemed to take in the darkness. "I think I know who it is."

So, she chose to meet in a public park late into the night to talk about someone following her? He rubbed his nine o'clock stubble. "Why would someone follow you?"

Karen shook her head, the fear in her eyes palpable. "Jacob lied to you the other night."

Christian leaned in. "Lied about what?"

"Landström."

He squeezed his eyes shut, wishing he could forget the name of that society. When his father passed, he expected that connection to be severed. But every damn day, it haunted him. "He promised he'd stay away from them."

"He had already joined when we saw you at White's."

Christian's heart contracted. His thoughts drifted to the woman he had gone home with, and that empty room in the morning. Quickly, he refocused. "I should've known. That place was too good to be true. Why does he do these things? It's like he's on self-destruct mode while everyone else is protecting him."

"Please don't tell him I told you. He thinks so highly of you."

A sinking feeling weighed Christian down as he watched all his work unravel before his eyes, but there was only a couple of days to go before the trial. "If he's in, he's theirs. There's nothing I can do about his membership. But the trial can still happen. Do you think he can hold it together long enough?"

"He's not fully in yet." She licked her bottom lip. "He's being initiated. But strange things are happening."

"Like what?"

Her eyes were weary. "The other day, I woke up to strange sounds outside our house. At first, I was scared, naturally, but I decided to check it out. A dead cat was on our doorstep, its blood smeared—" Her voice choked.

He pressed his back into the bench. "After false rumors get squashed, attacks continue like little evil echoes," he said, attempting to allay her fears.

"Dead cats on my doorstep?"

The echo of her raised voice trailed through the air.

"If you think the Society is behind it, talk to them."

She shook her head. "Women aren't allowed in there." She kept shaking it until she abruptly stopped. "I want to be debt-free from the most powerful club in the country."

"What debt?" Christian could almost smell her fear. "Clubs are meant to protect their own," he said in his most soothing voice. "They take care of their members; that's what they all do. We all need the clubs to operate like this. If Landström Society is treating Jacob differently, you can lodge an official complaint."

She faced him for the first time. "You have contacts there. Can you talk to them? I'll pay you in cash in an offshore account, or in points if that's what you want. We also have property. I'll give you whatever you need."

Christian looked at her. Someone had targeted Jacob, and it was spilling onto her. That much was clear.

"When he got involved with the Society," she said, "they told him he'd have to be initiated." She inhaled briefly. "I don't know what they'll make him do."

All the muscles in Christian's body tightened. "My father had been a lifelong member, but when he died, the contract died with him. I'm no longer a beneficiary of his membership."

She gave an indecisive nod, as though she was unsure she was allowed to know about the members.

"He was," he said, hoping to shore up her confidence. "Apart from being an absent father, around but not really there, I never saw anything dodgy they made him do."

"Maybe your father didn't give them rope to hang himself with," she said. "But you know Jacob. He's always been a little naive."

He shifted on the bench. "Vulnerable."

She nodded. "That Society has power that no one else does. They can make anybody do anything."

The hair on his arm rose. "Dead cats often turn out to be kids playing pranks. Or psychos playing sick games."

"You and I both know it's them."

Tension drilled between his shoulder blades. He wasn't even sure how much he could trust Karen. "Did you call the press?"

"Of course not. Wouldn't do any good anyway. Can you please talk to them?"

"What do you think they really want, besides Jacob?"

"Your proprietary algorithms."

His head dropped back. Of course. Christian's own proprietary algorithms were the only thing blocking the Q-scores. "I'll see what I can do."

"From you, that means a lot." She gave him a powerless smile. "I don't want Jacob to back himself into a corner and do something stupid."

"Nor do I."

Even though the trial was days away, and he had secured a hideaway for the prosecution, faceless members could still get to Jacob. He put on his glasses and switched on augmented reality. "I'll arrange for you and Jacob to stay in a hotel until the trial." He scrolled through a list of hotels and clicked on a concrete building with a letter X above the revolving door. "Booked. I'll send you this hotel's address. You and Jacob need to get there tonight."

The worry crease between her brows softened. She nodded. "Check in with me as soon as you get settled in."

CHAPTER 6

C̲HRISTINE P̲OULSEN, WHO PREFERRED THAT EVERYONE CALL HER Stine, trudged into the back office of the Hall of Records, coffee mug in hand. Her head felt as though a bowling ball was rolling around inside it, and she couldn't wait to climb into her chair and lay her head down. But Lorelei Lindbergh's annoying voice blared from a radio at the back of the room, something about the Q-score points, and the buzz drilled into her ears.

"Hvad helvede!" *What the hell?*

No matter how hard she tried, she couldn't get herself to schlep across the office and turn off the noise. She set her mug on her desk, plonked into her chair, and yawned.

Her computer screen's bright light flashed on her face. She squinted. Whoever put her on the daytime schedule would pay. "Harald, I know it was you. Your time will come."

Shielding her keyboard with her torso, she typed in her password. By the time she reached the twentieth character, she regretted choosing the manual input method. If she could go back in time and select the other box next to the secure voice input, she would have. She typed the last character and pressed enter.

The computer beeped in error.

She squeezed her eyes. Denying reality was cold comfort. Grumbling, she reached for her leather handbag and pulled out a plastic pouch filled with white powder. L-theanine. Best white stuff on the planet. She dumped a heaped scoop into her black coffee. It floated on the liquid's surface like white snow on the Baltic Sea. She swigged it down and retried the password.

The computer beeped again and threw up a red and white No Enter icon.

Seeing it felt like the hand of fate had reached through her screen and flicked a rubberband at her cheek. "Hvad helvede!"

She hit the video icon.

Within seconds, Henrik's sand-colored face appeared on her screen. His thick eyelashes fanned his eyes. "Hey, Henrik. I'm having a problem with access."

"We're testing a new cross-platform they want to install."

Her neck muscles tensed. She needed access to the records to do her job, and to fulfill her intelligence brief. This block in the system wasn't cutting it. "Why wasn't I told about this?" She straightened in her chair. "I'm only the head of this place."

"We have a couple of new people—"

"New hires?"

"They want to give full access to the public."

Her cheeks heated. Everyone would get in except her, it seemed. She tapped on her desk.

The buzzing radio in the background drilled another hole into her, but this time into her taut nerves.

"Give me a moment, would you, Henrik?"

Stine marched toward the sound of Lorelei Lindbergh's voice, that poodle barking about the Prime Minister's agenda for bringing paper back to the Hall of Records—as if they didn't have enough to deal with already. She hit the off button, turned around, and returned to her chair.

Giving in-house-only access had been problematic, with many

kinks still clogging up the system. The Hall of Records was already stretched too thin due to the energy conservation policies. Stine sank into her chair. "Henrik, we already grant twenty-four-hour access. People can come in and make their requests anytime."

Henrik jerked up. "That's for in-person only."

She stretched her neck. "What more do they want?"

"They want to give access to the remote regions of the country. That means everything has to be available online."

"It does?" She blinked, letting the thought of Henrik's level of stupidity pass over her. Maintaining stability in an already strained system was stupid too. "I don't like it. If access is expanded—"

"We're only in the testing phase." Henrik gulped. "Our report will come out in a month, so I'm surprised you couldn't get in. Let me try something." His fingertip chatter finished his sentence. The tapping stopped, and he looked at Stine, his eyes softer. "Reset it and try again."

"Reset my password? You have to be kidding me."

"Get the system to choose a temporary password and change it later."

Unease brushed over her. No way was she going to let the system choose for her. She typed an-easy-to-remember 12345, making a mental note to change the password as soon as she got off the line with Bozo the clown. She pressed enter.

The database popped up. She was in.

Yellow flags flooded her screen—each labeled Landström Estate.

"Is everything okay?" Henrik said.

"Hold on."

She clicked on a flag.

A large No Enter sign took over her screen.

A steely calm took over. She had installed an alert system on her computer when Intelligence first assigned her to the Hall of Records. It flagged changes in the records and identified which documents had been changed. In this case, Landström Estate kicked off the alert.

If their records were blocked, missing, or worse, other records were likely affected. Something was up. She could sniff the stench all the way from the next country, but good practice required an independent source to corroborate her discovery. So annoying. "Henrik, can you do a search for the Landström Estate? I want to know if their records pop up for you."

His fingertip taps poured through the speakers. "Huh. I tried a couple of different records. I'm locked out of Landström ones only."

"Do you think the records could be blocked due to the testing?"

"Impossible," he said. "Landström records will be on active and archival servers."

"So, we have a bigger problem."

"Let me do some checks." Henrik's eyes sharpened. "Maybe the tests caused interference. Hey, Stine, how did you know to look for the Landström Estate Records?"

She suppressed an eye flutter. "It's like your national museum, isn't it?"

"I suppose. They've been around long enough, but—"

"I use their records to test my access."

He sucked in his breath. "I'll get back to you as soon as I know something."

Satisfied that Henrik accepted her cover story, she closed the video feed, but the tension had lodged itself in her neck. She tapped on her wooden desk. Her SÄPO assignment was to report any unauthorized change of records. She should've asked for a precise definition of change, and she made another mental note. "Something is up."

The wall clock displayed 9:32 a.m. Harald had to be by now.

She stood up from her desk and paused. The last time she met him, he brushed her off. Bastard. She tugged her shirt. This time, she'd allude to the dangers of the new system, or some nonsense, and he would have to take her warning seriously. Who cares if it isn't about the blocked records. She wasn't there to convince him of anything. She needed intel about what was really going on with the Hall of Records and whether other plans were drifting down the bureaucratic pipeline.

She strode toward exit door four, the one leading to the Ministry of Interior.

"Payback, Harald. I'm coming," she mumbled.

STINE PUSHED OPEN the double doors and strode into the marbled entrance of the Ministry of Interior. Only a bare-bones, face-to-face meeting with Harald would do, not a useless video call. As she tossed her bag onto the X-ray machine, she clenched her other hand into a fist and pressed it under the scanner.

A guard sauntered over. "Christine Poulsen?"

Another new one. The turnover was getting ridiculous. "I know that's what my ID says but call me Stine."

"Stine. One moment."

He turned around and motioned to a tall, slim woman at the far end of the foyer. Her shiny black hair brushed her shoulder.

Stine knew her by Ulla, and she lived with her brother in a two-bedroom flat in Marieberg. Ulla started working at the Hall three months earlier.

"I'm here to see Harald," Stine said. "Nor her."

"The switchboard manager would like to talk to you."

The switchboard glowed red, a nuclear bomb ready to explode. Stine's fingers twitched against her thigh.

"I've never seen the switchboard this active," Ulla said. "I was going to come over, but the desk is so busy I couldn't escape."

"I came to talk to Harald."

Ulla nodded. "The callers are saying they can't access historical records."

A low boil raged inside Stine. Missing records. Blocked access. And why did this new manager think Stine was here? To talk to her? Hardly. "Tech is working to release the historical records, and I've come to talk to Harald."

The woman's lips scrunched together. "He's not here."

"We have a growing crisis," Stine said, pressing the point. "Where is he?"

Ulla gave a half shrug. "He's stepping down in a month."

"I don't care. He's still in service to the people of this country."

"Maybe you can talk to his private secretary?"

"I'm done with this."

Stine shot back to the entrance and flipped open her secure phone. "Message for Bjorn. We have a situation. Please call me as soon as you get this message."

CHAPTER 7

CHRISTIAN NAVIGATED THROUGH THE DENSE, MOSSY FOREST
floor, his finger resting on the trigger of a semiautomatic rifle. The
blood-red moon cast an eerie glow on the surroundings, illumi-
nating the towering trees of the exclusive Grove Redwood Forest.
Despite being in the virtual realm, he couldn't shake off the sense
of unease as he crept over dead leaves and scanned the area for
signs of danger.

Schroeder crouched behind a towering tree, its wide trunk
offering enough shade for three adults. Only three minutes left in
his weekly game with Schroeder and Stormykitten. Christian
peered through the gun's viewfinder, scanning the area for signs of
movement. Suddenly, a beep blared in his ear, and a profile box
materialized, seemingly rupturing the forest wall.

Against a massive redwood tree, a man with a static face
smiled at him. Christian blinked.

The face belonged to Dan, Christian's reliable and anxious
VIP client, who often pursued hair-brained schemes of noble
deeds to boost his public image as a funeral director. Those
lifestyles no longer existed, something he had reminded Dan of
several times already. He refocused on the game.

Two minutes left to go.

A bell rang out again. Dan.

Christian groaned and loosened his grip on the toy gun. "Answer, Dan," he said into the mic.

Living-breathing Dan popped up, his teeth digging into his finger. As soon as he noticed Christian, he flicked down his hand. "Today was meant to be my big day."

Christian lowered the gun. "What?" Through his headset's peephole, he glanced at the date on his watch face. Oh yes. Dan must be talking about the deed they had booked into SVT2 news, set to air during prime time. "Today *is* your big day."

Dan stepped in front of a blender filled with strawberries and white goop. "You haven't heard?"

"Heard what?"

"Switch on the news."

Thirty seconds left on the game clock.

Christian stepped back, his avatar mirroring his movement, and a dry leaf crunched in the virtual world. He couldn't even get in a full game before the world fell apart. "Give me a moment, Dan." He pressed the walkie-talkie. "Work's calling, guys. I'm afraid it's game over."

"But we almost won this time!" Schroeder poked his head out from behind the tree. "And in record time."

"Don't you have a court case to prepare?" Christian said.

"I should be doing some work, too," Stormykitten said.

After news spread about a player having a heart attack during the ultrarealistic combat game, Shock Warfare, they decided to move over to heart-friendlier virtual reality paintball. He and Schroeder had been playing for months when Stormy joined, and it occurred to Christian he had never asked Stormy what she did for a living in all that time. "What kind of work do you do?"

"Journalism."

"Oh." Christian wished he hadn't asked but clicked on

Stormy's profile anyway. The occupation line was blank. "Do you work for one of the British papers?"

She sucked in a sharp breath. "Not exactly. Maybe I'll tell you about it one day."

For the first time that he could remember, a cagey response succeeded in silencing him. "Intriguing. Okay! I'll catch up in another round."

Christian logged out of the game and pointed at the blue plus sign underneath Dan's face. A blank window popped up.

"I'm putting your window beside..." He air-dragged the windows side by side. "...SVT2 lunch hour news."

Lorelei Lindbergh stood in front of a black iron gate, her auburn hair whipped by the breeze. A plume of smoke sullied the summer sky above her.

Christian smirked. When you needed her, she was absent; when you didn't need her, she was in your face. He resized the screen, and the caption appeared.

Lorelei Lindberg reporting from Landström Estate.

An alarm rang through him, and he narrowed in on the smokey cloud on his AR screen. The time read 12:18 p.m. He'd been playing with Stormy and Schroeder for an hour, and Jacob had checked in with him from X hotel right before their game. The tension in his shoulders eased.

The Landström Society guys would stop at nothing to postpone the trial that would expose them, but Jacob was safe. "When did this supposed fire happen?"

"Supposed? The Estate got burned to a crispy strip of bacon last night," Dan said.

"It's Lorelei Lindbergh, queen of fake. Could be CGI footage for all we know."

"Looks real to me."

"Ten to one, it's CGI."

"Personally—" Dan's eyes moved rapid-fire—"that place should've been gone a long time ago," he said in a low voice.

Christian smiled, feeling the same, but he dared not voice it. Not in front of a client. The best course was the middle course. "I hear you, Dan, but Landström is the oldest club in the country."

"Is anyone even in that club anymore? Wait. Are you thinking of working with them?"

"I'm a lot of things, but I'm not insane."

"That's good to hear because everyone would hate you for it. I mean, I know their Q-score has skyrocketed since the fire, but it's all for show."

Christian's gut hardened. He shook his head, and his avatar reflected him. "Note: Check LS's Q-score."

"Who me?" Dan asked.

"Not you. Me."

"Oh." Dan draped his hand over the blender. "I haven't sent them any pity points. Let them sink, I say. They have no business existing." Dan froze. "This isn't being recorded, is it?"

"Everything said between us is confidential."

"Whew."

"But, I can't control who might be listening in," Christian cautioned.

A look of worry shadowed Dan's face. His blender motored into action, its grungy pitch drowned Dan's wheeze, and its blades pulverized his breakfast into a pink liquid.

Christian shifted his focus to the television screen.

It all began last night when rumors swirled around the Landström Society.

Lorelei Lindbergh's voice sounded resolute. He rubbed his

sweaty hands against his jeans. Karen. Jacob. The initiation. Karen had said she was worried Jacob would do something stupid. Jacob was persuadable. He shook his head. Nah, not Jacob. It would take more than a match to burn that place down, but this was a whopper rumor. Why hadn't Max called him? Christian needed space to assess what was real, and what wasn't. And Dan's face plastered all over his screen wasn't helping. He needed his AR glasses.

"Christian?" Dan's voice boomed. "You're a bit quiet."

Christian's breath caught in his throat, and his foot bumped into the coffee table. "I'm just taking it in," he said, zeroing in on Dan. "Hey, look at that." He drifted toward the kitchen in a stealthy move designed to prevent Dan's suspicions from perking up. "Just got a message from Alma over at Sverige Dagligen. Must be about your GD news item. I think it's best to reschedule, don't you?"

"I suppose."

Christian's outstretched fingers combed the cool marble countertop for his AR glasses. Empty. He drifted to the other side of the room.

"Hey, Christian. Your avatar's floating around the screen. You okay?"

He came to the bookshelf and pinched his glasses. "Looking for my diary so I can chat with Alma. Your story is too important to be canceled. I'll work it out. I should probably take her call now. Let's talk later, Dan."

He ripped off his gaming headset and switched on the flatscreen television, Lorelei's face in the box.

He snapped on his AR glasses and logged into his Nyström Image Architects account.

Dozens of messages crammed his inbox. Max had sent several about the Landström fire, and not one had he seen or heard. Where had he been? He groaned. Eating a juicy cheeseburger at

NY Bistro with Schroeder and watching football in 3D Cinemax. That's where. He covered his eyes with his hand.

Lorelei Lindbergh droned through the flatscreen's speakers.

Firefighters battled the blaze through the night and managed to salvage some artifacts. But Sweden's oldest and only gentleman's club, home to the Landström Society, hosts of royalty and dignitaries throughout its 300-year history, is now but a smoldering building of ash.

Unconfirmed reports indicate faulty wiring. Shortly, we will hear from the Society's spokesperson. Stay with us for developments.

Lightheaded, he stepped closer to the flatscreen. Lorelei Lindbergh, still outside the Estate's grounds, interviewed a firefighter, soot-stained creases around his eyes. That was real. Check. However, the building—all its charred wood and burning red bricks—remained hidden. He opened a browser window in his glasses. "Search for Landström Estate fire."

> BLAZE RAVAGED 300-YEAR NATIONAL TREASURE.
>
> LANDSTRÖM ESTATE BLAZE UNDER CONTROL.
>
> LANDSTRÖM SOCIETY RELIEVED NO ONE HURT.

His stomach churned. He had been out of the office for too long, talking to people who couldn't give him anything. He picked up the remote and clicked on the first article.

A pastel drawing of the Estate popped up, and underneath it, black text. His breath stalled. He clicked the next article.

Up popped a pastel-colored illustration of the Landström Estate. He clicked on the next article. The same.

A blip on the internet, perhaps? He scrolled down and read through the comments section.

Reader after reader protested the lack of authentic, real-time pictures; many trashed the Hall of Records.

He turned away from the screen. Having visited the Estate several times with his father, he knew the grounds well. He set the remote down. "I'll go see it for myself."

Disbelief lingered in him. The trial was in three days. Would the Landström Society have gone so far as to burn down their own beloved Estate? Anything was possible. If they knew that Jacob was the star witness to the upcoming trial, they'd create a fake fire and then pin it on Jacob. Anything to stop the trial. Anything. He lifted his glasses.

When the Q-score game started its testing phase, Jacob's mathematical prowess had noticed blips in the algorithm. He tracked them and analyzed the step-by-step anomalies. It took him months to see the pattern. He showed Christian how he traced the blips caused by a mathematical error. Only it wasn't an error. It was deliberate. That was the day the earth stood still.

Working together, they tracked down the source code developer—a member of the Landström Society.

Inadvertently, Jacob had discovered that the Landström Society had developed a mathematical formula that temporarily interrupted their own Q-scores algorithm and turned it into a type of assassin's shooting game that targeted people. Once the target succumbed to a cliff of doom, the Q-scores game reverted.

Christian had the original source code from his father, but he didn't know about the blip. The day Jacob discovered the blip, Christian could see that Landström intended to do far more than just play an assassin's game, and Jacob's blip discovery was the match that ignited the hydrogen-oxygen combo.

The trial needed to happen. It had to expose the Landström Society. People's lives were at stake, but that was just the start.

Early in the Q-score testing phase, Christian had seen innocent people destroyed—memories he locked away in the recesses
of his mind—like when an innocent family man was falsely
charged with murder. It had created a kind of PTSD in him.

He shook his head. It pushed him to use the Q-score source
code to create Octopus—his own propriety algorithm to protect
himself and his clients.

Some of his clients deserved punishment, sure, but picking
who to fix and who not to fix in a game rigged from the start
would complicate matters. He'd been using it in Quant PR to
mitigate the damage the assassin game caused ever since.

He glanced at his watch. Two p.m. He could make it up to the
Estate in an hour, but if he was going there, he'd make the hour-
long trip count.

Karen had said they wanted his algorithms. His propriety
algorithms. Maybe it was time to make them an offer. He reached
behind the back of his virtual reality games cabinet and soft-
pressed the wall panel.

A door slid open, revealing a narrow compartment locked by a
digital code containing a safe secured by a digital lock.

He punched in the nine-digit code.

The safe clicked open.

A black plastic device, no bigger than his index finger, lay
cushioned in electric blue velvet. It contained his older propriety
algorithms.

His fingers tingled as he lifted the RMD from the holding
bracket.

They wanted him to join them so they could get their hands on
his newer, up-to-date propriety algorithms—the only thing
blocking them from total control of the Q-score system. The up-
to-date algorithms, along with the Q-score source code, were in
safekeeping—a place no one would think to look—and he could

agree to temporarily work with them. This RMD would bring them to the table, and, most importantly, they'd leave Jacob alone.

He stuffed it into his pocket and pushed the wall panel back in place. First, he'd drop it off at the Landström Estate—a burning pile of ash or not—and then they'd come to the table.

Meanwhile, the trial would start, and Jacob would be the star witness. There was no stopping it. He laced up his thick-soled, steel-toed boots, and stood five inches taller in the world.

CHAPTER 8

CHRISTIAN GRIPPED THE WHEEL AND DROVE UP THE E4 TOWARD Upplands-Väsby, the location of the stately headquarters of the Landström Estate, carrying the remote memory device nestled deep inside his pocket. This leverage could turn Lindström's ire away from Jacob and onto him.

The car's silver bonnet beamed sun rays into his eyes. He flipped on his sunglasses.

An hour later, a haze blighted the sky, and the air began to smell like a bonfire gone wrong. Fire engines crammed along the edge of the country lane; their mud-caked tires were like Oreo cookies dripping in white chocolate. Police cars were stationed on the opposite side.

Tension pricked the surface of his skin. He slowed his car.

Up ahead, a security station stood at the entrance of the Landström Estate, Lorelei Lindbergh and her crew nowhere to be seen.

The guard popped up inside the security station and waved him over.

His engine purred to a halt, and he rolled down his window.

The acid smell of burned wood clawed his face.

The guard's his lips barely moved while his murmur trailed out through a slit in the plastic barrier. "This is private property."

"I'm from the Landström Society," Christian said, mirroring the guard. "I've come to look at the property and report back on its progress."

"Your ID."

Taking a gamble on whether his pass was still valid, Christian held his arm out the window.

The scanner beeped. "Christian Karlsson." The guard glanced at Christian and lowered the scanner. "Park just inside the gate. Walk up to the house from there."

"Yes, sir."

He rolled the window up.

The manor came into full view. Its royal yellow facade was stripped to nothing but damaged brick. He switched off the engine. The once elegant, Baroque mansion lay before him, and it teetered, at last, on a crippled foundation.

The Estate's iron gate jarred into motion, and he drove onto the gravel path. Christian couldn't help but remember his first visit to the estate when he was ten years old.

Christian and his father had entered the Landström Society Estate, the garden much the same today as it was back then. They were greeted by a much younger Viktor and Harald. Christian noticed that they looked at him as if he was already part of their group.

His father led the way as they walked through the grand hallways of the Estate, with paintings and sculptures lining the walls. The Estate had a rich history spanning over 300 years, and it showed in every detail of its grandeur.

As they walked, Christian heard snippets of conversation from the other members. They talked about something called the "Project," and how it was progressing smoothly. Christian didn't understand what they were referring to, but he could tell it was something important.

In a corner of the room, Christian's father engaged in a conversation with Viktor and Harald about business and the economy. Meanwhile, Christian observed the other members, who conversed in hushed tones about what seemed like secret matters.

He overheard one member say, "The Landström Society has been preparing for this for a long time. It's all coming together perfectly."

Another member replied, "Yes, and with the new blood, we'll be able to accelerate the Project."

Christian had no idea what they were talking about, but their words sent a chill down his spine. He began feeling ignored and out of place, like an outsider in this exclusive group.

As the evening wore on, Christian couldn't shake off the feeling that something was off about the Landström Society. He felt like he was being watched and judged, and he couldn't wait to leave.

When they finally left the Estate, Christian's father seemed pleased with the evening's events, but Christian couldn't help but feel uneasy. He couldn't shake off the feeling that the Landström Society was a secret and exclusive group, and he decided then that he wanted nothing to do with it.

A tear moistened his eyes. He had to get inside that building to drop off the RMD in the library, the room where knowledge was exchanged. He parked and walked up the path.

A heavy-set SOCO-suited man trampled over fire hoses and trundled toward him, an electronic notebook in hand. "Hold up!"

"I'm from the Landström Society." The lie rolled off his tongue with more finesse this time. "I've been asked to assess the situation and report back."

Up close, Christian could see bags layered under the heavy-set man's eyes.

"It's highly irregular to be here alone. We've barely had a chance—"

"If it were up to me, I'd have waited at least a week," Christian said.

Slate roof tiles crashed to the ground behind them. On instinct, they ducked.

"It's too dangerous."

"It won't take long."

Firefighters swarmed around them, every crew member laser-focused on the burned-out building that, no doubt, they had worked through the night to get under control.

The manager eyed Christian. "Everyone's busy. Give us one hour."

"You're overworked, and you don't need someone like me making extra demands on your overstretched crews. I don't need an escort."

He shook his head. "No way are you going inside. You shouldn't even be here. Stay away from the building."

"How long have you been working on it?"

"Since Monday."

That was the night Christian was with Jacob and Karen at White's. "But the news—" he said before cutting himself off. If he was from Landström, he'd have known. "But the news reported on it last night, which means you did a great job keeping it quiet. What's your avatar?"

The manager's radio scratched to life. "Johann, we need you here."

The SOCO-suited manager reached for his phone. "Landström Society sent you, did you say?" He shook the tablet; it brightened. "A quick signature, please."

Christian pressed his thumb to the screen.

"Dr. Smoke is my avatar." He inspected the thumbprint and

flipped the tablet closed. "You have an hour." He tossed Christian a face mask. "Find me before you leave."

Johann sloshed through a puddle and joined the crowd of fire-fighters, occupied by yet another crisis.

Heat surrounding him, Christian climbed blackened concrete steps.

A faint smell of burned flesh stung his nostrils.

He snapped the mask over his face and entered.

Carbon particles hung in the air like fruit flies. Smoke residue clustered like cobwebs on every surface. He treaded the warped ground and stepped over a smoldering beam.

He came to what used to be the library and knocked a charred stump out of the way. It disintegrated to black dust. A twine of fireproof fabric lined a deep hole in the ground—the compartment he was looking for was fully exposed.

He brushed aside ash floating in front of him and beamed his camera's light through the dark room.

Surprisingly, the antique floor porcelain vase still stood in the center of the library, looking like a white mermaid in an ocean of ash. They'd had it for decades. He nudged it with his foot.

It scraped against the floor, giving his foot little resistance. They'd notice their porcelain vase missing, and in its place would be the RMD.

He glanced at his watch. A few minutes more and Dr. Smoke would come looking for him.

He pulled off his jersey shirt and slipped it around the vase. Planting his feet firmly on the ground, he tucked the wrapped-up vase under his arm.

A metal clang echoed from within the vase. There was always something these guys were hiding, and in the most obvious places. He pulled out the RMD from his jeans pocket, marked with his initials.

The vase's base had left behind a perfect circle, preserving a patch of the shiny floorboards.

His mouth went dry. Once he dropped the RMD in that circle, the game was on. He could work with the most loathed Society in the country for a year, tops. It probably wouldn't be a full year because Landström Society would be exposed in court well before then. He dropped the digital drive.

It landed smack in the middle of the vase's burned outline.

He slid on his glasses. "Send Dr. Smoke a hundred points," he said into the mic.

A bell dinged, confirming the transfer. He highlighted the transfer on the leaderboard.

Now the Society would know he had been here.

The negotiation had begun.

HE CARRIED the vase out the door, the mask fluting against his nose, and hiked down the gravel path.

Firefighters crossed in front of him, their heads down.

Sweat dripped down the side of his face. He clicked open the trunk and tipped the vase. A small set of keys dropped out.

The smoldering Estate crackled behind him, as though it was alive. Those burned-out walls concealed more hidden compartments than anyone knew, a treasure trove of secrets.

He glanced at his watch. He'd been here long enough. The next best thing to a lengthy search for hidden compartments was the building's blueprints.

Next stop, the Hall of Records.

CHAPTER 9

STINE LOGGED BROKEN TABLETS AT THE RECEPTION COUNTER, huffing over how careless the public was at handling these tech machines. No one seemed to care that all the money to replace them would eventually come out of their taxpayer krone or Q-points if the opposition had their way.

The phone beside her sirened, ricocheting off the marble walls and stucco ceiling. Agnetha, her dutiful full-timer, rushed over and reached underneath the counter. "I'm afraid those records are inaccessible," she spoke into the receiver. "If you leave your name and number—" Agnetha stared at the receiver. "They cut me off."

"What do we expect?" Stine grumbled.

The phone blared again, along with the phone in Agnetha's pocket.

They stared at each other.

Stine switched on one of the salvaged tablets on the browse bar and searched for the latest headlines.

BLAZE RAVAGED 300-YEAR LANDSTRÖM
ESTATE NATIONAL TREASURE.

Stine cupped her face. Their records were blocked, a battle she had been fighting. Now, this.

"The public is going to go apeshit, Agnetha. Brace yourself."

Agnetha's face held the look of a frightened little rabbit in a dark forest. "What are we going to say?"

"The truth. Blame it on the Ministry of Interior; it's his fault."

The voices of two women trailed through the hall.

Stine slowly pivoted in their direction. One wore a sleeveless red top with matching nail varnish. The other was in a white safari shirt, jeans, and sneakers. Her wrinkled shirt looked thrown on.

"Can I help you?" Stine asked the duo.

"We're here to get records on the Landström Estate."

"What company do you work for?"

"SVT," Red Top said, her tone prideful.

Sweden's national broadcaster. "How come that doesn't surprise me," Stine said. "Send an email to the Ministry of Interior and tell him the records are blocked."

"That will take forever. We need records now."

Safari Shirt stepped up to the counter. "We could bring the cameras down here and report on the Hall of Records." Her singsong tone exuded sarcasm.

"Tell me," Stine said. "Who funds SVT?"

Safari-woman squinted. "What does that have to do with anything?"

"Who funds the Hall of Records?"

She tried to stare down Stine, but Stine straightened up taller. "Do you think the Minister of Interior would be happy with the Minister of Communications after such a broadcast?"

Safari-woman seemed to consider the scenario. "We are a free press, and government self-scrutiny is always healthy. Shows the government being impartial."

"Shows it, but is it?"

"That's a philosophical discussion."

"No, it's not."

Safari folded her arms.

Stine knew she was breaking the first rule of strategy—look forward and reason backward. Her responses were too knee-jerk, but she hadn't the time to consider the broad ramifications of the breaking news story. This runaround gave her a minute. She took a deep breath.

More people, media types, pushed through the door.

Conflict surrounded her.

What was the outcome she wanted? To get these people out of the Hall of Records immediately. What was the best way to get there?

She already knew conflict was inevitable. And she was already fed up. She flipped on the intercom. "All TV personnel, can you go to the right-hand side of the room."

Two stranded-looking people stood in the middle of the hall.

Stine covered the mic. "Agnetha, can you please attend to those members of the public," she said in a low voice.

Agnetha ushered them toward a browser bar terminal.

"The system is down, I'm afraid," Stine said. "If you come back tomorrow—"

Among the crowd, several voices erupted.

"You can't do this!"

"How come they get to stay?"

"Tomorrow?"

"Yes, tomorrow, or go online and make your requests."

Agnetha looked at Stine.

Shoveling in the bureaucracy problem would cinch the last cries. Stine hated using it, but these people weren't interested in the truth anyway. "While you're making your requests, consider emailing the Minister of Interior and let him know how irate you are."

The last visitor grumbled on his way out the door.

"They were using the Hall of Records for an extended coffee break, wouldn't you say, Agnetha?"

"Yeah, it looked like that to me. I swear I smelled booze on quite a few of them." Agnetha had a look of worry on her face. "Maybe we should warn the Minister of potential repercussions?"

"What do you mean?"

"Half those people were from the media. We could get blow-back. Bad reports."

Though Stine didn't want to admit it, Agnetha was right. She grabbed her entrance pass. "Forward calls to voicemail. I'm going to have a word with Harald."

Stine huffed down the passageway and up the stairs, thinking one thing: Harald's excuses had better be good.

STINE BURST into Harald's office.

The heavy door crashed against the wall. Harald bounced in his chair, his hand cradling his phone. "What's the meaning of this?"

How dare he ask *her* a question. She claimed the space near the dusty, musty, old man's bookshelves, smack in his line of sight —no room for excuses there—and pointed at her phone. "I'm sure you've seen this. Everyone has." She lowered the phone. "Except me."

A king to his throne, he lowered himself on his high-back leather chair and spoke into his phone in a low voice. "I'll call you back."

Slipping on a mask of calm, he laid the phone on his desk.

His stoic manner hammered her frustration into a white-hot missile. "We have a situation."

"Please close the door."

She paced the carpet. "We're holding back the tide out there, and you, you—"

"It's under control."

She halted midstride. The last time she was in this building, he had been out to lunch. "This isn't my idea of control. Why wasn't I told about this?"

A smug look spread across his face. "How was anyone supposed to predict this kind of breaking story?"

She slowly closed her eyes. "I'm not talking about the fire." She opened them just as slowly. "I'm talking about the blocked records."

"We didn't think—"

She took a step back. "Didn't think?"

"We didn't think it would disturb the flow of information."

His lack of foresight took the wind out of her. A twelve-year-old would've made better outcome calculations. She leaned in.

The silver name plate on his desk glinted in the light, as if to remind her she stood in front of an elected official, elected by the good people of Sweden.

She pulled back. "And I haven't been able to explain why the records are missing, to myself or anyone else."

He stood up. His gray hair, parted on the side, matched his characteristic three-piece suit. "We were caught unawares by the fire, as was the whole country."

"I'm not talking about the fire, Harald. We need access to those records. Tech is coming up empty." She sucked in her breath. "I am the public face of the Hall, and the Ministry, and this is no way to maintain the public's trust."

"If it's points you're worried about, we can replenish them."

She loathed the points system, but she was part of it, like everyone else. "No, well, yes, that too. But that's not—"

"The event caught us all unawares."

He may be old, but this man didn't look like the careless type.

"That's it? Overwhelmed? What am I supposed to tell people, the ones who are storming my bastille?"

He sighed. "Okay." He planted his knuckles on the desk. "The truth is, we were testing security measures, in case of an emergency, but the technology ended up sealing all the Estate records." He spoke without a twitch, without a blink. "We tested it on the Landström Estate archive, never once thinking something like this would happen. Please understand."

She admired his explanation, as much as she admired a liar. "That was good."

There was a light knock at the door.

"Come in."

A woman from Ulla's staff held the door ajar. "Ulla emailed you the press statement. It's ready for your approval."

"Can you cc that to me?" Stine said.

Harald nodded his agreement.

Stine's phone beeped.

Press Statement

The blaze at the Landström Estate is nothing short of a tragedy to one of Sweden's historic architectural treasures. Authorities are doing all they can to find evidence that can confirm the circumstances surrounding the blaze.

As far as we know, no one was harmed on the Estate. However, authorities, together with fire crews on the scene, are still trying to ascertain the cause of the fire. Due to the prevalence of CGI and other digital re-rendering products, they have requested all historical records on the Landström Estate be paused until further notice.

As soon as developments become known to us, The

Ministry of Interior will provide further information to the public.

"You should've given this to Agnetha to write," Stine said. "She'd have done a better job."

He straightened his back. "That'll do," Harald said to the assistant.

He signed the document with a thumbprint and handed the tablet back. "Email this to all of the news outlets." He turned to Stine. "That should slow the calls down while we wait for the official fire report."

Stine scanned the deep red carpet. He seemed too calm for a full-blown crisis, but maybe that's exactly what this crisis needed. Calm. She nodded. "I'll work into the next shift. Want to make sure we do it right," she said.

"I'll get points sent to you."

The door closed with a soft click.

ON HER WAY back to the Hall of Records, Stine's phone buzzed. It wasn't Bjorn. He still hadn't called. Frustration mounted inside her. "Hi, Agnetha. I'm on my way."

"A patron wants to talk to you," Agnetha said. "He's also looking for records on the Landström Estate."

"Have him fill out a form like everyone else."

"He wants to talk to the boss."

Stine pursed her lips. "Two minutes."

She drew in a deep breath and strode toward the double doors, pushing down her frustration. The double doors swung behind her.

She halted.

A man stood in the empty hall, but even with his back to her, she'd know him anywhere. His wavy hair, broad shoulders, fingers tapping the digital browse bar. There he was. The one and only Christian Karlsson.

She had dreamed of a day like this, one where he'd show up and tell her he'd made a horrible mistake. That they'd had something special, then promptly drop to his knees and beg her forgiveness. Six years too late wasn't going to cut it, and she'd be damned if she'd let him see her rattled. She tugged on her blouse and stepped into the Hall. Her heels clacked in a measured tone against the marble floor.

He turned and locked eyes on her. "Stine?" his voice wavered.

Doubly good. She stood in front of him. "Christian. Fancy seeing you here."

His cheeks burned crimson. "I thought you went back to Copenhagen."

She never expected to be here either. "Clearly, I stayed. What brings you in?"

A film of sweat glistened on his forehead. "The Landström Estate. I'm doing work on it, but the records seem—"

"Since when did you start working on buildings?"

"I just want the blueprints; surely the Hall can provide that record."

She noted his defensive tone. Protective manner. He was hiding something; it didn't take a spy to see that. On top of it all, he lied about everything. It wasn't even unusual for him. Sure, lies were normal. People lied to conceal, to protect, sometimes both. The question was, why? And who was *he* protecting? Himself or someone else? "I thought you worked for some PR firm."

"It's for a client."

She tucked her hair behind her ear. "You're working for Landström Society?"

He shook his head. "Someone else. I can't disclose."

Stine tilted a browser bar's screen in her direction. "What records do you require, precisely?"

"I need the history of the property, who owned it, blueprints, that sort of thing."

She typed in her personal ID, one finger keystroke at a time, and pressed enter. The main database popped up.

A red and white No Enter sign appeared, the same colors as her country's flag, and this time it brought with it a longing to go back home. "I'm afraid your access is denied, Christian."

He shook his head, short and sharp. "Or maybe you mistyped."

A wave of nausea swept through her. His dig resurrected painful memories she had long buried. Living with him had been like living under KGB surveillance. Nothing she did was ever correct. "Nothing's changed, has it?"

He stepped back and folded his hands. "I just want to get information, and I'll be gone."

She lowered her hands away from the keyboard. "It'll take time."

"How long?"

"As long as it takes."

He shook his head. "I can't believe you're working here. You weren't the most organized person. What, with all your bizarre conspiracy theories pinned on the wall. Our wall." His gaze swept the walls inside the Hall.

Agnetha sailed up to the browse bar behind Christian, dust rag in hand.

Agnetha never dusted the marble table tops, but there she was. Where she found that rag was anyone's guess.

"I grew up," Stine said in a raised voice loud enough for Agnetha to hear. "People change, Christian. But perhaps not in your case. You're as arrogant as ever."

His glasses in his shirt pocket chimed. He turned his back to her and propped his glasses over his eyes.

Apart from that tiny bit of dried-up sweat on his forehead, had it not occurred to him he had wronged *her*? Maybe he forgot about it all; conveniently suppressed it. She couldn't believe she used to love this guy. Used to love him. Henrik was a God in comparison.

"Does Torn know you called me?" Christian said to the person on the line. "I know where they are; no need to send me the address. I'll be back in the office and update you. Don't tell Torn anything until I get there."

He turned back around, his face tight. He shoved his glasses into his pocket.

"I see you're in a rush," she said. "Leave your number, and my assistant will contact you when the records open up."

"So they were closed, and you knew it." He lifted his glasses halfway out of his pocket and spoke into the mic. "Send Christine Poulsen at the Hall of Records my contact number. Expire it in thirty days." He dropped his glasses back down. "Shouldn't take longer than that for the Hall of Records to sort itself out, right?"

She lifted her chin. "The Minister of Interior will make sure of it."

He shoved open the exit doors and disappeared like a mirage in the desert heat.

Agnetha sidled up to Stine. "An old boyfriend?"

Stine sucked in her breath. "He isn't as good-looking as he used to be."

"If he's free—"

"He's all yours." Stine glanced at Agnetha. "I'm going to go see Henrik. We need to sort this shit out."

CHAPTER 10

CHRISTIAN STOOD IN FRONT OF A GRAY HIGH-RISE AND STARED AT the neon yellow letter X lit by one bare bulb, as if staring at it would make it go away. He needed to get inside those concrete walls, but his legs held firm to the pavement, a what-now weighing him down over what he might find behind the windows. The X flickered above the revolving door.

The heat of the summer air crawled across his skin. He had booked Room 1005, a safe haven, for Karen and Jacob, and he couldn't imagine why they needed to see him now, a day before trial.

His AR glasses buzzed. It was Stormykitten. He swiped the call away and pushed against the revolving door.

At the bank of elevators, he pressed the call button. The button stiffened.

The queue at the reservation desk—the dispenser of activation passes for the elevators—was a dozen people long. Standing in that queue would take more time than if he just climbed the ten flights. He pushed the doors open to the stairwell.

Legs aching and breathless, he stood in front of Room 1005 and knocked.

Quickened footsteps bled through the door. Karen cracked open the door, and her frazzled curls fanned her face. She wore a white T-shirt and ripped jeans.

"What's going on? Where's Jacob?"

"Thank God you're here." She swung the door open. "Jacob's inside."

Parking a multitude of questions at the door, he followed her swift steps past the sofa and into the bedroom. He treaded the beige carpet, every step chilling his spine. Jacob was nowhere in sight.

A bird swept past the open window, and a warm breeze brushed his cheek.

His blood galloped into his heart. That window was meant to be sealed. He stepped back. "What's going on here, Karen? If I don't get an explanation now, I'm out of here."

"Christian?"

Jacob's voice trailed inside the room with the warm air current.

"He stole a key from one of the housekeepers," Karen said in a low voice.

Christian inched closer to the open window, to Jacob's heavy breathing, and to the dreadful twenty-foot drop.

The fabric on Jacob's pant leg trembled.

Christian felt like a boulder weighed down his feet, but his body was so light he could fly. One unexpected move, and Jacob could fall. "It's me, buddy. What are you doing?"

"I needed to tell you—" Jacob's voice cracked.

Untrained for this sort of crisis, the best Christian could do was go along with Jacob's story and get him off that ledge. "Tell me inside."

"No point. I'm done."

"Nothing's this bad," Christian said. "No matter what you've done, no matter how bad you think it is, it can always be fixed."

"There's no fixing anything. Not this time."

On the other side of the room, Karen leaned against the wall, her black mascara streaking her cheeks.

"Have you called the police?"

She shook her head. "Couldn't risk it."

Christian wrestled back his tone. "Call them now."

She stared at him.

"What the hell is wrong with you? Call the police."

She scuttled out of the room.

He turned back to the open window. "Remember when I had that accident?" His attention drifted back to that time, rousing dark emotions. "You were with me the whole time. Of course, you remember."

Jacob nodded.

"My dad was in a state. I thought I was done, remember that?"

"You were a mess."

"Yeah, thought my life was over. Started drinking like my life depended on it. You were there for me through all of it. And the day I was cleared of reckless driving charges, and it all got sorted, you were there for me too. Take it from me; whatever the problem is, together, we can fix it."

"I did it, Christian," Jacob said. "I burned down the Landström Estate."

A chill spiraled through him. "Doesn't matter, Jacob. I'll fix it."

Karen's footsteps pattered in behind him.

"I'm done, Christian. Not even you can fix this."

Christian rubbed his mouth. "I went to the Estate, Jacob. I saw it. It would take more than a match to burn that place down. You couldn't have. I know you."

"People died, Christian. People died in the fire. I'm going to be charged with murder. There's no getting out of it. I'm as good as dead. Yeah, Christian. I burned it down. We're free. All of us are free."

Christian's mind skipped. He could barely move his lips. "What do you mean? We're not involved in the Landström Society. We're just going to trial to expose them for rigging the Q-scores. There is no way you could have burned down their Estate single-handedly. Come back inside."

"I didn't want to do it, but I had to do it. I had no choice." Jacob's trousers shook on the ledge. "Aren't you listening, Christian?" he said, a tone of desperation in his voice.

"Every word, my friend, every word." Christian tensed. "There haven't been any names on the feeds, or anything like that, and even if your name came out, you know it's manageable. I'll do whatever it takes to keep you safe, Jacob. Haven't I done that since our school days?"

Jacob sobbed. "Someone found out, and I panicked."

"You're talking to the person who can fix the problem," Christian said. His throat hitched, and his own desperation grew like a weed with every minute Jacob dangled on the edge of life. "Everyone has secrets, and no one has to know yours. Come inside and tell me what someone found out. We can go talk to them."

"Everyone's owned. Everyone. We're all pawns."

Anger sparked inside Christian. "I am not a pawn."

A bird squawked past.

"I tried, Christian. I really did."

"Try harder!"

"You're free, Christian. I'm sorry. Don't worry about me anymore."

"You're not going anywhere, Jacob. We need you. Karen, and I need you." Christian's heart softened his breath. "If you go, I don't know what I'll become."

"Just remember who you are, Christian. Never a pawn."

A gust blew through the window, and Jacob's sobs flew into the wind.

CHRISTIAN'S WORLD WENT WHITE.

The sound of a heavy thump echoed, and a high-pitched scream screeched through Stockholm.

Karen cradled herself, a tight ball on the floor, weeping.

He crouched down and lay next to her, his mind frozen. He didn't look for reasons, or fixes, or solutions. There were none. Sobs pelted him, beating power out of him, and his sorrow-filled wails were the sound of a broken-hearted man.

Through tear-filled eyes, he looked at Karen.

A stamp-sized tattoo, fresh red around its black edges, engraved her skin. A black cube. The Landström Estate had marked her.

A white-hot flame lit inside him and splintered his world. "What have you done, Karen?"

Her body shivering on the carpet, she wept louder.

He shoved her against the wall. It didn't matter what she said. They took Jacob. They might not have pushed him or held a gun to his head, but it was all the same. They took Jacob, and she was part of it.

His glasses vibrated against his chest.

Someone knew. Someone must have seen him come here. It had to be them.

A knot formed in his gut. Never again. Never again. For everything they had taken from him, he would make them pay. Each day would bring the Landström Society closer to destruction.

He sank into a dark stillness, letting it bury a part of him. Out from the void, a mountain of doom formed in his mind.

CHAPTER 11

Inside the Comms Hub, Kelly Blackwell gulped down air and her eyes shot open. Sweat dripped down her forehead.

"You all right?" Harry White handed her a pint glass filled with water. "You were out for a couple of hours there. I was getting worried."

She pushed against the armrest of the reclined leather chair, but her sweaty palms failed to grip.

"Take it easy," Harry said, bringing the glass closer.

She guzzled the water down in one take and exhaled. "You know our guy Christian Karlsson, the one I'm playing the paintball shooter game with?"

"Yeah, the one with the bio-device." Harry filled up the glass with fresh water. "You've been tracking him for a while now."

"I'm not sure what the hell happened. His heartbeat was racing, and then suddenly I plummeted. Next thing I know, I got sucked into a memory storage device."

"How did that happen?"

She shook her head. "I have no idea. All I could see in this vast white space was old, incomplete code."

"This is getting too dangerous for you. The last time you took on a code…you don't want to do that again."

"It wasn't a virus this time."

"What kind of code?"

She shrugged. "I didn't have a chance to record it. Next thing I know, I could hear a couple of men talking about bringing Christian in."

"Was it a police station?"

She wiped her forehead. "They didn't sound like police officers to me. These men's voices sounded deliberate and older, and they spoke formally, like last century formal. They spoke Swedish, and my bot translated." She took a sip of water. "One of them ordered someone else to destroy the storage device." She looked at Harry. "I was inside it when it started getting erased."

"Holy shit."

"Somehow, my mind-bot jumped back into his bio-device." She held her stomach. "I tried to log into Christian's AR glasses, but he had them switched off. It all happened so quickly."

Harry's mouth hung open, his eyes wide.

She licked her lips. I don't know him very well, just played a few games, as you know. We don't say much during the game, but he shoots well, and he has excellent strategies."

Harry closed his mouth. "What are you going to do?"

She lifted herself from the chair, and the room swirled. She gripped her head.

"Give yourself time to adjust," Harry said, guiding her to lean back on the recline.

"I can't do this remotely anymore," she said, holding her head in her hands. "I nearly got erased."

"I agree. You going to give it up, then? Wait for him to contact you?"

Unblinking, she probed Harry's face. "Since when have I ever given up?" She sat up and let her feet hit the solid ground. "For whatever reason, I contacted him, or my bot connected with him, and I've got to see this through."

Harry grinned and gave her a cheesy wink. "So, what're we doing, boss?"

She exhaled and pushed herself off the chair. "Get me on the next plane to Stockholm. By the time I land, I'd like my bot to have Christian's home address, all info you can find on the Landström Society, and a map of Stockholm. Then, call the PM to get me onto the MI5 contacts list. I'll need free access to on-the-ground surveillance equipment. Lots of it. I'll download it all when I land on Swedish soil."

"They're going to ask what mission this is for," Harry said.

Kelly stopped pacing. "Give me a minute."

Her bot travelled across the Thames River, entered the MI5 building, located the C room, and unlocked the live operation files. It scanned all of them until it identified one related to Scandinavia. "Found it. A bit old, but still active." She turned to Harry. "Tell them it's for Operation Dovetail."

"It's so cool you can do that."

She shrugged. "I don't like to scan MI5, that place is murky, but when needs must."

Harry slapped the table. "You'll have your downloadables by the time your plane hits the tarmac."

CHAPTER 12

"HARALD, MR. WE-HAVE-IT-UNDER-CONTROL. BJORN, MR. Missing-In-Action. Hm!" Stine slammed down the phone on her kitchen table. "It's my neck on the line!"

She kicked the kitchen table's steel leg. The whole thing stank, and she seemed to be the only one smelling it. No information, no data, not from Harald, not from Bjorn. At least Henrik was trying.

If no one else could do their jobs, she'd just have to do hers for all of them. She snapped on the television.

An advert for laundry detergent drowned out the chatter in her head while she brushed her teeth. She spat toothpaste into the bathroom sink and watched the pink foam wash down the drain, along with her last bit of irritation.

She poured stale coffee into a used mug and sat in front of her laptop. Movement was underway, and she'd be damned if they were going to leave her out in the cold. She scrolled through the news and stopped at the Sverige Dagligen's front page, the worst page because it gave meaning to the cliché, *on the same page*. Its purpose was to give the public a homogenized overview of current events, and it gave her nausea.

She selected the news features menu and landed on a one-thousand-word article. The lengthy pieces, designed to put the public to sleep, tended to contain intel messages in the lower paragraphs—intel updates on confidential operations so well hidden in the text not even the insomniacs noticed. She book-marked it and moved on.

She came to page ten, the Extras section, and an innocent-looking paragraph, loaded with numbers, repetitive words and phrases, caught her attention. She moved closer to the screen. If the black hats were operating clandestinely again, they communicated in the Extras section. She zeroed in on one snippet:

Midsummer Preparations

In recent weeks, there has been an unusually high amount of luggage left in storage at Arlanda International Airport. Now that Midsummer is upon us, more tourists will be passing through starting on 6 June, for the Midsummer celebrations. If you are one of those travelers, keep your Bjorn Bag or Louis Vuitton Suitcase safe and by your side at all times, or it will be collected by the authorities and possibly discarded. For extra security, visitors should tag their items with their names and addresses and store their luggage at the left luggage in Terminal 5 on level two for a small fee.

Stine sat back in her chair. Had it not been for several signs, she might've overlooked it. For one, it mislead the average reader into thinking that luggage holding facilities could only be located in Terminal 5 on level two. This was simply not true. Arlanda International housed luggage storage facilities on all levels. Levels tended to refer to bureaucracy, there being several levels. The top level, the Prime Minister himself, was Level Five.

Her skin tingled. Could the Prime Minister be involved? She scratched her jaw and refocused.

The snippet named Arlanda Airport—usually a drop location —but it could also mean travel, movement, flights, international connections, someone arriving, and someone else departing.

Midsummer could be read as the national holiday, but that was too obvious. It could be a deadline or the time of day an operation was meant to begin. Since Midsummer was mentioned three times, it was most significant. Arlanda was mentioned twice.

The hierarchy of importance was set, and she wrote:

Timing: 6 June 2032
Place: Arlanda Airport, level 2
Purpose: Prime Minister?

She looked at the section again. The biggest sign of all, the one that made her take notice, was the name, Bjorn. Her intel agency boss.

She wrote:

Timing: 6 June 2032
Place: Arlanda Airport, level 2
Purpose: Bjorn would arrive at 5 p.m. to pick up
the package from location 5 on level 2, something
having to do with the PM

But she wasn't sure. The decode didn't feel complete.

She tossed the pen and stretched her arms. Being desk-strapped in the Hall of Records for the last three years had rusted her ground surveillance skills. Worse, her crazy wall skills were downright withered. Her last complete crazy wall, the one where she cracked the code on the Olaf Palmer assassination, was when she was dating what's-his-face. That's probably why he left her, the bastard.

She opened her living room window, and the fresh air cooled her cheeks. There was only one way to get moving. That was to get moving. She shuffled into her slippers and made her way down the staircase to the basement.

She came to her assigned storage section and switched on the light.

Dusty plastic bags packed the single metal shelf. The bottom shelf held a box of corkboard squares and a toolbox. She finger-hooked the plastic bags and made her way up the stairs, carrying what she could.

Two trips up and down the stairs later, she shut the door and dusted her hands off. Her old conspiracy days were back. She smiled, grabbed a glass of wine, and dialed in a radio station playing rock music.

She took a sip of wine and opened the toolbox.

Red strings, pins, and multicolored pens.

One by one, she laid the tools on the floor. Her brain crackled with clues she'd gathered over the last few days. Ready to begin, she grabbed a sheet of paper and a black pen, and wrote down the first clue:

Minister of Interior
Harald.

Henrik. Bjorn. Archives. Missing Records. Dates. Times, and every factual bit of information she could remember got its dedicated sheet. She pinned them randomly on the wall.

With all clues pinned to the corkboard, she sipped more wine. It dripped onto her chin.

There was one last clue that nipped around the edge of her mind. She wiped her chin and grabbed the largest sheet of paper. In black marker and capital letters, she wrote PRIME MINISTER and pinned the sheet to the top of the board. She twirled the ball of red string.

"It's too soon to make connections, but what would Bjorn say? Start with who has the most power."

Somehow, her thoughts drifted to Christian, her personal button-pusher, and she brushed the intruding thought aside. She stood back and stared at her wall. "For a girl out of practice, not bad. Not bad at all."

Eventually, the clues would fall into place. For now, all she had to do was wait like a tiger in the bush.

CHAPTER 13

A WEEK OF CHRISTIAN'S LIFE SLIPPED BY SINCE JACOB'S PASSING. Nothing existed powerful enough to hold back the magnitude of loss spiraling inside of him. So, night after night, struggling to come to terms with what, how, and why Jacob's death had happened, he spent hours circling Stockholm in the back seat of a taxi, a bottle of schnapps in hand, filling up the dark. During these late night drives, he watched people under the city lights get on with their simple lives, and it soothed his heart and occupied his blurry mind.

Tonight was different, though. He had received a private, handwritten electronic message from the lead lawyer in the Nationalbanken trial that said:

> The trial has been suspended due to the untimely death of Jacob Rasmussen, the star witness...

It was over.

The words erupted in Christian's mind for the hundredth time, and his whole being bubbled like molten lava.

Christian's AR glasses buzzed against his chest. For a moment, he considered answering it. But talking to yet another client, a distraction, and spewing words that sounded as though he could fix their problem was doing him more harm than good.

He stared into the night sky, resuming his fantasies of death and destruction on the faceless Landström Society members caught and cornered by Octopus, crushed and cleaned by online vultures; the entire Landström Society demolished until there was not a whisper, not a soul.

The news of Jacob's death, confirmed officially by police, had engulfed social media, and he let it because there was something bigger he faced: the hole in his heart Jacob's passing left behind.

A news bulletin blared through the taxi's speakers:

IT IS NOW BELIEVED THAT ARSON MIGHT
BE A FACTOR IN THE FIRE AT THE
LANDSTRÖM ESTATE, THE FIRE CHIEF HAS
STATED. WE'LL BRING YOU THE LATEST
WHEN WE KNOW MORE.

Sickness swirled around Christian. He could almost feel the raging lava backing up, getting ready to turn on him and devour him whole. He opened the backseat window.

Air blew against his face, drying the sweat from his forehead.

It brought with it a fresh strategy.

He closed his eyes. An online reputation problem was too basic a punishment for the Society. It was better to pin Jacob's death on them. Direct and to the point. He inclined to the taxi driver. "Take me to Sveavägen."

Twenty minutes later, he walked onto Nyström's floor.

Max stood up from his chair. "Where've you been?"

Christian clutched his glasses. Unable to mouth the harsh words—Jacob died—because saying it would unleash... he'd rather not know. "Jacob Rasmussen..." he managed to say.

He clicked on the shared display.

"Who was his club?" Max asked.

"The Landström Society, sort of."

Max slow-lowered himself into his chair. "What do you mean sort of?"

Christian shook his head.

"Why did he get involved with them in the first place?" Max asked. "For all we know, he burned the Estate down himself."

Christian shot a fierce look at Max. "Don't ever say that again."

Max's chair hit the edge of the desk. "What? I don't understand."

"I'm going to redirect all the rumors to The Landström Estate," Christian fired off.

Max rolled forward and planted himself next to Christian. "Hold on. What are you about to do?"

Christian fired up the Octopus icon on the shared display. "I doubt anyone in the Landström Society would even notice. They probably haven't seen a computer their whole lives."

Max's eyes widened. "I know you're in shock, you're angry, but you'll regret it if you press that button."

The need to destroy everything pulsed through Christian's finger, his throat, his whole body.

"We have no proof it was them," Max pleaded. "If you press Octopus, you'll destroy this firm. Do you want that? What about all of us here?"

Christian lasered in on the Octopus icon. The anger, trapped inside him, begged for escape. His body shook, but the echo of Max's words of reason reached him like a soft, cool hand, tempering him.

His eyes softened, and he could see the edges of the display screen. If he set Octopus into action, he'd destroy not just the Landström Society, his only actual target, but also everyone here at Nyström. Society members would seek out the culprit before he even had a chance of running for shelter. Then they'd win. He blinked back tears.

The RMD at the burned-out Landström Estate was still in play, he thought. He stepped back from the screen.

Max exhaled. "We'll figure something out."

Christian cradled his head.

"Christian." Yolanda's voice came out of nowhere. "Torn wants to see you."

"I'll talk to him later."

"He said—"

He shot her a sharp look. "I can't right now!"

He stormed off the floor and sought shelter between the private bathroom walls.

He heaved, but he came up empty, and his stomach cramped. The pain weakened his knees, and he spat into the sink.

Tepid tap water cleansed his tongue and cooled his trapped heat.

A man in the mirror stared at him, his eyes sunken discs, his face stone. He barely recognized himself.

There were other ways to destroy them, ways that would take time. He could take pleasure in exploiting their weaknesses. For Jacob. For his father. For his own satisfaction. This man staring back at him, he knew, would find a way to plunge the Landström Society into chaos. Come what may. He wiped his face.

Torn crashed into the bathroom and stood back.

Christian shut off the water and yanked a towel off the rail.

"I got a call from a journalist this morning," Torn said. "Were you with Jacob Rasmusson when it happened?"

A chill went down Christian's spine. "Yeah."

Torn rubbed the back of his neck. "It could be a problem."

Christian dabbed his jaw with the towel. "Which vulture was it?"

"Who else."

Christian's blood pressure rose. "Lindbergh. I have her number. I'll handle it."

Torn shook his head, his face the look of a worried man. "We might have to suspend you until all this is cleared up."

Anger whirled through Christian, reigniting his fantasies. Too many people were holding him back, pinning him down. He had to find out who was behind Jacob's death and expose Landström Society that way. The only way to get that done was to get inside Landström itself. He wiped his forehead.

The RMD containing his old algorithms was still in play, and Landström must've received them by now. A week was just the right amount of time to prepare for their call, a week and a bucketload of Q-points. He placed the damp towel next to the sink.

The new plan reset in his mind and all his righteous rage gathered itself. "Good idea," Christian said. "A week should do it."

Torn nodded quietly, and his brow creased.

Justice and peace shuffled in and dampened the fire inside Christian, but only for an intermittent second.

CHAPTER 14

CHRISTIAN CLOSED THE LAUNDRY ROOM'S DOOR, CLUTCHING AN empty clothes basket. He tucked it under his arm, balanced it against his hip, and began the climb out of the basement.

His watch rang, and the sound bounced off the stairwell's brick walls. He paused on the step. It could be Landström. It had been a couple of weeks since he dropped the algorithms at the burned out Estate, but he still heard nothing from them. He squeezed the basket tighter against his hip and looked at his lit-up watch.

It was his club.

He breathed deep, put the basket down, and pressed accept. "Hey, Ulrich," he said, forcing himself to sound brighter than he felt.

"Have you checked your points?" Ulrich said.

"This morning." He tucked in his chin. "Is it urgent? I'm doing laundry."

"Quite."

"Give me a moment."

He raced up the second flight of stairs, dropped the basket, and flipped on his AR glasses. He logged into the Q-score leader-board. His points had dropped by 90,000 from this morning.

He tensed. How did that happen? Didn't matter right now. One big rumor would blow him right down the ladder. "I'll get on it."

"Your associations with that Society," Ulrich said, "are getting out."

"What associations?"

"That you might be working with the Society because of the fire."

Dan! Had to be that blabbermouth Dan who couldn't keep his mouth shut. "I'm not working for them," Christian said. "Nor do I intend to work for them. Ever."

"We've tried to counter the rumors, but it's not working. I'm afraid I'm going to have to warn you. This is the second warning. I don't want to call you again."

"What do you mean?"

"Third time, and we'll have to suspend your membership."

Urgency mounted inside Christian, building in him like a tidal wave. The RMD he had left inside the Estate hadn't baited Land-ström, as he expected it would. Maybe the firefighters tossed it or disregarded it—likely given the lax security around the Estate. He still needed to get inside the Society. Plus, he needed to save his own ass online. Now. "My membership will remain, Ulrich. I'll sort it out."

He closed the line and rushed to the kitchen. He logged onto his vitals hub and typed his name into the Player Spotlight search bar.

His name appeared alongside the Landström Society in dozens of posts, just as Ulrich had said. Then he came to a photo of him coming out of the Landström Society's Meeting House in Central Stockholm.

Christian slumped on the chair. That meeting happened what

felt like ages ago. Who was releasing photos of him coming out of that Meeting House now? "Who else could it be?" he mumbled, knowingly.

But vultures were vultures and they were pouncing, and he needed to clean up. Fastest way to contain them was to admit a little something because a basic admission tended to hack speculation. His fingertips sprinted across the keyboard:

**So what? Aren't people allowed
to have meetings in this city?**

He read it softly to himself. It was too simple. It had too much food for the vultures. They'd latch onto his *so what* and run with it. Lesson 101 in vulture management: you don't write to the vultures. You send a message to the audience. He tapped on the table. He could turn this minor crisis into an opportunity to get Landström to pay attention. He deleted the draft and started again:

**Yes, I met with the Landström Society.
There's no crime in that.
Everyone deserves to be heard.
I was there on behalf of a client.
That is all.**

He dropped back. They'd sniff his irritation, and he'd be in dcfcnsc mode for the next three days. Fed up with overthinking, he opened a fresh post and typed the first words that came to mind:

**Fuck off.
And you can tell that to Landström Society too.**

Fire lit in his belly. The post would get attention, especially

Landström's, and that's what he wanted, but it also risked him being blown down to Tier 2. He glanced at his points. He had enough spending points to get back to Tier 1.

A wave of energy surged through him. He stared at the simple demand. It would also get Ulrich's attention, and he'd be kicked out of his club as soon as he pressed send. To pull this off, he needed backup. He pulled away from the send key.

Max and the team were real people with real accounts and real addresses. Not like most of the vultures. If the vultures attacked him, and surely they would, he and the team had a case of gang warfare. He could then report the vultures for online assault, and the police could track the assailants. If the vultures were indeed people, and not AI bots, he could find their identities and prosecute for...he wasn't sure what...but the threat felt good.

If they turned out to be bots, he had no recourse. Bots weren't human, but the police could track the people behind the bots and shut them down. Within twenty-four hours, this entire mess would be mopped up. Sure, he'd be kicked out of his club, but as soon as his points climbed, Ulrich would be back.

More importantly, someone from Landström would come knocking. He needed Max and the gang onboard.

He opened a new window, attached the link of his draft post to Max, and pressed send. He grabbed a coffee, giving Max a few minutes to see it.

Fifteen minutes later, he dialed Max.

Max's voice mmm'd down the line. "No one will have sympathy with what you just wrote."

"I only need twenty-four hours. Back me up. Tell the team. I'll deposit 500,000 points to hire extras who can help. In the meantime, put Octopus program 2 into action, and swap me with Ulrich Persson."

"Isn't he in your club?"

"Yes. But program 2 won't hurt Ulrich. Just replace my avatar with his for the next twenty-four hours—he has plenty of good deeds to go around, plenty—and let O2 do its thing. He won't get hurt. He's a Tier 1, thanks to me. As soon as his points materialize on my Q-score, pull O2, and Ulrich will return to normal. Nothing lost."

"But nothing gained either," Max said.

Christian knew Ulrich didn't deserve to be a T1, but Max could never know. Ulrich was one of those clients who deserved to be a T2 at best. "Nothing lost," Christian reiterated. "Ulrich is the head of the best good deeds club in the country. He's a busy man with many good deeds in the pipeline."

"I'll get on it," Max said.

Within half an hour, Max and the team's posts appeared on the vitals feed:

Snapshot25: Wish I could say that.
A man can't have a basic meeting in peace anymore.

KatMeowRina: Finally! Someone is standing up
to these negative people!

Christian's points on the Q-score leaderboard stopped bleeding.

His watch rang.

The call displayed an unknown caller ID.

For the phone troll, he readied his fiercest voice and pressed the green call-accept button.

"Christian Karlsson?"

"Who's this?"

"Transferring you to Viktor Hansson now."

Confused, he squelched his urge to yell.

"Thanks for taking the call," Viktor said.

Christian's belly tightened. Though he had been aiming for

someone at Landström to call him for weeks now, he couldn't steady his nerves. "What's this about, Viktor?"

"We've been contemplating our online reputation, what with the fire and your comment today. None of it is doing us any favors. I think it's time we try to rectify the situation."

"You're calling me to fix your reputation?" Christian heard his own sarcasm, and he didn't care. So this was how they'd play the game. "Today is my laundry day."

Viktor cleared his throat. "Not only that. I recognize we also need to repair our relationship with you."

"Why? I'm not in the club. Who cares?"

"You're a Tier 1 person with lots of clout. And a former member."

"Former honorary member, correct."

"Let's meet," Viktor said.

Unease circled around Christian.

"We have mutual interests to discuss," Viktor added.

Rarely were they this forthcoming, least of all Viktor. "I have nothing to gain by meeting you," Christian said.

"We know you were close to Jacob Rasmussen, and his untimely death must've shaken you. He was an initiate of the Society, as you know, and as with all good societies, we look out for our own. We hunted down the people who messed with Jacob."

"What do you mean, messed with?"

"His harassers. We hunted them down, and the punishment is coming to them. They're the reason for his untimely death."

Christian narrowed his focus. Viktor didn't mention the RMD containing the algorithms at all. "You can go after them yourselves. You're very capable. Why do you want me involved?"

"Come on, Christian. This isn't the sort of thing we can discuss over the line. We need to meet in person. You know that."

His skin spiked as if needles bore into several dermal layers.

The trial was dead, but getting justice for Jacob and getting inside Landström was the new game, he reminded himself. He scratched his itchy scalp and crossed his arms over his chest. "This is about Jacob, and only Jacob. Agreed?"

Viktor's silence affirmed.

The Jacob incident had pounded Christian's nerves into thin wires, so if his instincts were screaming inside him, he couldn't feel them. But if there was a chance at finding out who was behind Jacob's demise, he couldn't pass it up. "Shall we meet at the Meeting House?" Christian said.

"Naturally."

Christian closed the line and logged into his Nyström account. He transferred 500,000 points from his Q-scores account, the currency Max needed to bring him back into Tier 1. His reputation, his Tier, justice for Jacob—all would be sewn up by the end of next week.

CHAPTER 15

CHRISTIAN SAT ON THE EDGE OF AN UPHOLSTERED SOFA IN A private members' room of the Landström Meeting House. He listened out for footsteps coming up the stairs or shuffling feet outside the door. Nothing. The quiet unsettled him.

The grandfather clock in the downstairs hallway chimed, breaking the eerie silence. A door squeaked open. Heavy footsteps plodded up the stairs.

Viktor was on his way at last. Christian leaned back on the sofa, straightened his shirt, and crossed his legs.

In walked a gentleman carrying a briefcase. His silent and measured manner announced his high-level position in the Society. He took up the empty chair across from Christian.

"And when will Viktor arrive?" Christian asked.

The gentleman's nose twitched as though he smelled cut grass plucked from the grooves of someone's shoes. "He won't be coming."

Christian dug his feet into the carpet.

The gentleman laid his briefcase on the table. "I'm here in his stead to go through the paperwork."

"Paperwork for what?"

The gentleman snapped open the briefcase. "You've gotten yourself into quite a mess."

"I'm here to discuss a very important matter with Viktor," Christian said.

The gentleman sighed, put on his reading glasses, and pulled papers from the case. "If we are to work together, we have to do a background check."

"You already know my background," Christian said. "My father was a member. I was told we'd be discussing what happened to Jacob."

The gentleman glanced at Christian; his oiled hair glistened under the light. "Things have changed since we last spoke. Things have changed considerably."

Indignation lit inside Christian. He rested an elbow on his knee. "How so?"

The gentleman scanned a page. "As of an hour ago, you are without a club, your Q-score is in Tier 3, your points are bleeding, and your job is all but gone." He lowered the page and raised his glasses, resting them on his forehead. "You have no relationship to speak of with your ex-girlfriend who hates you. And the trial you worked so hard for is suspended." He shot a sharp look at Christian. "Despite all your skills, your fun and games with the Q-score leaderboard, you couldn't save yourself, let alone Jacob. You also stole a vase from the Estate. Add it all together, and you're a liability."

The man cut Christian down with his acid-laced words, but Christian wouldn't let them touch his skin. He barricaded his anger behind his most serene face. "I called to talk to Viktor, not you."

The gentleman continued, "Landström Society operates as one."

Christian's face tightened. "My points will revert to Tier 1 within twenty-four hours, my club membership will be reinstated, and my job is still mine. I'm on leave." He shifted. "The trial won't happen now; I'll give you that. And, if you want the vase back, just ask me for it."

"We still haven't received your father's things." He pulled out Viktor's ledger book. "Viktor sent you a copy of the inventory."

"After Jacob died, I didn't see the rush." Christian clammed his hands. "I've had other priorities, like finding out who pushed Jacob to his death. I intend to find who it is."

"We know you want justice for Jacob, but you also know we only work with members and initiates, and Viktor, as the new leader of the Society, is having trouble approving your temporary membership to grant you access to the network. If the members discover we allowed such a low-status individual to enter the Society, they will revolt."

Stunned, Christian felt like a barge set adrift to sink. "So, what's this meeting all about, then?"

A look of disgust shadowed the man's translucent-like face. "You are still part of the bloodline, whether or not we like it." He sighed. "There is one way to get the justice you seek. The only way. The members already voted on it. Viktor doesn't like it, but he has no choice either."

Christian stared into the man's eyes; the blue irises had long since faded to gray.

"A game," the man said.

Christian pulled back. "A game?"

"It's the only way. You'll get access to the network, you can interview whomever you like, and you can investigate to your heart's content. Only through the game will you get your justice."

"What's the catch? There's always a catch."

"You will be an initiate."

Christian crossed his arms.

"And Viktor Hansson will be your chief opponent in the

game. The good news is he was a very good friend of your father's, as you know, so it will be a fair game."

Christian straightened his back. "I want guarantees."

The man's mouth flinched. "For the duration of the game, you will come under the aegis of the Landström Society. Just like your father."

Hearing that was a bitter pill on Christian's tongue, but in twenty-four hours, that would all change. "You do know that everyone wants to see the Landström Society fade into oblivion?"

The gentleman sat stone-faced momentarily before he continued, "We've survived three hundred years, two world wars, hundreds of battles, scandals, and an assassination. This latest scandal involving the Estate is a mere blip. We will undoubtedly weather this storm."

Jacob was the only decent person Christian knew, and now that Jacob was gone, he almost didn't care anymore. Getting justice for him was all that mattered, and with it, exposing these guys for who they were. Decency was the last thing these guys knew anything about. If they were decent, he wouldn't be sitting here pleading for justice.

"What's involved in this game?" he asked, narrowing his eyes.

The gentleman lifted his chin. "It's a game you are adept at, although after watching your performance these last few days, it makes one wonder. It's a game using the Q-scores, plus other measures."

Christian recalled his meeting with Karen in the park that night, how she said they were after his algorithms. "Other measures being dead cats and such?"

The gentleman's eyebrow arched. "Consider it an initiation of sorts."

Christian possessed the Q-score source code. He also had Octopus, he had Max, and he had himself. If this game brought him closer to the man who drove Jacob to his death, he'd do it. "When do we begin?"

"First smart choice you've made in quite a while." The stately man pulled a fountain pen from his inside breast pocket. "Sign here."

Christian read the one sentence printed in the center of the A4 sheet of paper.

**Christian Karlsson hereby agrees to play
The Arcadian Match.**

If this game was the only obstacle in his way to getting what he was here for... he scribbled his signature, nearly ripping the page with the sharp tip of the fountain pen.

The stately man cupped the papers. "We're throwing a party this evening. Go home, put your best on, and come back. There, we will tell you the rules of the game."

"I'll be here."

The gentleman rose from his chair. "Good. Because if you don't show up, you might as well leave Sweden for good, and go find a cave in the Andes." The gentleman walked to the door. "I'll tell Viktor that you've agreed."

"And your name?" Christian asked.

"You can call me Gamemaster."

CHAPTER 16

CHRISTIAN STOOD IN THE HALLWAY OF HIS APARTMENT AND glimpsed Gamemaster's entry pass to the party.

He bristled at the sight of the card. Soon, he'd hear the rules of this game, but was all this worth it?

The trial had been suspended indefinitely, and he seemed further than ever from exposing Landström Society as the ones behind the Q-scores that had ruined innocent people's lives. Worst of all, Jacob was dead. He closed his eyes.

For a second, he saw himself on a plane headed for England. Landing in London, he could work in traditional public relations, and maybe Stormykitten had a contact or two he could use. She was based in London, and he always liked that city. And getting lost in the bustling metropolis of London, with its nine million residents would be easy. But the tentacles of the Landström Society reached into all corners of most cities, and without allies and resources at his disposal, he'd be worse off. He opened his eyes.

Gamemaster had given Christian an ultimatum: compete in the game or leave Sweden. If he left, he'd have to keep running for a long time. Gamemaster had mentioned the Andes, but Christian knew what he really meant. There was nowhere he could run. No, he had to face the game and expose them.

That goal in mind, he'd stay put and face the deep dive into the web of influence and power Landström Society had woven. That was the ticket to the most promising chance to escape their grasp and get the justice Jacob deserved. He stuffed the invite into his dinner jacket's inside pocket and called for a cab.

The cab drove over Riksbron Bridge, and the city's bright lights reflected on the river.

Minutes closer to the Landström Society Meeting House, his body buzzed as though an alarm deep inside him shot off. He felt he was going in blind. He gripped the inside of the car doorhandle. Then, he remembered he had its source code. And Max and the crew. He release the handle and leaned back.

He arrived at the Meeting House. His confidence quaked as he stepped into the dark summer night and stood in front their lair.

VOICES BUZZED on the other side of the door. He knocked once, twice, three times.

The butler opened the door, and a roar of voices spilled into the square.

Christian flashed Gamemaster's entry pass.

"Good to see you again, Mr. Karlsson. We are celebrating the new leader's appointment," the butler said. "Please, this way."

He stepped into a dimly lit entryway. He trailed behind the butler, his coattails acting like a kind of homing device.

They passed the parlor room, and he glimpsed men in black ties and dinner jackets, and ladies in long, glittery dresses. Their chatter, the distant clang of crystal, and the scent of rose hit his senses all at once. Their faces were veiled in white masks as they sipped on champagne.

"I believe you're wanted in the library," the butler said.

The butler guided him to a closed door and knocked three times.

"Enter," a man's voice said from the other side of the door.

Inside the stately room stood Gamemaster, Harald, Viktor, and two other members, one a portly man puffing on a cigar, and the other in a polka-dot bow tie. All were unmasked.

"The man of the hour has arrived," Gamemaster said.

Christian's toes cringed in his black lace-up shoes.

"I must say, I am impressed." The portly man blew a cloud of smoke, obscuring his face. "You're the first who dares play this game."

"Yes, it's caused quite a stir in the Society, hasn't it?" Harald said.

Christian shook his head. "It's just a game."

The men laughed.

"Do you know what Arcadia is, Christian?" Harald asked. "In Greek mythology, Arcadia is a virgin wilderness, home of Pan, the boy who never wanted to be a man." He peered at Christian. "Utopia itself, some might say, the craved for, but forever unattainable."

"We shall see," the portly man said.

Gamemaster stepped forward, a sheet of paper in his hand. "Shall we begin?"

Christian scanned the faces. "Let's."

"The goal is simple. Gather as many points as you can over the next thirty days," Gamemaster said. "The man with the most points at the end will be declared the winner. Simple."

"And the winner gets what?" Christian asked.

Gamemaster smiled. "The grand prize is leadership of the Society, along with all the power and loyalty that goes with it." He said the last part, waving his hand in the air.

The portly man laughed. "Can I play?"

A server entered the room and held out a tray of red wine, white wine, and champagne. Christian grabbed a flute and downed the pale gold liquid. Bubbles zipped down his throat.

Gamemaster turned to another page. "Let's cover the rules of the Arcadian Match." He cleared his throat. "Rule one: Murder is forbidden. You can't kill your opponent. In the case of untimely death, an autopsy will be performed."

Christian felt chills crawl down his spine. What kind of game required the specification of not murdering your opponent? "Untimely death, as in a heart attack?" he asked hastily.

Gamemaster looked up from the paper. "We will know the truth." He looked at Viktor first, then at Christian. "The second rule is to never speak about the Arcadian Match to anyone outside the Society."

The other members hummed in agreement.

"Now." Gamemaster glanced at Harald. "The Landström Society respects the national Q-score system, and it is the scorekeeper."

Excitement bubbled inside Christian. His victory was all but assured, he thought. He sipped on his champagne.

"The public will come to know of both of you, and they will affect your credit score rating." Gamemaster looked at Viktor and Christian over his glasses. "Remember rule number two."

Gamemaster refocused on the page in his hands. "We also have a private in-house scoring system—one that Society members are privy to. At the end of the match, both scores are tallied. Whoever has the most points is declared the winner."

Christian lowered his champagne. "So, this game is based on our reputations?"

Gamemaster nodded. "Partly." He steadied his gaze on Christian. "The other half is about what you're willing to do to win. That's what the Society members will judge you on."

Christian placed his champagne on the fireplace mantel. This rule felt like a license to commit petty crime. "Does the Society intervene if either of us gets in trouble with the law?"

"No. The law of the land prevails."

"So, we're on our own?"

"Yes," the portly man said, smiling.

Christian felt the tension build in his shoulders. He didn't care to gain ultimate power over this Society or any other. He was here for Jacob and to take down the man who drove him to his death—a man who could be inside this very room. He scanned the man's faces.

"On your own," Gamemaster confirmed, nodding.

Tension gripped Christian's chest. "What happens to the winner and the loser?"

"We're getting there," Gamemaster said. "If your opponent drops out first, the remaining will be the automatic winner."

"So, we can push the other one out?"

"Forfeiting one's place, particularly for the greater good, is a gentlemanly thing to do. The Society will look it at favorably, but I would consider that one of many strategies."

Viktor and Christian glanced at one another.

"This could get ugly," the man with the polka-dot bow tie said.

"All is fair in love and war," the portly one said.

"In the event of a tie, the Society will vote," Gamemaster said. "Harald will be the deciding vote." He flipped over the page. It was blank. "Questions?"

"And the loser? What happens to the loser of this game?"

The Gamemaster's lips puckered, and he drew a deep breath. "The loser will be banished from the Society, and he will not be helped by a single Society member for the next five years. Any outstanding legal charges will have to be faced alone."

Sweat sprinkled Christian's palms, and fear beat in his heart. "What if I just walk away now?"

"I never took you for a masochist. Shallow. Misguided. A little stupid perhaps—"

"That's not his fault," Harald said.

"No, I suppose not. The truth of the matter is, Christian, you're locked into this Game. You accepted the terms when you signed the paper and stepped through our front door. If you leave Sweden, the Society will have no choice but to retaliate swiftly. Trust me when I say you do not want to know what will happen to you. Better that you are your charming, resourceful self and try to beat this thing."

The bubbly turned in Christian's stomach. That was more than just an idle threat. If he tried to run, he knew he'd end up like Jacob. Dead.

"And the winner?" Viktor asked.

Gamemaster rubbed his hands. "At the end of the game, the winner will go on an all-expenses paid holiday for one week, and in that time, the official records will be cleared for the winner. Any misdeed that occurred during the game will be all but forgotten upon his return. He will then take complete control of the Landström Society, and all its power, including its affiliates." He clapped his hands. "Now, before we depart, Harald would like to give each of you a gift."

"Any other questions?"

Christian shook his head.

"Good," Gamemaster said. "As Harald is the deciding vote, neither of you may contact him. There will be points deducted should that happen."

Harald stepped forward. "This code will give you access to the journalist Lorelei Lindbergh. It's good for three uses." He handed Christian and Viktor a piece of paper. "Each of you has a different code, a code which she is bound to honor."

Christian unfolded his sheet of paper. The code was 0099. He folded it back up and stuffed it in his trouser pocket.

Viktor laid his paper on the table beside him.

Gamemaster then handed each of them a box. "Inside the box is what you must wear when you are in the public eye with her. It signals to the members that you are with the Society."

Christian opened his box. A bright yellow bow tie was cushioned in sky-blue satin-lining. He'd look like a duck wearing that thing, he thought. "Must I?"

Gamemaster opened his mouth to say something but sucked in his breath. "That is all."

The server opened the door, and the men started to file out of the room.

Viktor tapped Christian's arm. "May I have a word?"

Christian dropped behind Harald, Viktor at his side.

"I'm sorry about all of this, Viktor. If anyone challenged my position, I'd feel the same way."

Viktor pulled in his chin. "It isn't ideal. The impact on the Society…" He sighed. "But, I must honor the rules as they are. How did you come to hear of the Arcadian Match exactly?"

"Gamemaster suggested it."

Viktor's eyes swept the ground. "I propose we make a pact. The winner secretly looks after the loser."

"A deal within a deal?"

Viktor nodded and smiled.

He was an old friend of Christian's late father. What harm would there be in that? "Agreed," Christian said.

CHRISTIAN AND VIKTOR moved into the parlor, and the room seemed to boil with confusion and excitement.

They flanked Gamemaster, who stood at the head of the crowd.

"The contenders have both agreed to the rules," Gamemaster

announced. "All Society activity is suspended until the end of the Arcadian Match in thirty days. You are free to place your bets."

Crystal clanked, and a swell of voices filled the air.

The members shouted out their bets.

After a few minutes, it was clear the odds were on Viktor.

The cigar-smoking member sidled up next to Christian. "I like unpredictable bets. Keeps things exciting."

Christian looked at the betting board. They placed only one bet on him. "Is that your unpredictable bet?"

The member puff his cigar. "I don't mind losing the money, but please don't make me regret it. Give us a good show."

He patted Christian's back.

Gamemaster raised his hand above the teeming crowd. "Harald, do you want to place a bet?"

Harald shook his head. "Best if I remain neutral."

"Ah, yes," Gamemaster said. He held up his glass of champagne. "Attention, please."

He tapped a silver spoon against the crystal flute. A high-pitched ring echoed above the voices. "I'd like to remind all members who have placed bets that you are not allowed to help the challengers. If such an act is discovered, you will be expelled immediately, resulting in negative points."

Murmurs rose.

He glanced at the bets board. "All bets are in. The Arcadian Match has now begun," Gamemaster announced. "May the best man win."

Christian's knees wobbled. Viktor was a middle-aged man who had been working in the Society for at least ten years, knew all their rules, and what made the members tick. Christian shunned them every chance he got, and he was certain that word of his disdain for them had spread. He was lucky to have an ally at all, the cigar-smoking portly man standing next to him, but he wasn't a staunch ally. His only staunch ally was Max, an outsider.

The portly man turned to Christian. "Arcadia is paradise precisely because it is hell." He pumped his cigar and blew out smoke. "Remember that, Christian."

The smoke clogged Christian's lungs. "Thanks for the advice."

He shuffled out of the Meeting House and surrendered to the night air, drawing in a long, deep breath. He needed Max up to speed with this game as soon as possible. He put on his glasses and opened a text box.

> My points are restored. Back in Tier 1.
> Thanks for overseeing O2. Call me. Let's
> meet for a beer tomorrow.

He pressed send.

CHAPTER 17

ADRENALINE RUSHED THROUGH CHRISTIAN'S FINGERS AS HE grabbed his car's fob from the key cabinet. His meetup with Max was at Melanders in Östermalmshallen in half an hour, and he'd be instructing him on how to activate O3. He'd need to do a couple of manual inputs to the algorithm to get it to work, but with a bit of help from IT, he'd manage.

The pair of keys that had tumbled out of the Landström Estate vase hung off the bottom hook. Unlabeled, unknown. They might've once opened a door somewhere inside the Landström Estate, but the fire had caused so much damage it was hard to imagine they'd be of much use now. Maybe he could trade them for something else down the line. He closed the cabinet.

His front doorbell rang.

Schroeder stood at the door, holding a large metal box with a red wax seal over the keyhole. "A courier from Westland Storage Company dropped this for you."

"I hope it wasn't too much trouble signing for it."

Schroeder shook his head, shuffled in, and placed the box on the parquet floor.

He gave a cool smile, in the hopes it would deter Schroeder's fluffy chit-chat. "There's been a lot of work going on. You know what it's like."

"Clients. I get it."

"Thanks for taking it in."

Schroeder shrugged. "He said it was too important to leave in the hallway." He leaned toward Christian. "All those things they say about you on the feeds, I don't believe it for a second."

A high-pitched ring echoed in Christian's ear. "Half the stuff on the feeds is garbage. I should know." He clutched the keys. "How did the paintball game go last week?"

Schroeder cocked his head and stepped into the hall.

Grateful that Schroeder took the hint, he closed the door behind them. The lock clicked.

"Stormykitten shot down three opponents," Schroeder said. "She's amazing. We won. Where did you meet her?"

"Just online," he said to Schroeder. "Love to chat more, but I need to meet a colleague. Maybe we can catch up later."

———

CHRISTIAN SAT IN THE BOOTH, waiting for Max to return from the gents. He waved to the server and ordered a couple of beers.

Max sauntered back, pulling a handkerchief from the pocket of his brown corduroy trousers. He wiped his hands and stuffed the handkerchief in his back pocket. "I hate this no-paper thing. Ever since they implemented that policy, going out has been a nightmare for me." He sat down across from Christian. "Oh, I forgot to tell you. Some woman was calling for you the other day. Stine?"

"What did you say?"

"You weren't there. That's it. Who is she?"

"An ex."

Max laughed. "We've all been there. Why d'you two break up?"

"She was a conspiracy nut who thought everything was going to shit. She was always talking about how the world was falling apart." He rolled his eyes skyward. "Wouldn't stop. I couldn't take it anymore."

Max laughed.

The server laid the beer on the table and brought out the payment reader.

Christian stretched out his palm.

"I picked up the tab on the way back," Max said.

Christian rubbed his hand over his stubble. "You didn't have to do that."

Max dawdled, tracing a line in the wood with his finger. "Torn's been a little tense these days over the Jacob situation. He might extend your break." Max looked at him. "Do you have a plan?"

Christian could feel himself about to break rule number two. Max was an outsider, and his computer setup was fortified to the hilt. No way would they know he told Max anything. The urge nudged him forward. "I'm working on getting justice for Jacob."

"You talking to lawyers?"

Christian shook his head. "No. The Landström Society is involved. I'm dealing with them direct. I have to play a game."

Max sat up with a glint in his eyes. "What kind of game?"

"Do me a favor and look into Arcadian Match—that's the name of the game. You might have to search old text or digitally scanned rare books. See if such a game even exists." He smiled at Max. "Next, I need you to activate O3 and apply it to Viktor Hansson."

"Who?" Max said.

Christian smiled again. "Exactly. Viktor Hansson."

Max eagerly grabbed his beer and sipped it. He licked off his foam mustache. "Go on."

"Viktor has no public profile. He's a blank slate as far as the public is concerned. No media accounts, no personality, no branding."

"Is this guy even alive?"

Christian sipped on his bitter refreshment. "Sometimes I wonder that myself." He lowered the glass on the table. "Set up a fresh account on him. Don't skip out on anything. Next, order an augmented reality scene. Make it intriguing, something that would encourage the public to ask questions about him. No police involvement."

"Do we have photos of this Viktor guy? Date of birth? Historical records? We can't just make it all up. Ethical standards and all that."

Christian shook his head. "Still working on his birthday. But don't worry, I'll get what we need. We'll base all this on a solid foundation."

"The Hall of Records must have something."

Christian sighed, remembering his run-in with Stine. "They're having trouble with their system."

"Typical." Max tilted his head and frowned, looking as though he'd stepped into a bed of quicksand. "Anyway, how did you get mixed up with this Viktor guy? Wait, let me guess. You slept with his wife, and he's out for revenge."

"If only it were that simple." Christian laughed nervously. "Remember how I went to the Landström Society to find out if they were behind Jacob's cliff of doom?"

Max nodded eagerly.

Christian shifted his gaze to his beer. "Viktor Hansson, the new leader of the Society, has it in for me for having the audacity to protect Jacob."

Max's eyebrows knitted into a frown. "So, he accuses you of

all sorts, and then roped you into this game?" Max shook his head and sipped his beer. "The world is getting ugly."

"It could get worse. So, I need to get ahead of him, it. But only you, or rather Nyström, have access to my octopus algorithms. We'll use it regularly over the next thirty days."

Max stared at Christian and splayed his hands on the table. "Torn could find out about this."

"I'll send you cash so you don't go through accounts," Christian added.

Max's face softened, and he looked at his half finished beer. "I'll see what I can do."

Their AR glasses buzzed.

Christian put on his glasses and clicked on his feed.

His jaw tightened.

"What's wrong?" Max flipped on his own AR glasses and scrolled through the feeds. "Holy shit." He stared wide-eyed at Christian. "Someone posted a picture of us sitting here. And now you're wanted on manslaughter charges?"

Christian reeled. He couldn't help but think that this was part of the game—Viktor's grand opening move. No, this wasn't just Viktor's move. This was the Landström Society's move. Just as they had done with Jacob, they were out to destroy him.

Max pulled off his glasses and shoved them into his pocket. "This is a dirty game, but something else is going on."

"Not even a day into the game," Christian said, "and Viktor's coming out swinging."

Max pulled his handkerchief from his back pocket and wiped his hands as if getting ready for a fight. "Looks like he's out to destroy you, but this is our business. This is what we do; we manage reputations. And you have the best algorithms in the business. Whatever game this is, we're going to win."

"My sentiments, exactly," Christian said. "But my points will start dropping like acid rain from the sky, so activate Octopus program 2 as soon as you get back to the office. Don't use Ulrich this time. Change donors regularly. I need to keep my points buoyant."

"You got it."

"I'll send you info about Hansson as soon as I can, and then we'll switch to program 3. Really important we expose him for who he is."

Max downed the last of his beer. "Send me the cash, and I'll get it done."

He placed his empty beer glass down and walked out the exit.

People in the bar glanced over and lifted their phones. They snapped photos of Christian, now alone in the booth, as though they were looking at a circus seal.

There was a quick route to ending the manslaughter charge speculation, and it involved Lorelei Lindbergh. Enough of being this afternoon's entertainment, he left the table, put on his AR glasses, and stepped outside.

He clicked on the SVT2 program schedule. The guest lineup had been booked months in advance, but he knew Lorelei well enough to know she'd move a mountain to get his exclusive. One broadcast blast could set the record straight and put Viktor in his place. He speed dialed Lorelei Lindberg's private line, stored in his contact list the last time they met in the hotel on Skt. Andreas.

Her voicemail picked up.

"Lorelei, Christian Karlsson here. I have an exclusive for you. Did you see the rumors about me on the feeds? I can come in to talk, maybe even do a broadcast. Your viewers will love it."

Next, he called the switchboard.

"SVT2 switchboard. How can I direct your call?"

"Message for Lorelei Lindbergh."

"You and a million other Swedes."

"She knows who I am."

"That narrows it down by half."

"My name is Christian Karlsson. I have an exclusive for her. I left her a message on her voicemail. See that she gets it."

He reached into his pocket and pulled out the code number Harald had gifted him at Landström House. 0099. He crumpled it and tossed it to the ground.

CHAPTER 18

HIERARCHY UPHELD ORDER. HIERARCHY AVERTED BLOWBACK. Hierarchy was the reason Stine sat inside the water-cooled air of Stockholm Central Station, waiting for Bjorn.

Her foot impatiently tapped the concrete floor as though it had a life all its very own. She had received a message from him a couple of days ago—God knows what took him so long. Too slow for her liking, but they had hierarchy. For good reason, too.

She couldn't shake the feeling of unease as she thought about former Swedish Prime Minister Olof Palme. The ruling party at the time, along with the opposition parties and SÄPO itself had broken the hierarchy when they ignored the Geneva Convention in their investigation of his assassination. Breaking the Geneva Convention was far more embarrassing to all of them than the murder itself.

SÄPO claimed their primary task was to promptly investigate crimes related to national security, but it seemed they were lagging behind. Though they had instilled new protocols since then, the pace was still sluggish. She squeezed her knee, anxious about what else they might be overlooking.

Though she wasn't on the bottom rung of the intel hierarchy

(that position was held by the cleaners), she'd been in a holding position for the last three years. She had a good command of Swedish, but her Danish accent came through no matter how hard she tried to cover it up. Maybe that was why she got stuck at the Hall of Records desk job. Her foot stilled.

SÄPO rules stated she needed authorization to act, but no one had returned her calls. In her desperation, she called Bjorn over fifty times. So, she was sitting here on the promise of a meet. At least she got through.

The server stood beside her, electronic tablet in hand. She ordered fizzy water with a slice of lemon.

She remembered discussing the Olof Palme assassination in online conspiracy forums while dating What's-His-Face. A wry smile broke through the tension on her face. It was then that she caught the attention of Bjorn, or whoever he really was, and before she knew it, she was being interviewed at SÄPO. Though he never confirmed her theory, she emerged from the SÄPO training program, run by Bjorn, and she was mostly polished. She leaned back in the chair, straightening her posture.

Unlike most other Swedish organizations with flat hierarchical structures where no one cared who the boss was (unless they needed a pay raise), SÄPO was the opposite. In SÄPO, everyone knew the boss, and everyone followed the hierarchy. If agents broke the hierarchy, the consequences echoed for decades.

The server arrived with the fizzy water. The slice of lemon had sunk to the bottom of the glass. She took a sip.

She wasn't going to ask Bjorn for a full step up the ladder. He probably wouldn't grant it to her anyway. She'd aim a little lower. Permission to take action in one single operation—the operation involving the Landström Estate.

She had to be careful, though. When the Soviets warned the Swedish Government of Palme's potential assassination, they got the initial blame. Messengers could become scapegoats if it suited an agenda.

A man sporting a beige raincoat and a leather briefcase pulled up a chair across from her. The lines on his forehead and the smooth hollow of his cheeks gave him an air of distinction, as though he had traveled business class his whole life. Other than that, nothing else showed from his steel-blue eyes. He was a SÄPO man.

"I was expecting Bjorn," she said.

"We haven't met," he said without skipping a beat. "Let me introduce myself. I'm Mr. Eriksson."

Eriksson wasn't his name, but from now on, Mr. Eriksson is what Stine would call him. "Where is Bjorn?"

"He's operating elsewhere for the time being."

Operations always won the don't-ask argument. "When was he activated?"

"Sometime last week."

A surface vein throbbed above the corner of his mouth—his heart's mirror. "When the Landström Estate went up in flames, by any chance?"

His vein pumped a little faster. "That wasn't the reason."

Classic. "I have reason to believe that the Landström Estate could be connected to a surge of unwanted activity at the Hall of Records," Stine countered.

He blinked. "I studied your file, carefully, before I came." Eriksson pulled out a tablet from his briefcase. "It says here you have a tendency to jump to conclusions. Impulsivity issues."

"I got all high marks on all exams. It's the only reason I'm here."

He raised a hand and let his finger caress the corner of his lips as though he had just finished eating.

"Give me access to more sophisticated equipment, and I can prove what I suspect."

Eriksson laughed. "You have it the wrong way around. You prove you can do it, and then you get access to the goodies."

She wiggled her tight jaw. "I need proper equipment."

He pulled back. "I'm sorry to disappoint you, but that is only for personnel on the next level. Send me your reports, and we'll assess from there."

"I suspect black hats operating."

"How do you know they are black hats?"

"Anyone with a single working eye could see as much."

"Did you document your findings?"

Stine's cheeks warmed. She wished she could hide her face, but that would be too obvious. She had to power on even though he now knew he got the better of her. "It wasn't opportune."

"How come no one else reported this? You're the only one who is picking anything up?"

Words vanished from her mind.

"Try again."

"Someone I know may be personally involved," she said at last.

"Your request is denied."

"Why?"

"You're emotionally involved," Eriksson said in a measured tone. "It explains why you broke protocol several times already. Lucky for you, they were only minor infractions. Second, your incessant calls pulled me away from far more important operations. Not the best way to start our relationship. You will cease all surveillance. Immediately."

Stine went to speak.

"Your access privileges will also be suspended."

Stine's eyes widened. "What?"

"Two weeks," Eriksson said sternly.

Stine shook her head. "You can't."

"Three?" Eriksson questioned, his voice teetering with disdain.

Stine felt like she was a child being reprimanded. Being denied access to data, limitless storage, and formidable processing power was daunting, but it wasn't as painful a loss as pride. She bunched her lips.

"As with all things in life, there is an order we must follow." Eriksson wiped his dry face with his hand. "If you choose to do something stupid like make a spectacle of yourself in front of the media, I won't protect you. Bjorn won't protect you. In fact, I'll feed the jackals information about you to feast on. We'll let the Q-scores do the rest."

Stine shuddered. "I'll use the time to contemplate."

Eriksson pinched his chin. "Excellent choice." He picked up his briefcase. "Go back to the Hall of Records. Do your job and nothing else."

She watched him drift back into the crowd. A national security issue was at stake. She could feel it in her bones. Whoever that Eriksson person was, she'd have to get around him.

⎯⎯⎯⎯⎯

AT TWO O'CLOCK in the afternoon, Stine stared at her evidence wall, and the feeling of agitation rose in her as she replayed the meeting with Eriksson. Where was Bjorn?

Bjorn placed her in the Hall of Records to keep an eye on the movement of the records. She's reporting according to her brief, so why hadn't he notified her that Eriksson had taken over? She grabbed her secure cell phone from the bedside table and direct-dialed Bjorn. She waited for the line to connect.

After the fourth ring, she heard four tones increasing in pitch as a female voice on the line said, "The phone you are trying to

reach is not in service. Please check the number, then dial again."
Then the call ended.

Stine was stewing. Had Bjorn been made a 404, or was he out
of action by choice? She shook the thought from her mind.

If she dug around SÄPO to find him, especially without safe-
guards, word would spread quicker than a fire in a parched forest.
She switched on Talk Sveriges Radio and let the pointless chatter
fill the empty space around her.

She stared at the wall calendar. Two weeks. Eriksson said two
weeks. Why not one week? Why not a whole month?

She mouthed the word and muttered to herself, "Suspended."

Eriksson pushed her off this case on technicalities, and she
should've asked for more clarity. It was too late now. Stine tossed
off the duvet, trundled to her living room, and snapped open her
laptop.

She called up the SÄPO employee database and inputted her
ID. Her screen blinked, and she heard a short beep.

Access denied.

"That's weird," she said, biting her lower lip.

She punched in her ID again, and her finger hovered over the
enter key. SÄPO's foremost and subtlest spy was their website.
Every log-in was automatically tracked, numerous logins would
raise a help desk ticket of suspicion. Eventually, Eriksson would
learn she wasn't riding out her holiday in the hilltops of Norway.
The risk of detection was inevitable if she pressed the return key.
She shut the screen, not in defeat, but with calculated risk
assessment.

Leaning back in her chair, she steepled her hands as she
reflected on the sequence of events that led to her temporary
suspension.

Bjorn hadn't turned up for the meeting. Poor communication
skills described everyone else, but not Bjorn. Did he authorize her
suspension? Though it was a possibility, Bjorn would have

warned her. While his inexplicable absence caused alarm bells to ring in her head, Stine forced herself to refocus on the primary issue.

Eriksson.

He had been vague about her suspension. Too many phone calls to Bjorn? That was not conduct worthy of a suspension. She broke protocol? How exactly? Eriksson, she concluded, had made up his mind to suspend her well before he arrived at their meeting.

The question was why.

Bjorn once said anything that happens in the spy world is never personal. Never a truer statement was made. Spies are agents being moved around by people who know more. Fortunately, Bjorn taught Stine how to play the spy game well.

First step: identify the game.

Bjorn had said you can know the game if you analyze the opponent's moves.

Second step: break down the opponent's actions into their constituent parts.

Third: narrow down what the action could mean. After all, they wouldn't have made a move if it didn't get them to their endgame.

Final step: match it all together, and you will get a strong hypothesis of their endgame. With enough of their moves, you might eventually identify the real chess player—before it's too late.

Stine shot up from her chair and paced the living room. Identifying the game was easy. It certainly wasn't a win-win game because players of a win-win game tended to be the fair-minded sort, and Eriksson was not fair-minded. He was a shark. She saw his calculating steel-blue eyes. But it wasn't a negative-sum game because she was still on salary, still alive. Indeed, they were both still alive. The lose-lose negative sum game ensured mutual destruction. Even sharks were self-preserving.

It had to be a zero-sum game in play. Only one side could win.

Next. The action. Most sharks were unpredictable, but Eriksson came from SÄPO. The odds were high that the game Eriksson was playing originated from within SÄPO. This meant he would make the most efficient moves to get to his endgame. Also, he had access to some of the most sophisticated equipment.

She glanced at her laptop on the kitchen table. She had none.

She kneaded her tense muscles at the back of her neck and stretched. A pop sounded in her ears, and with it, a release of tension.

Eriksson probably saw her as a minor obstacle. Possibly even weak.

If they saw her as weak, Sun Tzu's Art of War prescribed an excellent strategy:

> "Appear weak when you are strong, and
> strong when you are weak."

If they viewed her as an obstacle, an obstacle to what? What had she been tracking at the time of her suspension?

Landström Estate and the missing records. They didn't want her to track the records.

A tingling sensation crept up her arms.

Hypothesis one: she was gathering information they didn't want her to find.

She reached for her laptop and opened her search history from two days earlier. SÄPO was probably already tracking her online activity. Indeed, they probably already hacked it. They knew she was looking at Landström and the records, making the connections. She leaned back.

Advantages existed to being suspended. Namely, the shackles were off. She wouldn't have to wait for permission to act now. Her analysis-decision-action process could run smoothly and seamlessly. However, having no access to data or the latest equipment put her at a heavy disadvantage.

She glanced at her evidence wall. She stood before what looked like a map of the London Underground, but something was missing. She couldn't name it but could feel it was waiting to be found. The greater the pressure to recall, the deeper a memory burrows, Bjorn had said. That something wanted to be pinned in the right spot on the wall, but pressuring herself wouldn't get her any answers.

Her stomach grumbled, right on time, and she shuffled into the kitchen.

Except for a tub of week-old beetroot salad, a jar of pickled herring that would last a lifetime, and a stick of salami, the shelves held barely a crumb. Images of her favorite pastry played on her mind, those sweet but sour strawberries on a bed of almond ricotta custard nestled on a butter-packed, flaky pastry case. The taste of midsummer.

Her skin tingled. Summer. She grabbed the salami and rushed back to the wall.

She tore off a bite of the salami and chewed as she calculated the timings. Midsummer was four weeks away. She scribbled the starting date on a piece of paper and pinned it to the wall.

End date Midsummer?

SÄPO was always on high alert for all national holidays, especially midsummer, the biggest national holiday in Sweden.

If Eriksson was a black hat, it would make sense that he'd want her out of the way on that day. If he extended her suspension by two extra weeks, she'd know for sure.

She grabbed a sticky note:

Eriksson: Black Hat ?

She pinned the note to her evidence wall and grabbed another note.

Hypothesis:
Black hats/Midsummer.

This zero-sum game required one side to win and the other to lose. What did the records have to do with Landström Society?
Where was Bjorn?
So many questions and not enough answers.
She stepped away, picked up her tablet, opened the Art of War, and read the first passage her eyes landed on:

> Now the general who wins a battle makes
> many calculations in his temple ere the
> battle is fought.
> The general who loses a battle makes but
> few calculations beforehand. Thus do
> many calculations lead to victory, and
> few calculations to defeat: how much
> more no calculation at all! It is by atten-
> tion to this point that I can foresee who
> is likely to win or lose.

CHAPTER 19

KELLY BLACKWELL WALKED PAST THE SHOP WINDOWS IN CENTRAL Stockholm and caught a reflection of her straight-edged bob—a last-minute decision before leaving London. Considering the time pressure her hairdresser had to work with, he did a great job. She smiled.

Her bot buzzed as she approached a shop window displaying mannequins dressed in wedding gowns. She stopped. In the soft glow of her mind's eye, she saw the physical location matched the one Harry had sent through earlier. She pressed the shop's bell.

Top of her surveillance equipment list was a tracker, the innocuous kind that can attach to anyone and anything. She refocused, cupped her hand against the glass, and peered through the grate.

Pink chiffon fabric hung from the ceiling, and vanilla almond-colored puffy dresses hung on cushioned hangers from clothes racks. It all looked like a Cinderella's den. Kelly pressed the bell again.

At last, the door released, and she stepped inside.

Dulcet notes of Bach streamed from hidden speakers. She passed yards of metallic charmeuse folded neatly on the shelf and came to a security door blocked by a mannequin in a pistachio-colored bridesmaid dress. She knocked.

Behind the door, heels clicked in tempo, coming up the stairs.

A woman opened the door, breathlessly. Her honey-colored highlights swayed in her blown-out hair. "Kelly Blackwell. Nice to meet you. I'm Marcia. I've been expecting you. I saw you in the cameras, but the hairstyle threw me off. I put in a call, and Harry White said you had made a last-minute change. It's a flattering look. Please, come this way."

Kelly followed her down the stairs into a room that looked like it hid a diamond vault somewhere in the back.

Marcia pressed a button underneath the counter. "Lewis, Kelly Blackwell will be joining you shortly." She gestured to the door behind her. "Ms. Blackwell, Lewis will see to your needs."

Marcia placed her finger on a scanner, and a wall slid open to another back room. It was triple the size of the showroom upstairs. Glass cabinets were packed with listening devices, spy cameras, and watches. A valet mannequin, decorated with a long leather jacket, stood off to the side.

Kelly's mouth watered. The room had all the trimmings of a professional spy shop.

A man in a three-piece suit stood behind a marble counter. "I'm Lewis. How may I help you?"

"It's a discovery job. I'll know what I'm looking for when I find it. Do you know the Landström Society?"

Lewis raised an eyebrow. "Everyone knows Landström Society. If they are involved, may I suggest spy cameras, hidden cameras, voice recorders, time slip recorders, night vision goggles, and GPS beacons? Slipping a GPS beacon into a pocket is straightforward enough. And since most use fingerprint impression keys, it's all secured to you once you imprint it."

"I'll take it all. Plus, a dozen burner phones, a bionic listening device, and a mobile hotspot."

"We have new bait and trap equipment you might be interested in."

"Sounds good, but I'm going to need something more along the lines of a truth serum."

Lewis pulled down a blue box from the shelf behind him and opened it, lifting a silky royal blue wrap. Inside was an EpiPen. "It contains a careful balance of barbiturates and scopolamine, rendering the user particularly candid."

"Your equipment is impeccable."

"Will you also be needing extras?"

Kelly's brow scrunched. "What are extras?"

"A pair of AR glasses that will get you onto the Q-score leaderboard and paper for incidentals." He pulled out a ream of paper. "This paper dissolves."

Kelly scanned Lewis. He appeared thoroughly human, but she was beginning to have doubts. Or, maybe this country was trying to create nonhuman humans. "Since the printing press, we've had paper," she said. "But Sweden wants to do away with it now. I get it."

Lewis cocked his head." For ecological reasons."

This really was a different country, Kelly thought. "It so happens, Lewis, I don't need paper, and I don't need AR glasses either."

His eyebrows twitched. "If there's nothing else?"

"I will need an outfit. Black jeans, shirt, boots. I need to look like I came out of a VR paintball gaming session. And then I'll need nontraceable cash."

He smiled. "I suggest you stick to Q-score points as your primary payment option. Makes it easier. We can open you a visitor's account."

"Q-score points?"

"Ah, I see," Lewis said. "A lot of visitors get confused about it. It's a national scoring system that we use to rate each other and pay for things. But you're a visitor, a tourist if you will, so I can get you a temporary spot in Tier 1, the highest tier on the scoreboard. It gives extra privileges."

Kelly massaged her earlobe. "Are you saying I'm going to have to log into some scoreboard so I can pay for dinner?"

Lewis nodded. "And you'll have to be on your best behavior while you're there; otherwise, your points will be deducted."

Tension rose in Kelly at the thought of dealing with yet another AI system. She huffed. "What sort of game is this?" She held her hand up. "Doesn't matter. I've dealt with these AI systems before. Just give me the URL, and I'll deal with it."

He pulled a sheet from the ream and peeled back a protective layer. "Once the paper is exposed to oxygen, we have ten minutes before it dissolves." He scribbled down the URL address and handed it to her. She read it, and her bot logged it with a soft click.

"Don't you want to type it into your—" Lewis surveyed her as demurely as he could. "Do you have AR glasses or a phone or tablet or something?"

She finger-tapped her temple. "I have all I need."

He logged onto his tablet. "I'll register you and send you the URL. What would you like your username to be?"

"Stormykitten."

Lewis set up the account in Tier 1, passed her the URL on another sheet of dissolving paper, and tallied the bill. "And who shall I bill?"

She stroked the corner of her mouth. The only good thing about huge bureaucracies was that accounting was deliberately opaque. By the time MI5 got the bill, she'd be back in London and would approve it herself. "The British Government."

Kelly stepped out of the bridal shop, holding a duffel bag of equipment and dressed in dusty black jeans and boots to match. She would've preferred the four-inch heels, but there was a high probability she'd have to start running, so she settled for the two-inch heel, thick as a brick.

She logged into her bot and scanned for Christian.

One address popped up in her mind's eye: 4500 Lugen-strassgarten.

CHAPTER 20

IN THE REARVIEW MIRROR, CHRISTIAN GLIMPSED THE HAGGARD look in his eyes. It didn't matter what he looked like; he wasn't going to be on air today. All he needed was the promise of a ten-minute slot on Good Morning, Sweden—the highest-rated television show for the last ten years, outranking A New Day at every turn.

The secret to Good Morning, Sweden's success? Its spotlight anchor, Lorelei Lindbergh, with her hound dog nose for a story and her kitten purr voice. Even though Christian never willingly watched the show, it seemed to hum along on a screen somewhere. If you didn't watch Lorelei Lindbergh in the a.m., you would hear about what she said by lunch.

Lindbergh started from a lowly position within a studio, likely as a runner. However, after emerging from the Me Too movement and standing up to her aggressor (who subsequently sank into obscurity), she quickly rose to the status of a celebrity broadcaster. While some doubted the authenticity of her quick ascent to fame, the narrative certainly made for a compelling story.

Ever since then, she reported on exclusive stories that somehow made their way to her. The show attracted ten million weekly viewers between the ages of twenty and fifty, and she'd won numerous awards for breaking stories on the nightly news. Offscreen, the lines on her forehead were deeper. Christian had slept with her more than once, as did many others, he suspected.

He turned into Tegeluddsvägen, followed the signs to the subterranean parking lot underneath the SVT building, and parked his car in a visitor spot.

Elevator doors opened into a white lobby dotted with TV screens on the wall behind the reception desk. The switchboard, lit red, was barraged with calls, challenging the operator.

She redirected two calls, and Christian didn't feel like waiting anymore. He tapped the white wooden counter with his car key to nab her attention.

Startled, her head sprang up.

"I have an appointment with Lorelei Lindbergh. It's Christian Karlsson, and it's urgent."

She nodded and called through. "Lorelei's assistant will be right down."

The back of his thighs tingled in anticipation. He sat next to an inert TV monitor mounted on an iron pedestal like a dark stallion wearing blinders, ready to kick off.

A young brunette greeted him. "Christian?"

He stood up.

"I'm Lorelei's assistant. I'll take you up to the boardroom. It's only one flight of stairs." She spun around, and the clickety-clack of her heels against the floor tiles led him up a spiral staircase.

She opened the door to a stoic conference room. Lorelei Lindbergh sat next to a suited colleague. On screen, Lorelei's smooth forehead put her in her mid-thirties, and her rock-solid brand as a survivor, with a capital S, was always sitting in the back of viewers' minds. In person, her forehead lines ran deep.

"Coffee and water are in the corner if you need them," the assistant said before shutting the door.

A mix of alcohol and stress toured Christian's mind; he needed more than just black coffee. "I was meant to meet with Lorelei."

"I'm Erik, the producer," the colleague said. "I hope you don't mind. Grab yourself a coffee, and we can get started."

Christian shuffled toward the coffee station against the bare wall and poured black liquid into a ceramic mug.

After polite introductions around the table, Christian sat down, cradling the mug and setting it in front of him like a miniature checkpoint Charlie on the vast wooden table. "I'm flattered you took time out of your busy schedule to see me."

"I always leave a slot open for the unexpected," Lorelei said.

She leaned back in her chair. "What's your exclusive about, Mr. Karlsson?"

The stark question was like being shot at point blank. Indeed, he was just about registering that he was sitting in a boardroom across from Lorelei Lindbergh in the cold light of day. The entire journey had been too silky smooth. "You can call me Christian, Lorelei."

Lorelei glanced at Erik, and she leaned into the high gloss-lacquered table. "Christian, we're on the clock here. So, what's this all about? You have five minutes to explain."

"I must get on the air and talk about the Jacob Rasmussen case. I don't expect to go on air today, but I need to get ahead of the rumors. You might've seen the feeds."

She swooped her wavy hair back, and her jutting chin reflected in the high-shine table. "That's a massive story."

"He's not ready, Lorelei, and we're not ready," Erik said. "We have no idea what he's going to say, nor have we vetted him. Then there's the footage, and the Hall of Records is—"

"I don't need footage," Christian said.

"I can't agree to this," Erik countered.

A broadcast could clear up this accusation in seconds. Christian needed to secure a spot, even if it was a few days into the week. He could hold off the rumors with O2, but he needed to get on the air, talk to the nation, and let them decide. "You can do your vetting, and I can do a preinterview."

"Why should we let you on air?" Erik crossed his hands over his chest. "Of all the people in Sweden, with your points dropping, it would set a bad precedence."

Christian glanced at Lorelei.

She dropped her gaze and tucked in her chin.

The last thing he wanted to do was use the code Gamemaster had given him to activate Lorelei, as using it would tie him to Landström forever more. But it was a choice that could lead to his bigger goal. Expose Landström. "Code 0099," he said.

Lorelei shot Christian a hard look. "If you don't deliver, I will personally destroy you."

Christian had zero doubt of that, but she'd have to get in line. Knowing she was part of the Landström network satisfied a small portion of him. He was finally uncovering Landström's secret network. In time, he'd know enough about the Society to bring them all down.

Erik's gaze swiveled between Lorelei and Christian. "What's going on here? This isn't a good idea. At all."

"It's just an intro, and we should get on the air before SVT4 gets it," Lorelei said, allaying Erik's confusion. "And it's an exclusive discussion with Christian Karlsson, the biggest suspect in Sweden in the last two years. Our Q-scores will skyrocket."

Christian's forehead heated, and perspiration sprinkled his brow. "Shouldn't we prep?"

"No one is ever ready," Lorelei said.

Christian recalled Harald's instructions: he must wear a yellow bow tie. "I'm not dressed for it."

Lorelei looked at Christian. "We are the biggest TV broadcaster in Sweden and are ready for every eventuality. I think we can manage your wardrobe."

Erik flattened his hands on the table as if surrendering. "Lorelei, I trust your instincts."

She pressed a button on the phone in the middle of the table. "Come in and escort Mr. Karlsson to the Broadcast Room."

Before Christian could raise a question, her assistant whisked into the room.

Lorelei lifted her chin. "Tell media to put a reel together of Landström Estate stock footage before the fire. That's what we'll open with. Then, get my latest report and use the burned-out Estate for the closing."

The assistant nodded and promptly ushered Christian out the door. She whisked him up a flight of stairs, and he followed behind, like a plastic bag in the wind.

———————

A READY-MADE public audience sat in the bleachers along the walls of the broadcast room. White noise chatter echoed off the walls, and coffee aroma suffused the air.

Christian's stomach flinched with waves of nausea. He followed the assistant and checked in on his Q-score to curtail the growing queasiness mounting in his stomach. His position had dropped to Tier3 since the manslaughter announcement this morning. He was bleeding points faster than Jacob ever did. He tripped over a thick cable on the floor.

"You okay?" the assistant asked.

The cable roped one studio camera to another, and the ground he walked on looked covered in black snakes. He nodded and turned off the AR mode in his glasses.

A technician propped Christian up on a sofa like a puppet.

A make-up girl fluttered around him like a butterfly with a powder puff, straightening his hair as she went along. She blotted his forehead with a micro-cloth, and her gentle touch soothed his nerves.

A sound technician attached a lavalier mic to his collar. He tapped on the mic. A sharp, screechy sound tore through the room.

Christian winced.

"Good to go," she said.

A technician positioned a teleprompter at Christian's eye level and nodded. A camera operator rolled in a camera-stallion like the one Christian saw in the lobby—but this one had glowing red eyes. "We're ready to go in ten," he shouted.

Christian's heart hammered in his chest.

Lorelei sat in the chair opposite. "Are you ready?"

Maybe it was good for him to be on air now, stop his points bleeding, and stop his nerves shaking. Before he could say yes, he blurted *no*.

"Just focus on me," Lorelei said, her tone hurried.

"I prefer being behind the scenes," Christian said. "I'm not a natural at having a cozy conversation in front of five million pairs of eyes."

"Don't think about it." She scooted in. "Would you like a benzo to calm your nerves?"

"There is one thing I need."

She squinted.

"A yellow bow tie."

"If it makes you feel better, why not?" Lorelei snapped her fingers at the makeup girl, who was in gossip with one of the camera operators. "Have wardrobe bring down a yellow bow tie. Quick. And bring a jug of water. Make it look pretty."

The make-up artist buzzed away.

Lorelei cast her eye over Christian. "I know we're going on

cold, but take it from me, you're prepped and ready. Count yourself lucky."

A white spotlight flipped on, its heat bearing down on him,
coiling around him like a python.

Sweat poured down his chest.

The make-up girl returned to the stage, carrying a yellow bow
tie. She fastened it around his neck and clasped it tight.

His air passage felt constricted and his cheeks burned.

She blotted his forehead. "Extra color for the cameras makes
you look even better."

Silence descended over the broadcasting room. The lights
dimmed, shading the sea of faces in the ready-made audience.

"In three, two, one—" the cameraman pointed at Lorelei.

A floor camera rolled in closer.

On cue, Lorelei looked straight into the camera.

"We've come to you with an emergency breaking exclusive.
Christian Karlsson, the man accused of manslaughter, the first
person to be accused of such a crime since the Q-scores began, is
here to tell us what happened in his own words."

A whoosh of fabric ruffled through the air. A single cough
sounded from the audience. Then a hypnotic silence captured him.

He began.

"Thank you for having me on so quickly, Lorelei." He cleared
his throat and glanced at the camera. "My name is Christian
Karlsson, and I work in Quant PR. A few weeks ago, I started
working with Jacob Rasmusson. He also happened to be an old
school friend. He was getting attacked by online vultures, vicious
online vultures."

The audience let out a collective murmur.

"I worked with him day and night as his friend, his supporter.
I believed in him. I had known him for a few years and was trou-
bled to hear he encountered hard times."

A deep cough echoed across the room.

"We all face those moments in life, but in Jacob's case it was one tragedy after another. His beloved dog had died. A few weeks later, his sick mother died. He was out of a job, and his club had dropped him. He had a long history of being bullied, and life was harsh on him. But he was a mathematical genius, and sadly, the world never got to hear his voice."

The audience seemed to breathe in the room.

"I couldn't let my friend suffer. And he was suffering. Couldn't sleep. Barely ate. His wife called to tell me he was walking around the house late at night. One night he called me, crying. I've never heard a man sobbing like he had. Said he didn't want the life anymore. He was tired. I tried to talk him out of what I knew he was thinking. But he made me promise I'd never forget him. That's why I'm here."

Several sniffles streamed from the audience.

"I had to honor my word. I was there for Jacob in his final hour, trying to stop him from doing what I knew he was about to do. Anyone here would have done the same."

The silence deafened him.

He laced his fingers and bowed his head. "The rumors online are just that. Rumors. I was there trying to stop my friend from taking his life. That's all I was there for, but someone is trying to make it sound like manslaughter."

Lorelei Lindbergh's voice cracked. "This is a harrowing story. One we never would have known had you not come to share it with us." She faced the camera. "We will take a break, and when we come back, we will hear more about the special friendship Christian lost."

The camera's red eye shut down, and the overhead lights went on.

"That was good," Lorelei said. "That was very good. You even had me going for a while. You need a break?"

"The gents."

A technician guided Christian to the second door along a bricked hallway. He locked the cubicle door and slipped on his AR glasses.

In the space of those twenty minutes, he had gained nearly 50,000 points, climbing back up Tier 2.

A lightness floated through him, and ecstasy exploded in his mind. This was the first major score in the Match, and he didn't even have to employ Octopus or put Max and the team into play. Was a broadcast all it took?

Then, he sensed another part of him, deep, so deep, it stirred. "It's just a game," he murmured.

He slipped the glasses back into his pocket and strolled back to the broadcasting room, ready for more.

KELLY STEPPED through the double doors of the communal Gaming Room and stepped into a low-lit room. It reminded her of the echo chambers in London, minus the quiet.

Television screens lined the wall, and game consoles and cockpit seats covered the floor. The odor of aged sweat surrounded her. She rubbed her neck.

Her bot flashed 4500 Lugenstrassgarten in her mind's eye, also confirmed by the desk clerk.

She dropped back. Why was she here? Of course! Her bot needed a console to download the information Harry had sent through. She took up a seat in front of a games console.

Blotting out the gamers' spitting bullets, Kelly psyched herself up for the deep dive and focused on the dark screen in front of her.

Steadying her breath, she softened her gaze, her inner focus.

Her bot unlocked a file Harry sent through. The filed opened with a brief conversation between two men. Something about an invitation. "Thanks, Torn," the other man said.

Pictures of the Landström House ran past. She saw footage of a burned Estate, its address, history, ownership, and blueprints. The video flipped to a man exiting the Landström Meeting house —the man was Christian Karlsson. His phone details, personal address, age, weight, and description streamed along his photo.

He was holding a yellow bow tie, his face a mix of worry and determination.

With Christian's identity confirmed, Kelly pulled her focus back into the room, swirled around and stepped away from the console, her head heavy.

The sound of bullets sprayed the air.

She jumped. The gamer on the next row was killing a terrorist. She exhaled. She got what her bot needed and made her way to the exit.

> LORELEI LINDBERGH WILL CONTINUE
> BRINGING YOU THE BREAKING EXCLUSIVE.

Good Morning Sweden played on several TV screens on the walls, and a ticker tape banner ran across the bottom of the screen:

> BOMBSHELL EXCLUSIVE LIVE. CHRISTIAN
> KARLSSON SPEAKS TO LORELEI LINDBERGH.

Kelly froze.

Lorelei Lindberg's face appeared close-up on the screen, and fake concern crinkled her eyes. A montage of historical images of the Landström Estate splashed across the screen—the same as Kelly's bot had streamed to her.

The camera cut back to the studio and panned out. Next to Lorelei Lindbergh sat Christian in a yellow bow tie.

Kelly's face drained. No matter what country she was in, the media was always corrupt, always controlled. She didn't have to think twice about it. If it weren't for Kelly, England would be just like the rest. She pulled out a burner phone and dialed Christian Karlsson's personal line. His voicemail picked up.

"It's a setup. Get out of there," she said.

She looked back up at the screen, hoping he'd pull his phone from his pocket. He didn't so much as flinch. Either he didn't get her message, or he was ignoring his phone.

A man came onto the stage and sat across from Christian. "I have my own version of how it all happened," he said.

Kelly's eyes widened, as though her eyes helped her recognize the voice. But she already knew. It belonged to Torn, the man from the digital conversation. "Identify Torn on the TV."

Kelly's bot identified him as Christian's boss at Nyström Image Architects.

She didn't care who he was. Torn was in on the Landström Society trap. Kelly shot out of the game room and hailed a taxi. "Take me to SVT where Good Morning Sweden, or whatever the hell it is, is broadcasted."

The driver switched into first gear and rested his hand on his lidded coffee mug in the cradle. He lowered his glasses over his eyes. "Stormykitten, we don't talk like that here in this cab."

"How do you know my name?"

"It's on the Q-score leaderboard." He waited for a gap in the traffic. "But you're a tourist, so I'll let it pass."

She scooted up. Two could play this game. "I'll give you triple points if you get me there in five minutes," she said.

The driver swigged down the coffee and slammed on the gas.

CHAPTER 21

CHRISTIAN WATCHED, DUMBFOUNDED, AS TORN WALKED ONTO THE stage. In front of him hurried a technician with a pair of head-phones half-cocked on her head.

Christian suppressed the urge to jump up from his chair and greet Torn but couldn't decide on what-the-hell-are-you-doing-here or good-to-see-you. Didn't Torn see Christian was cleaning up his reputation, and that it would ultimately benefit Nyström Image Architects? Maybe Torn was there to back him up. He settled in his chair and waited.

The technician stooped in front of Christian. "You have a message," she whispered.

Dread lined his stomach. "From whom?"

She shrugged. "I was just told to tell you: it's a setup."

She stepped away.

Where had he heard that before? Oh yes. Who else? Stine. She was back to her conspiracy theories.

He glanced over at Torn. Not once had he looked his way. Not a good sign, but if Christian bowed out now, it would send the wrong impression to every pair of eyes watching. No matter what

Torn planned to say, Christian could handle it. He squeezed his restless thighs and bolted his feet to the floor.

"Thank you for coming over on such short notice," Lorelei told Torn. "We're grateful you could join us."

Torn straightened his back. "Thanks for having me."

"You're here to tell us about Christian Karlsson," Lorelei said. "After all, you've worked with him for…"

"Two years."

"A little over that," Christian interjected.

Without turning his head, Torn nodded. "Yes, now that I think about it. Time flies."

"What is Christian like to work with?"

"Christian is a combination of brilliant and reliable, rare qualities in the PR world. He's devoted to his clients, our clients."

Lorelei stole a quick glance at Christian.

"He has rescued many of our clients from Tier 3 status, so much so that we started considering him for partnership. But then, his father passed away last year."

The audience sighed.

"It changed him," Torn continued. "I gave him time off, but he refused to take it."

"I'm sorry, but that's just not accurate," Christian cut in. "At least not how I remembered it."

"You probably don't remember," Torn said, glimpsing the floor near Christian. "But that's understandable. Your father had just died, and you were in grief."

"Grief is a challenging emotion," Lorelei said.

Torn nodded. "I thought it better he take time off, but he insisted on taking on the Landström Society as a client."

Christian's nerves tightened up a notch. Whatever respect Christian had for Torn skidded to an abrupt halt at that moment. "That's just not the case, Torn."

"Grief makes people see things in a very strange way," Torn

said. "His late father was a member of that club, so I guess he wanted to be part of it. I never knew it would come to this, though."

The camera zoomed in on Lorelei's mock sympathy. "We'd like to bring in our studio psychologist to discuss the effects of grief. I'm sure many of our viewers would like to understand how it can affect mental health. But first, we'll play a video Torn brought in."

Christian's hands tingled. His thoughts drifted back to the message. Stine rarely, if ever, watched television. In fact, she downright hated it, but today, she must've been tuned into this broadcast along with millions of others. So, why was she going out of her way to get a message to him? Why? Maybe she was on to something. "What video is this?"

The studio blacked out. The video played.

A hooded figure trundling up to the Landström Estate, carrying a gas tank away from the Landström Estate. A fire burned behind him. The video played it again.

The audience whispered, their voices of confusion growing.

Despite no clear identification that the hooded figure was Christian, the implication that he was the Estate's arsonist was clear. He gripped the edge of the sofa.

Stine was right. Lorelei was a Landström contact, and clearly, Torn was one of them too. It explained why Torn had the Landström Society's invite on the day Jacob's online reputation was being trashed. The whole thing was a setup.

A plump woman jaunted onto the stage.

Great, he thought. A psychologist with an eating disorder. Damned if he would let her hog the stage and turn this entire show into a circus. This was *his* opportunity to set a trap of his own. If he confessed to burning down the Landström Estate, he'd steal Torn's thunder, and the police would get involved. They'd ask official questions, and Christian could bring Landström

Society into the fray. One way or another, he was going to expose those mass manipulators, and lead the oncoming investigation, via the back door, to Jacob and the Q-scores. It was a long shot, and it was only possible as long as he confessed here and now.

Christian puffed his chest. "Let's do away with all this buildup, shall we?" he said. "I'm the one who burned down the Landström Estate. Yes. It was me. What can I say? I was filled with grief. As Torn said, I was completely and utterly confused. I laid my father to rest and had no idea what I was doing."

The broadcast room fell into silence.

"The charges said nothing about arson," Lorelei said.

"You mean the rumors, don't you?" Christian said.

"Yes, rumors," Lorelei looked at Torn. "The rumors mentioned manslaughter."

"I might as well also say that all those rumors about me causing Jacob's death, yes, I confess."

Christian faced Lorelei, and he saw a twinkle in her eye. He knew that she knew none of this was admissible in a court. "Yes, Jacob's death was all down to me too."

She fumbled with her tablet. "You heard it here first, folks. We'll be right back."

The cameras pulled back and their red lights went dark. The overhead lights on the audience brightened.

Lorelei narrowed her eyes at Christian. "This is not what we agreed."

"You have the exclusive you wanted. And because you're in with Landström, you must heed their call."

She reeled back.

Torn shot up from his chair.

Christian grabbed his arm and led him backstage. "Who told you to come here?"

Torn yanked his arm free. "I came here to distance ourselves from you."

"Viktor Hansson sent you here, didn't he?"

Torn froze. "Who?"

"You're working with him. Why?"

Torn held a firm gaze. "I came for the sake of the firm." His voice clipped. "And the partners all agreed. You made yourself look like a fool, and we have to distance ourselves from you."

"TV is just a stage."

Torn scoffed. "But some people do believe it. You did what you had to do; I get it. But you're taking your chances, and I did what I had to do to save the company."

"I did what I had to do for the firm, too," Christian said.

Torn straightened his tie. "Not the best choice, Christian."

He crossed the broadcasting room and stormed out the exit door.

Christian flipped open his AR glasses and logged on to the Q-score leaderboard.

More rumors circulated about Jacob having an accident, and that Christian might've caused it. His points were dropping again, and he was approaching Tier 3.

For the next thirty days, his points, Tier status, and reputation would be dire. The only way to protect himself was to stop caring. "It's just a game," he murmured.

He logged off the leaderboard and transferred ten thousand points to Max's personal account, bringing himself firmly into Tier 3 territory, alongside deadbeat parents, petty thieves, and other riffraff. "Text Max," he said.

A window popped up.

Christian: Saboteur got to Torn.

> Max: Hey, man. That was a disaster. Dropped a Tier during the show, but we got you back up. Confirm, I got the points transfer.

> Christian: Start the O3 on Viktor Hansson.

> Max: Still need his DOB and photo.

> Christian: Will get it to you asap.

> Max: FYI. Protests have started down where you are. You sure know how to draw a crowd.

KELLY EXITED the taxi in front of a brown brick building, the signage identifying it as SVT.

The receptionist behind the lobby desk was startled as Kelly entered the lobby. "Are you the new make-up girl?"

Kelly brushed her hair back. "No. I need to speak to Christian Karlsson."

The receptionist scanned the roster.

"He's the one Lorelei is interviewing right now." Kelly pointed at the monitor. "He's the guest—" She cut herself short. With a prepared story, she would've easily gotten past this brain-dead chick.

"I'm afraid we can't do that."

"It's important. I have information related to the Landström Estate. They both need to know before Christian makes a fool of Lorelei Lindbergh. You don't want Lorelei to be embarrassed, do you?"

A look of worry shadowed the receptionist's face.

"I can go up to see him myself," Kelly said.

The receptionist stood up from her seat. "I'm afraid I can't allow you to go up there."

Names get recorded. Actions get logged. Red flags got waved. Security was the last thing Kelly needed. "Perhaps one of your people can deliver a message to Mr. Karlsson?" she suggested.

The receptionist readied her hands over the keyboard. "What's your name?"

"Leave it blank."

CHRISTIAN HITCHED his hip against the balcony railing and peered down into the lobby of SVT.

Heat whirled up from a gang of black hoodies who floated together like crocodiles on the prowl. Scrawled on their protest signs, Christian made out the words justice and Landström—two words that had no business being near each other. The public hated Landström Society, so these so-called protesters were likely bought and paid for by them. But even though they were Landström's paid cheerleaders, they were still dangerous.

He backed away, retracing his steps, lightly dampening his leather shoes against the stone floor.

A throng of people spilled out of the broadcasting studio and fanned along the railing, among them Lorelei Lindbergh.

A man in a hoodie pointed up at him. "There he is!"

"Get him!" Another yelled. "Landström deserves justice!"

The mob swarmed the spiral staircase's fortified plastic barrier, their gloved fists and boots punching and kicking it.

Christian's heartbeat surged. He darted for the escape.

The exit door swung open, and two security guards stepped onto the balcony. "We're not here to hurt you, Christian. The police will arrive soon." The guard spoke calmly.

He rushed the guards.

They grabbed him and tackled him to the floor. His head hit the stone ground with a bang. They held him there. "You going to keep calm?"

The stone cooled Christian's hot cheeks. With no other choice, he nodded.

They dragged him to his feet.

The jostling crowd cheered. "Justice for Landström! Justice for Landström!"

Lorelei Lindbergh snapped her fingers at a cameraman. "Get in there!"

A sound technician hoisted a boom mic over the balcony and steered it to the center of the room. It bobbed like a furry fishing pole above the rabble.

A cameraman descended the stairs, beaming the camera light at Christian. "We're live!"

Christian wiped the sweat from his jaw. He descended step by step, the security guards on either side of him, until he stood behind the cracked plastic barrier—the only thing keeping the mob from launching at him and tearing him apart.

The mob bubbled silently.

Christian's pulse raced as the guards removed the barrier. He stepped onto the lobby floor.

A female protester's frosty stare, framed by her razor-edge black bob, captured his attention.

A wild-eyed protester shoved the barrier out of the way and attacked Christian.

The crowd surged.

Christian backtracked up the stairs. The attacker grabbed his leg and dragged him down.

They tussled on the steps.

Metal doors clanked. Riot guards shouted, batons in hand,

their biceps pumped for a fight. They pulled the attacker off Christian.

A dozen more riot officers shuttled into the lobby and surrounded Christian on all sides.

"Stand back!"

Christian welcomed the shield.

An officer stepped forward, his face protected by a hardened plastic mask. "Mr. Karlsson, you're under arrest for arson of the Landström Estate. We will escort you out of the building and into a police car."

The mob raced toward them. A riot officer teetered back.

"Arrest the lot!" someone yelled out.

Riot police began to round up the mob, both inside and outside the building, and they scattered.

Through a narrow gap between the officers, Christian glimpsed the girl with the razor-edge bob. She glanced at him through her thick strands of dark hair, then eyed the cameras along the staircase, the boom mic above her. The camera lights glinted in her eyes.

A riot officer turned to her, and she spoke into his ear.

Christian stood motionless. Who was she, and what was she saying to the riot officer? The other riot police guarded the protesters, who were now filing into windowless police vans.

"Let her through!" the riot officer announced. "Officer Blackwell is going to escort Christian Karlsson to the station."

She squeezed through the narrow gap and slapped handcuffs on Christian's wrists.

"Who are you?" Christian demanded.

"We are releasing you into the custody of a SÄPO agent, Kelly Blackwell. Place your fingerprint here to confirm."

"Kelly Blackwell? SÄPO?" Christian said.

Eyes straight ahead, she said, "Don't say a word," in a low voice.

Even if he tried, not a single word could escape his mouth. She was the journalist Kelly Blackwell, his virtual reality team member, Stormykitten. Not SÄPO. Christian pressed his thumb into the electronic pad.

"Thank you, officers," she said. "I'll take it from here."

CHAPTER 22

INSIDE THE LANDSTRÖM SOCIETY MEETING HOUSE, GAMEMASTER stood transfixed in front of two television screens. Beside him smirked the burly, cigar-smoking member who had placed a bet on Christian winning the Arcadian Match—the only one to do so.

On one screen, they watched Christian exit the burned down Landström Estate, carrying the vase wrapped up in his shirt. On the second screen was a video of a hooded man exiting the burned down Landström Estate, taking the same trail as Christian, only the hooded man was carrying a kerosene tank. The timestamp read two days later.

"The lighting will change to nighttime, and Christian's face will be transposed onto the hooded figure," Gamemaster said.

"Astonishing," the member said. "Well, he did step right into this one, didn't he?"

The Gamemaster turned to the member. "I must say, when he admitted to burning down the Estate, live on TV, despite the charges not being made public, it was a little unnerving. Almost as if someone prepared him for the next public accusation."

The member shrugged. "It is weird, I agree." He ashed his cigar. "So, the hoody retraced Christian's footsteps, carrying a kerosene tank, looking uber suspicious, and our production company will transpose the two footages, fix the lighting, and make it look as though Christian was walking away from the fire?"

"Yes."

The member puffed his cigar. "Looks a little bit obvious, don't you think?"

Gamemaster looked at the member. "Sometimes we have to do the police's work for them."

Lorelei Lindbergh flashed onto the screen, cutting into the deep fake video demonstration. Across from her sat a young woman wearing black office trousers, sneakers, and tousled blond hair. She looked like she was trying to make the 90s grunge era into something respectable.

The caption read Stine Poulsen, Head of Hall of Records.

"Poulsen." The member wrinkled his nose. "Isn't that a Danish name?"

Gamemaster nodded. "I believe Harald works with her."

The member slapped money down in front of Gamemaster. "I don't know if it's wishful thinking on my part, but it still looks like Christian is going to win. So, I'd like to up my bet."

The Gamemaster pushed the money back at him. "Bets are closed."

CHAPTER 23

CHRISTIAN FOLLOWED KELLY INTO THE SUBTERRANEAN GARAGE, and he welcomed the cool air. It soothed his blistered nerves and gave him space to breathe. "Thanks for that back there, whoever you are."

He pulled a fob out of his pocket and double-clicked it. A car beeped in the distance.

"Where can I take you?"

"Good, you have a car, but give me the key," she said.

He looked at her. "It's my car. I'm driving."

"Christian, it's me. Kelly Blackwell. Stormykitten."

"I know." His head dropped back, releasing the pent-up tension in his neck and shoulders. "Why are you here? How did you find me? Don't you live in London?"

She nodded. "Let's get out of here, and I'll tell you what I know."

"I'm driving."

"They can't see you driving me," she said, holding out her palm. "Give me the key."

Christian huffed and relinquished his grip, reluctantly, of the fob. "Don't make me regret it."

Kelly scooted into the driver's seat and adjusted the sides and rearview mirrors. Positioning her hands at nine and three on the steering wheel, she revved up the engine and studied the scene in the rearview mirror. "Let's go to your place."

He started to give her the address.

She raised her hand. "No need. I already have it."

Christian stared at her. "How much *do* you know? And how?"

"A lot, but not everything." She backed out of the tight space. "I need you to fill in some areas for me, and then maybe I can piece the rest together."

She drove out of the garage and turned left. The sun struck the white bonnet and beamed into his eyes. He squinted and quickly put on his AR glasses. "Sunglasses mode," he said.

She drove along Oxenstiernsgatan at a steady 50 km per hour.

They drove along the road, not a word being uttered between them.

Their silence gestated a myriad of questions, and they all tumbled through his mind. "Who are you really?" Christian said.

"I could ask you the same thing, Christian."

He faced her. "Why did you come to the TV station?"

She glanced at him before returning her attention to the road. "It doesn't take a genius to work out you're in trouble."

"And why are you so interested?"

"All I can say is that you're involved in something that involves me, and it's linked to the Landström Estate." Her hand tightened on the wheel. "Can you please take off that ridiculous bow tie."

He pulled it off. "Better? Now, start to answer my questions."

"About a year ago, you connected to our... equipment in London. We received a recording you sent."

"I didn't send anything to you."

"You have a biotracker, don't you?"

He extended his hand. "You mean this?" He lowered and

leaned his arm against the passenger door. "It's not a biotracker. It's a biochip. I had it embedded years ago. I make payments with it, and it keeps my health stats and—"

She sighed. "If it has a chip, it's a tracker in my book. Can we please stay focused?"

"Whatever," he said.

"You just splashed yourself all over the national news. Take it from me. I know how twisted the news can get." She made a right turn. "Do you know what that means? Everyone's thinking you're a pyromaniac criminal on a rampage. From what I gather, your Q-score points should be in the doldrums by now."

He sank into his seat, and the cushion seemed to push him back. He had promised himself he wouldn't look at his Q-scores, he reminded himself. "I have my scores under control, don't worry about that. I need to know— First of all, how do you know where we're going? You don't have any glasses on."

"I don't need glasses, and I don't need a biochip in my palm." She glanced at him. "My chip is in my brain."

He scrunched half his face like a cockeyed pirate. "You got that thing embedded in your brain?"

She inhaled. "It's a long story. Can we stay focused? You just admitted on national television that you burned down a protected national treasure. You do realize that?"

"I can handle it."

"Whoever is after you will run with it." She halted in front of his apartment block and put the car in neutral. "Are you not listening to anything I just said?" Her gaze locked onto a bird soaring in the sky. "What are you involved in, Christian? Why are you being accused of things you and I both know you didn't do?"

"Why are you so interested?" he shot back.

"Because you contacted me."

"So you say." It came out harsher than he intended. "Here in

Sweden, we run on reputation, and someone has my reputation on the line. That means, if they win this game, I face certain death."

"What game? You mean the Q-scores? Your life is on the line?" Kelly stared at him. "You people are so caught up in this game of yours, you don't even know what's real anymore."

"I know what's real, and I'm handling it."

She turned her attention back to the stationary road.

He opened the car door.

An oncoming car beeped. "Watch where you're going!" hollered the driver, shaking his fist.

Kelly reached over and pinned Christian to the seat. "You're not paying attention. Whoever is playing with you, and I suspect it's the Landström Society, will blame the arson on you."

"I hope they do."

She released the pressure on his shoulder as though the wind got knocked out of her. "You mean you want that? Well, if I were them and was out to ruin you, I'd do the same." She shook her head. "Why did you say it if it isn't true? Unless, it is true."

"It isn't true." He rubbed his forehead, thinking about Jacob, about how to best expose Landström, about the mess his life was becoming. "If they decide to use my false confession against me —if they're that stupid—I can prove I wasn't anywhere near the building the night it caught fire. An investigation will start that'll dig into who they are and what they're capable of."

"They can make a deep fake video of you doing it," she said. "Then the accusation would be made to be true. And, if you're in prison, what good are you?"

"I'm not worried. The truth will come out, one way or another."

"My bot has seen so much shit going on here, and a lot of good people have been ruined."

Boy, that was one thing he did know. It was the whole reason he was playing this Arcadian Match at all, but how advanced was this bot of hers that she could see innocent people being ruined? "I work with tech and algorithms all day. I know the limitations, and there are plenty of firewalls and passwords on every website. You can't possibly know—"

Kelly smirked. "My bot has seen plenty."

"Your bot."

She turned to him. "I don't know what you're doing or why you're doing it, but get ready for the arson accusations." She stepped out of the car. "I'll send your biotracker my contact details. When you're ready, call me."

"Can I call you a taxi?"

She gestured behind them. "I called them ten minutes ago."

"I didn't hear you do that."

She pointed to her head and grinned. "My bot."

The taxi drove up and she stepped inside the backseat.

He huffed. No way could there be anything more advanced than his algorithms, he thought, watching her taxi travel in the direction of central Stockholm.

As he steered toward his building's entrance, his glasses dinged. Her direct private email sat in his inbox. Maybe there was something more advanced, he thought, or maybe she was just different.

Underneath her email was a message from Max.

He was asking for Viktor Hansson's personal data to activate O3. He also needed extra code for Program 6 because the office systems were updated.

The weight of to-do's piled on top of Christian, and he could feel the stress in his neck, arms, and legs. He'd have to get his updated algorithms out of their safe place and somehow get Viktor's DOB details. If Kelly did indeed possess a super advanced chip, she might come in handy with locating Viktor Hansson's data. Maybe even with the Q-scores. He stepped inside his building, the urge to check his Q-scores stronger than ever.

He unlocked his front door, and a sense of safety surged inside him. Everything: his sofa, his coffee table, his coffee-stained mug in the kitchen sink, was as he had left it. He dropped his keys in the bowl and tossed the yellow bowtie on the counter.

Looking over his apartment, he glimpsed the junk box on the coffee table Schroeder had left. It looked like a blackened tree stump smack in the middle of his bright minimalist living room — the makings of a surreal painting. He'd have to open it, especially because it may contain the information Max needed, and hopefully more too. Anything he could use against Viktor and Torn and the whole Landström lot would be a bonus. But now was not the time.

He popped open the fridge, grabbed a beer, sank into the sofa, and let the cushions enfold him like a cozy blanket.

CHAPTER 24

STINE SAT BESIDE HENRIK IN THE BASEMENT OF THE HALL OF Records, searching for a way to release the records to the public. The Landström Estate had just become a bigger event, especially after that idiot, her ex-boyfriend Christian appeared on national television, admitting to burning it down. He was a lot of things, but he was not an arsonist. And those manslaughter charges. A hoax for all she knew.

Henrik slammed his fist on the table with a look of defeat in his eyes. "We tried everything, and every avenue is blocked."

"There is one more place we haven't looked."

He glanced at her sideways.

"The Minister of Interior's server."

Henrik ran his hand through his hair. "No way. If we get caught..." he said, shaking his head.

In former days, tiny things like staples gave agents away. Cyber espionage changed all that. Biomarkers identified agents, playful game phone apps traced and tracked, and foreign hackers turned them in, sometimes inadvertently, but who cared about the how. Fortunately, silent warfare countermeasures existed, and so did Henrik. "We are under the aegis of the Minister of Interior. You can get us in. I know you can."

"Why don't we just wait to get the proper permission?"

She scooted closer to Henrik. His aftershave was laced with his salty sweat. "Do you think they'll give it?"

"No, which is why we should leave and wait to get the order from Harald."

If she were on her own, she'd be wearing contouring makeup to blur her face's bone structure for the computer's camera, but with Henrik's help, she could be in and out in ten minutes, under the cyberguise of a Tina Baum, deceased in 1926, just as Bjorn had taught her. All the Ministers were linked to SÄPO directly. If she got onto Harald's desktop, she was in SÄPO. "I just need to get into Harald's computer because he would have the history trail of what really happened to the Landström records."

"It could be anywhere on his computer," Henrik said with a hint of openness in his tone, a sign of being open to negotiation. "It'll take too long to search."

"We could narrow the time frame, and filter out files and documents older than six months. If we don't find anything, we shut it down. No one has to know."

"I agree it is strange that the Landström records went offline right as the Landström Estate got burned. And I don't like when I'm told to set up a software test only to have it backfire. Looks bad on me. But I can't be part of this." He scooted up to the keyboard and started typing. "I may have to leave the room for, say, half an hour."

She smiled. "You had nothing to do with anything."

Henrik typed in the final code and called up Harald Severonsson's account. A few clicks later, they were staring at his desktop.

Henrik shot up from his chair. "I'm going to the cafeteria. You need anything?"

"Take your time."

Her skin tingled. She had free access to all accounts the Minister of Interior held. "I'm going to get you now, Harald."

Ghostlike in his machine, she searched for his link to SÄPO. There it was.

She entwined her fingers, then inputted her alias, Tina Morten. As Tina, she broke through the barrier, manned by border patrol algorithms, and bypassed the cyber data capture system.

A search field popped up.

She typed *alias Bjorn* and boom...found out where he lived, his real name, his aliases, and whether he had indeed been assigned a different mission. These searches never ran smoothly, but clues were always handy, even if they led to a dead end.

Her index finger hovered over the return key. Beads of sweat peppered her upper lip. She took a deep breath, exhaled, and pressed the return key.

There was no going back.

She was in.

Bjorn. Return. Error.
Christian Karlsson. Return. Error.
Special Agents.

She sighed. That type of direct name search was useless. They'd never list them like that. She highlighted the lot and pressed delete. She typed:

General Directors. Return.

Ten names popped up alongside their profile pictures, none of whom looked like Bjorn. If the direct method didn't work, a side entrance might.

Christine Poulsen, Danish. Return.

A page popped up with her name and an early photo taken before she entered the training program. They listed her as part of the Administration Department. She scanned a summary paragraph next to her profile picture. As fascinating as it was to read her own record, she couldn't spare the time. She scrolled down the page, searching for the name of her direct supervisor.

There it was.

Supervisor name: Andreas Neumann.

"So, that's your real name, Bjorn. Nice to meet you at last."
She clicked on the link.

Andreas's profile pic showed a headshot of him. Side-parted light brown hair, brown eyes, square-ish face. That was Bjorn. And his bio link also contained all his contact details. Jackpot.

She screenshotted the webpage, exited the site, and exhaled.

She had all the info she needed, and no one knew anything. She rolled her shoulders, letting the feeling of victory cascade down her shoulders.

With his bona fide contact details, straight off SÄPO itself, she could track down Andreas Neumann, whom she had known as Bjorn, and that was exactly what she was going to do.

CHAPTER 25

CHRISTIAN MOVED INTO POSITION OVER THE METAL JUNK BOX. The Landström Society's insignia emblazoned the lid. It felt bumpy to the touch. He tested the door handle; it held firm—as it should've.

He crossed into the kitchen and swung open the key cabinet. He grabbed the junk box's key, yellowed with time.

An impulse to take another beer from the fridge spiked inside him. He was about to face whatever was inside that metal box, like facing a demon itself, and a beer wasn't going to help. He ignored the rippling dread, returned to the living room, key in hand.

His hands tingled as he inserted the key into the junk box. It clicked, and he nudged it open.

A thick yellow envelope rested inside. No label. Nothing.

He rubbed his palms. Getting it over and done with, he snatched up the envelope, flipped it around and pinched the wings. Its contents flowed onto the coffee table.

Among the documents was a page detailing his family's bloodline traced back to the 1700s, old photographs, aged Post-it notes, several handwritten letters, and the Landström members handbook. Bingo.

He flipped through the handbook—it was exactly the information he needed—and out fell a wad of folded pages.

Unfolding the oversized pages, he could see they were torn out of a ledger book—the kind Viktor had thumbed through when Christian was pleading with them to leave Jacob alone. He counted nine pages in total, and they contained a handwritten list of names and dates, all in fountain pen ink.

He leaned back on the sofa. This is what Viktor wanted. This is why Viktor was so perturbed at not having the papers returned to him. He zeroed his attention on the names.

His hands warmed as he flipped one page to another. Maybe these were the names of Landström Society's members. Maybe the names belonged to Landström's work contacts—like Lorelei Lindbergh. He skimmed down the list.

Her name wasn't on the list. There were only nine pages, and there were probably many more pages in the original ledger.

Maybe the names were their victims. He lowered the pages.

Whatever the list was, he knew he had hit a goldmine. He placed the torn-out ledger pages next to him as carefully as fragile eggs and scanned the rest of the documents. One sheet had an old font, as though it had been typed on a rusty typewriter.

He pulled it out.

It read like a resignation letter dated December 2002, signed by someone named Mr. Thomas Kolokov. It was on headed paper from the Center for Research and Science, and the address on the masthead was Geneva, Switzerland. In the upper right-hand corner of the paper was a bronze figurine with outstretched arms and a spiraling tail. On the opposite side, in the upper right-hand corner, was a bronze insignia he didn't recognize. It was rather ornate, like ribbons wafting in the wind.

His mind was blank. He looked closely at the paper and saw

the fibers and small indentations where it had been touched. Maybe it still held the oils of the fingers that touched it.

He slipped on his AR glasses. "Search for the Center for Research and Science or CRS in Geneva, Switzerland."

Faded images of Geneva, Switzerland, popped up, and he selected one picturing a building captioned as the CRS building.

He landed in a green field in virtual reality. He reached for his haptic gloves and switched on the EarthWatch app. He motioned his hands in the direction he wished the path to take.

He walked through a complex of modernistic buildings, one domed, the other a rectangular functional build. He strolled past the buildings and came to a statue in front of the entrance of a Hindu figurine.

"What are you doing in the middle of Switzerland?" he mused.

The scene turned to night, and another Hindu statue reflected off the front façade of the CRS building. He lifted his glasses and looked at the letterheaded paper. The same bronze insignia. He felt a breakthrough at last, but as quickly as it came, it also left. What did any of this have to do with Viktor or the Society?

He tapped on his mic. "Search for Thomas Kolokov, Geneva, Switzerland."

Search listings popped up, most of which named a psychologist Jacob Korsakoff from 19th-century Russia.

"What the hell?" He bookmarked one encyclopedia link, switched back to the EarthWatch, and walked back to the front of the figurine. "Identify and search this statue in relation to the Center of Research and Science.

"Shiva is a principal deity in the Hindu religion," the audio said, reading verbatim from generic text. "She is the goddess of cosmology and destruction, and she comes with a variety of interpretations. According to the history of this building, the Indian government donated this statue to the CRS between the mid-twentieth and twenty-first century."

"Why would they do that?"

"There are conflicting dates as to when it was donated. Some sites say 1960, and others say 2004."

"That's quite the span of time."

He continued to the back of one of the buildings and landed in a dreary car park. Painted on the building was a multicolored mural designed like a Legoland project.

"Find this mural and explain."

"This building was built by Le Corbusier, an architect influenced by Cubism functionality and minimalism. The mural painted on the side of the building is said to be of a particle collider housed inside one of the buildings."

"There was definitely an incoherent design in this building park," Christian said, shaking his head. "Street art and murals are imposed upon architectural structures, but why put this mural at the back of the building, as if to entertain a bunch of empty cars? Was it commissioned to cover up the concrete eyesore?"

The audio remained silent.

He walked toward a wooden globe. A Visitor Center sign was nailed above the door. He exited the path. "Find the history of the CRS logo."

He crash-landed into an archived discussion in a forum, seeing it unfold as if in real-time. The discussion was dated 2019.

> 666 IS IN THE CRS LOGO. DID YOU SEE
> THAT?

What a strange thing to say, Christian thought. He flipped up his glasses and looked again at the headed paper. No way did the shooting tail look like three sixes. He flipped the glasses back down over his eyes.

CRS SICKOS DESIGNED THE PARTICLE
ACCELERATORS WITH CHAOS IN MIND.
THAT'S ALL THEY CARE ABOUT. CHAOS. OF
COURSE THEY'D PUT 666 IN THEIR LOGO.

DON'T BE DAFT. SHIVA SYMBOLIZES THE
COSMIC DANCE AND THE LOGO SHOOTS
OFF ENERGY IN DIFFERENT DIRECTIONS.
YOU GUYS ARE A BUNCH OF NUTTERS.

Christian shook his head. CRS seemed to be a scientific research center, and that was all. "So many conspiracy theories," he mumbled. "Yep, a bunch of nutters."

The discussion reminded him of Stine, who used to be into this stuff. He was so glad he broke up with her when he did. He paused in midthought. Landström Society wasn't far from this line of thinking, though, he had to admit. All their codes and secrecy and stupid yellow bow ties. These people were made for each other.

He glanced at the clock in the upper corner of his glasses. Three hours had passed, and he was no closer to getting Viktor into the hot seat of the Arcadian Match. All this time wasted because of a resignation letter.

He lifted his AR glasses.

Who sent this letter? And what was he meant to find? He stretched his hands over the documents and perused the photographs, some black and white and some color, all faded. He shuffled through the unfamiliar faces, until he came to one he did know.

The strong cheekbones, intense blue eyes, a warm smile. Owing to the warm smile, he almost didn't recognize the man in the photograph, but it looked too much like the face Christian saw in the mirror every morning. The photograph was dated 1975, stamped with the same irregular logo matching the embossed symbol on the safe.

This was his father's face from a time before Christian was born. He'd never seen him so happy.

Christian's eyes stung, and he quickly wiped the wet from his eyes.

His father was standing next to a younger man. That man looked like Viktor.

A chill went through his body. They were friends all the way back then. In those documents had to be Viktor's data. His fingers scurried through the documents.

Nothing.

At least he had a photographic image of a young Viktor, and he could pass this to Max. As for the other stats... he didn't want to involve Kelly. Enough reputations were at risk. But she was a foreigner, and she could leave Sweden and this whole mess behind. He'd need to tell her everything, so could he risk it?

Did he have much of a choice?

He flipped on his AR glasses. "A message for Kelly Blackwell."

> Can we meet tomorrow at the Garten Café in front of the Opera House? Say around 1pm? Please confirm.

He laid his glasses on the table, picked up the Landström Society's member handbook, and started reading.

CHAPTER 26

A<small>T THE</small> G<small>ARTEN</small> C<small>AFÉ</small>, C<small>HRISTIAN</small> <small>SETTLED INTO HIS SEAT AT AN</small> outdoor table with a view of the Riksdag Parliament Building on one end and the Opera House on the other.

A server wearing AR glasses approached within seconds. He stood at the table, his hands clasped behind him, with a respectful smile on his lips. No funny looks, no sneering eyes, no sneaky snapshots. The quick service signaled the server knew Christian was a Tier 1. He'd check his score later.

Christian ordered two gin and tonics in honor of his soon-to-arrive guest Kelly Blackwell. The server bounced on his heel and left. A breezy gust of summer heat whipped his hair and just as quickly passed. He put his glasses on and called up his Q-scores Leaderboard.

Tier 1 status confirmed. It was a few points lower today—his graph probably dipped into a cliff of doom yesterday—but they recovered after the broadcast, and that's all that mattered.

The wind brushed his back, as if bolstering his confidence.

If Kelly's bot could access Viktor's private personal information—date of birth, childhood photos, hopefully, some offenses tucked away somewhere—O3 could get activated and land a blow on Viktor.

He rubbed his hands. If there's anything else her bot could do —like track down the Landström Network—that would be a bonus, but it didn't matter much at this point. His strategy was working. His O2 preserved his Tier 1 status, the drive of his up-to-date algorithms pillowed, snug and secure, within the Opera House. Viktor's personal information was within his grasp. the Arcadian Match was his for the win. He raised his AR glasses and rested them on the table.

The server placed two gin and tonics down. "In case you need to rate my service, my username is TovakKilt," he said, bowing.

An unfamiliar discomfort roiled inside Christian, a questioning he couldn't put words to. Where once he played the Q-scores, now they played him. He brushed the thought away and nodded.

The bitter-sweet drink coated his tongue and cooled his throat.

The serene river seemed to soak in the sun, and the water's surface twinkled here and there as though being kissed by fairies.

He watched a mother, father, and their two brooding teenagers trundle across Norrbro Bridge. Judging by their khaki shorts, white sneakers, and colorful t-shirts, he guessed they were American tourists.

Pointing at the Riksdag building, the father suddenly halted, and the brigade collided. Tense-filled faces exchanged words, and the father pivoted toward the building again. While the father admired the building's harmonious neo-classical edges and neo-Baroque charm, the mother stood hands on hips, the son draped himself over the railing, and the daughter scrolled through her phone.

Christian couldn't remember the last time he enjoyed the river's vista, the people, the architecture, and soaking in earth's gravity holding him steady. When the whole mess of this Match was over, and Landström was exposed for who they were, he promised himself he'd do this again.

"Didn't think you'd contact me so soon," Kelly said.

Christian snapped out of his daze.

She wore a white flowing summer dress, looking not at all like her last outfit that screamed hardened undercover cop, follower of the law. He preferred this new look because it softened her straight-edged bob.

She took a seat and slammed down a tablet. "After we talked, I dug into your family history." She opened a file on her tablet. "The records aren't fully locked down here. Did you know that?" She showed him his father's death certificate and then scrolled down. "There are two death certificates for your father."

He squinted as he scanned the screen. The black and white copies looked duped, but one recorded the cause of death as a heart attack and the other as a drowning. "My father died of a heart attack. This drowning one is a mistake, or it belongs to someone else," he said, shoving the tablet away. "Lars Karlsson is a common enough name."

"Same date of death, though?"

He shrugged. Maybe there was a corrupt algorithm in the Hall of Records, and Landström records were being concealed. "Stranger things have happened. The Hall of Records has been having problems with the Landström Society records." He leaned into the table. "Can your bot track records down?"

"Specifically Landström Society related records?"

He nodded. "My father was part of them."

"I can tell you that nothing is ever erased or blocked. I know this for a fact. But depending on how corrupted the algorithm is, it may take time. Why don't you just tell me what's going on? Are you any closer to finding out who is out to destroy you? A crazed client, perhaps?"

He didn't know what to say or how to answer that. He was

sitting across from a woman whose bot was more capable than his algorithms, and she was a natural at spotting a lie. He considered his words.

"There's only so much I can do if you don't tell me," she said.

He craved to tell her everything, not because he needed to cleanse his soul or let out some deep, dark secret or because she was a foreigner who could leave Sweden at any moment and not suffer any consequences. It was because he didn't want to be like his father, always pandering to that Society. Christian had decided long ago he was his own man. He thwarted their rules. "It's a man named Viktor Hansson, and he's head of Landström Society."

"Why does he want to take you down?"

The sun seemed to aim its rays at him at that moment, heating his cheeks. A droplet of fear had taken hold. He wanted to tell all, but the words wouldn't come. "I'm involved in something. For the next two weeks, he and I are in a kind of game."

Kelly glanced at the calm waters, but her focus wasn't there. "Sounds like a deadly game," she said, encouraging him.

A part of him clammed up. If they were manipulating the Hall of Records, God knows what damage they could do to him. "Do you think you can get personal intel on Viktor Hansson too? I'll give you points or cash. Name your price."

———————

KELLY STUDIED Christian as he pretended to watch people who crossed the bridge. He was physically sitting there, but his mind wasn't on those people. Something was nibbling at him. The sharpshooter in virtual reality she had come to know was losing focus, and she wasn't sure why.

"You said you were involved in a game. What kind of game?"

He looked at her briefly before reverting his gaze toward the bridge, this time to the river's surface. "You heard it on national television."

"The manslaughter rumors? That's the game?" She recalled what Lewis had said about how Swedes grade each other using the very public Q-score leaderboard. "The worst that can happen is your reputation dies. So what? Who cares?"

A look of horror shadowed his face. "You don't understand." He faced her. "Jacob was my best friend, and my public profile is being publicly hammered over bogus rumors."

"You're right. I don't understand how anyone can make all these claims and people believe them."

"It's not just one person making the claims. It's many!"

"People can say whatever they like. It's not true." She took his hand. "Courts decide who's guilty and who's not."

He exhaled, and his face relaxed.

Kelly shook her head. He wasn't being cooperative. A change of subject was in order. "What kind of tracker is this?"

She indicated toward his arm.

"It's not a tracker, Kelly," he said, his tone clipped. "It's a simple device that lets me pay for stuff. No way can they keep the amount of data that passes through this device. There aren't enough servers in the world."

She shook her head. "Not true either. Every time you pay for something, your location is pinpointed." She gestured at the two gin and tonics on the table. "Someone with know-how will see you sat down here."

He rose from his chair. "I have more important things to worry about, and I hope *they* do too. Maybe we can pick this up another time."

Her irritation stirred. "You asked for my help, and now you push me away. Talk about mixed signals."

He exhaled. "I appreciate your support, but honestly, this is a

game only I can play. Giving you more information than that
could put you at risk."

"I'm not bound by the Q-scores you guys live by."

"But I am." He pivoted toward the opera house and swung
back around. "Do you think you can email me the personal details
of Viktor Hansson by tonight?"

She let her arms drop onto her lap. He needed more than she
could give. "I'll send you what I find, but after that, I should probably get back to London."

"Good idea." Seeming to regret his abrupt manner, he closed
his eyes. "I'm sorry I'm not more forthcoming." He opened his
eyes and slipped a hand in his pocket. "My job is managing reputations. For someone like me, the Q-scores are a big deal, and the
game I'm involved in is an even bigger deal," he said, his tone
softened this time.

"I'm going to put all this down to you being under pressure,"
she said. "Do you have a friend you can talk to?"

"I have a very good colleague, Max. He's also helping me
out." He crossed his arms. "I'm under enormous pressure, I admit.
I apologize for snapping."

She glanced at him sideways and fought the urge to roll her
eyes. It took him a while to admit something about himself, but he
got there in the end.

"I see you need to go. I'll send you what I find," she said,
keeping her gaze locked on his eyes.

He returned her gaze, but only for a second. He rapped on the
back of his chair. "I'm headed to—" He pointed toward the
bridge.

Kelly sighed in frustration. Clearly, this private game Christian was playing weighed on him, but he didn't trust her enough
to tell her more. There was only so much she could do if he didn't
let her in. She tapped on the table and watched him scramble
across the bridge with his head down. She'd enjoy this last Stock-

holm summer evening here at the café. "One sparkling wine," she called out to the server.

Christian was almost on the far end of the bridge now. Beyond him, in the distance, loitered a journalist and his camera crew. A white bus drove up and parked across the mouth of the bridge, blocking half the road. An ambulance came up and parked behind the bus.

She stood up and tunneled her hands over her mouth. "Christian! The road's blocked! Christian!"

Kelly stood still, waiting for him to look up and see what was happening in front of him.

All other traffic on the bridge had disappeared, and the afternoon bustle died.

Goose bumps sprung up her arms. Something was about to happen.

CHAPTER 27

An almighty bang blasted through the serene afternoon.

A second of silence descended on Stockholm.

A dark gray cloud billowed into the sky.

A stampede of distant screams engulfed the city.

Voices roared out from behind, in front, above, and beside Kelly. She shot up from her chair.

Christian stood frozen on the bridge.

Another blast ripped through the air.

She ducked.

Out of nowhere, a wild-eyed crowd stampeded in all directions like panicking wildebeest, their weight pounding the tarmac, tearing through the barrier the ambulance and bus had created. The only one standing still in the mayhem was Christian.

Adrenaline surged through her body, and she ran to the bridge.

The crowd engulfed her, and she pushed through in the opposite direction, moving into the unknown and Christian moving farther away still.

The smell of hot rubber, gunpowder, and fear filled the air. Three fire engines drove up the other side of the bridge.

The crowd's wails sprang forth from bloodied faces, eyes glazed with terror, their heat suffocating.

Smoke spilled out over the river, stinging her eyes.

She wiped the tears and saw people jump the railing and swim across the moat toward Gamla Stan.

Firefighters stood on the edge of the crowd, their gloved hands pointing in one direction. The Riksdag. "Go that way!"

Kelly pushed ahead, covered by the crowd.

Christian appeared as if from a desert mirage, and she reached out to him.

He looked at her, his own face frozen in shock.

"What are you doing?" she pleaded. "Come on! We need to get out of here!" she yelled as loud as she could, but her voice was drowned in the chaos and Christian's oblivion.

ONLOOKERS GATHERED on the other side of the bridge, almost all on their phones, as they filmed the scene.

"Harry, I'm standing on Norrbro Bridge. Stockholm is under attack. I repeat, Stockholm is under attack."

She froze. Her own words paralyzed her, and she was instantly transported back to the time she received Christian's self-delete video. Her bot knew this was going to happen. Had it whittled this moment down to the most probable of all probabilities? And that after this moment, all other probabilities shattered? Anything was possible.

Her heart leapt. Now she understood how her bot communicated to her.

She was here to help Christian. His mission needed help, even if he didn't want to admit it, even if he thought he was the most capable man in the world, and he was. But his mission, whatever it was, called out for assistance because the world could not lose him, or this country.

"Kelly, you there?"

Harry's voice was but a distant sound. She plugged an ear with her finger. "I can't hear you."

Christian rushed into the crowd.

"I'll get back to you," she yelled, running after Christian. "Come back, Christian!"

She ran past a man with a bandage dangling down the side of his head. He wandered aimlessly down the bridge like a shell-shocked zombie in search of nothing. A woman raced toward Kelly, her cheek bleeding from a gash, her head shaking as though shooing away flies. "Get out of here!" Kelly heard her say. "Another bomb could go off."

The journalist and his crew Kelly had noticed earlier, ran to the zombie man.

Police officers barked commands through a megaphone. "The area is not secure. Go to the Riksdag for immediate attention. An ambulance is on standby."

A score of people ran toward the Riksdag. Traffic lined along the edge of the riverbank. Ambulance drivers weaved through the crowd, shouting directions to the nearest safe zone where people would find emergency workers, counsel, and water supplies. Yellow fluorescent jackets were laying down barriers on the road.

Kelly's heart thumped in her chest, the smell of gunpowder stinging her nostrils, and she followed Christian deeper as if he were being pulled like a magnet toward the emergency workers.

The ambulance lights flashed yellow, and the back doors stood wide open. Inside, a man lay on the stretcher covered by a blood-stained sheet. He was talking to someone on his AR glasses.

She finally caught up with Christian, gently touching his arm, and firmly coaxed him to look at her. "Let's get out of here, Christian. Let the emergency services handle this."

He turned to her, his eyes wide. "I need to get inside the Opera House."

Kelly nodded. "Listen to me. Right now, we need to get out of here." She pulled him along, and his feet seemed to float inches above the ground, dreamlike.

He planted himself on the tarmac. "We're going in the wrong direction."

"What's in that opera house that you need so badly?"

"My algorithms. That's where I stashed them."

He looked into her eyes, and all the hopelessness of the moment faded. He believed every word he said.

His AR glasses buzzed, and the vibration roused him from his shellshock trance. Life returned to his eyes.

"We'll get your algorithms later," Kelly said. "Right now, we need to find shelter."

* * *

Christian's head was still spinning from the explosion that had just rocked the city. He could hear the screams of people and the sound of glass shattering in the distance. Kelly had managed to pull him to safety behind a nearby building, but he could still see the chaos unfolding in front of him.

He rubbed his forehead and muttered. "Damn Viktor and this bloody game. So what, murder is okay as long as he doesn't kill me?"

Kelly looked at him, her eyes wide with disbelief. "What are you talking about?"

Christian shook his head, gesturing at the smoke-filled air and the people running in all directions. "This," he said. "This is his idea of a game. Pulling out the big guns, showing off. And now look, we're caught in the middle of it."

Kelly's eyes narrowed. "You think he's behind this?"

Christian nodded, his gaze fixed on the chaos. "Who else? I've already been set up for the homicide of my best friend, and the burning down of the Landström Estate." He waved his hand. "And now this. He's setting me up to take the fall for this bombing."

Kelly's expression softened. "I'm sorry, Christian. This is all so messed up."

Christian nodded grimly. "Exactly. And now, because of it, I'm going to be the scapegoat for this attack."

They stood in silence for a moment, watching as emergency services rushed to the scene. Christian knew they had to act fast if they were going to clear his name and stop Viktor's schemes once and for all.

"Come on," he said, grabbing Kelly's hand. "We need to get to the Opera building."

Kelly nodded, and they began to make their way through the chaos, dodging debris and avoiding the panicked crowd. Christian's mind raced as he tried to come up with a plan, but he still felt hesitant to reveal much more to Kelly. He didn't want to put her in danger, and he didn't know if he could trust her completely yet.

As they neared the Opera, Christian breathed a sigh of relief. They needed to find a way to take down Viktor and clear his name before it was too late.

CHAPTER 28

THE SOUND OF SIRENS AND SCREAMS ECHOED IN THE AIR, mingling with the roar of flames and the crashing of debris. Christian's heart pounded in his chest as he tried to steady his trembling hands. He knew he had to act fast if he wanted to stay ahead of his enemies.

He put on his glasses, which rung like a stoic and steady church bell leading the way out of the chaos. Christian brought them to his eyes, and his vision cleared as the augmented reality interface flickered to life. The screen was pitch black, but a message flashed in his field of view.

"Don't get too comfortable, Christian," a man said, his voice low and controlled. "If you think you licked it with that performance on SVT, think again. You're not going to get away that easily. Rumors can be true—and we have a video to prove it. Expect a gift at your flat."

The line went dead, and Christian felt a cold sweat break out on his forehead. He knew what the man meant by "gift". It was code for a threat, a warning that he was being watched.

His hands trembled, and he felt a wave of fear wash through

him "The Landström Society," he muttered under his breath. "They're behind this."

Kelly looked at him, her eyes wide with concern. "What's happening, Christian? Who was that on the phone?"

Christian took a deep breath and tried to steady himself. He couldn't let his fear show, not in front of Kelly. She was his partner, his ally in this dangerous game. He had to trust her.

"It's the Landström Society," he said, his voice low and urgent. "They're threatening me. They have a video that could ruin me."

Kelly's face hardened, and she put a hand on his arm. "We'll figure it out, Christian. We'll find a way to beat them."

Christian nodded, feeling a surge of gratitude for her support. He knew he couldn't do this alone. "Their gifts were nightmares," he said, his voice tight with emotion. "I had ensconced the list of names, Viktor's photograph, and all the other unidentified documents from the junk box inside his hidden compartment, so it's all safe. But they could plant their gift anywhere."

He took out his phone and called Schroeder.

"Hey, man. Where are you? Did you see what happened to Norrbro Bridge?"

"Yeah, it's nuts," he said, shielding the mic from the wails of the people around him. "Can you do me a favor? Keep an eye on my flat."

"Does this have to do with the rumors about you committing arson on the Landström Estate?"

They took the bait, but now more than ever, he needed his up-to-date algorithms to preserve his score on the Q-score leaderboard. "They're just rumors. Landström Society needs to blame someone."

"Why you?"

"Because I turned their rotten membership invitation down. I'll be home later. Can you keep an eye on my flat?"

"Sure thing." Christian tore off his glasses. Victory was one step closer. He looked at Kelly. "They took the bait."

"Who took what bait?"

He searched for an exit from the crowd. "Landström Society will start to spread the arson rumors that I burned down their Estate."

"Just as I said they would."

He nodded. "As you said." He found an opening in the crowd. "I need to hold back the points drop that is going to come my way."

"How?"

He pointed toward the opera house. "That's where I stashed my updated algorithms."

She followed behind. "What do your algorithms have to do with the arson rumors?"

"Max needs the algorithms to activate O3. That will replenish the points I will inevitably lose once the arson rumor picks up traction online. Then, when I get Viktor's personal information, with the help of your bot, I'll land him a blow."

"*If* there's something on Viktor my bot can find," she said.

His jaw tightened. "This is Sweden. Everything is online." He grabbed her hand. "This way."

He wound around the edges of the crowd, yards from the actor's entrance to the opera house. "I have to do this alone," he said to Kelly.

"I'll get to work on Viktor Hansson. Anything I find will be in your inbox when you get home."

He squeezed her arm and trekked to the back of the building.

CHAPTER 29

As soon as her doorbell rang, Stine scurried to the intercom. Bjorn, aka Andreas Neumann, stood in front of the security camera, briefcase in hand, scanning the street. All the efforts to track him down succeeded, and the opportunity to get answers to her questions finally arrived. She buzzed him in.

Not a word passed between them, but seeing him there, standing at her front door, seemed to liberate all her pent-up energy. She stepped aside and let him pass. "Where have you been?"

He exhaled and squeezed his tired eyes. "I was assigned a case that took up all my attention."

"Let me guess. Eriksson assigned you," she said.

Bjorn loosened the knot in his tie. "There's a war going on inside the Bureau. Eriksson is intent on taking over."

Stine carried in two tumblers filled with sparkling water and placed them on the table. "I guessed as much. I called you several times, and when Eriksson showed up, I knew something was up."

"Good thing you persevered." He sipped water. "Got anything stronger?"

She reached for a bottle of vodka. "Does that envelope have something to do with the Landström Society, by any chance?"

"The Landström Society is looking to merge all the social clubs under their control," he said, taking the shot glass of vodka that Stine had poured.

If Landström monopolized the social clubs, Stine reasoned, the Q-scores could be easily manipulated. "What proof do we have?"

Bjorn swigged back the vodka and opened his briefcase. He untied a large manila envelope and grainy, black-and-white images spilled out. One photo was of Harald, her boss, sitting at a table with a man slightly younger than him, the opposition party leader, and the most well-known social club leader, Ulrich Tokvej. The whole country knew Ulrich because he consistently ranked in the top five of Tier 1.

She picked up the photo. "Who's next to the Minister of Interior?"

"Viktor Hansson, the new leader of the Landström Society." Bjorn pointed at the timestamp in the lower left-hand corner of the image. It was taken at 11:15 p.m. Last night.

Tension built around Stine's shoulders. "After the bomb went off? Do they have something to do with it?"

"We believe Christian Karlsson might know. He's involved with them somehow. Did you see that broadcast he put out? He was wearing their signature yellow bow tie."

She'd been wanting to get Christian out of her life for good, but he always seemed to pop up like a bad rash. "I used to date him, you know."

"I know."

"Of course," she said. Bjorn recruited her during her conspiracy theorist days when she and Christian were living miserably together. "I don't think he's part of them. He hated that Society."

"Why would he appear as a member then?"

She shook her head. "I was surprised. And then, he confessed to all that stuff. Christian is a lot of things, but not that. He'd never confess in front of a live audience like that. It looks like someone had a gun to his head, if you ask me."

The look on Bjorn's face told her he concurred. "We believe the Prime Minister's position is at stake. The bridge bombing, we believe, is connected. The media is coming down hard on how the PM handled it. They're building dissent against him to get the public to push him out. Then, Landström Society will place their own puppet, the opposition party leader, in power."

"Hasn't the opposition been pushing to turn the Q-scores into the national currency?"

Bjorn nodded. "Once the PM is out, we can expect that agenda to take the forefront."

"And with the Q-scores under their control, they'll be omnipotent." A sense of dread folded over her. "We can't let that happen."

"And we won't. There is someone by the name of Kelly Blackwell. I'll send you her details, or rather, her IP address. She's already in Stockholm—"

"Her IP address? What is she, some kind of walking AI?"

He shook his head. "She's real, all right. Too real, some might say."

"Is she one of us?"

"She's not one of our agents, no. She's independent."

"So, we need to keep an eye on her?"

"She's more of an asset, but she's British and protected by her government." He stood up. "She, well, I'll let you discover for yourself."

She glanced at Bjorn sideways. "Who is she?"

Bjorn laughed. "That's what we're trying to figure out too,

and I'm not sure why they sent her. She's been meeting with Christian. In fact, she was at the bridge with him yesterday. Once we get a handle on her angle, we'll know how to manage her."

CHAPTER 30

YELLOW AND BLUE LIGHTS FLASHED AGAINST CHRISTIAN'S residential high-rise—the gift the caller had warned him about. He clamped a hand over his pocket, carrying the storage drive containing his up-to-date algorithms, as though he were carrying a loaded gun. He took a turn off the side of the building and entered the bike shed.

Not a secure nook in sight.

He pushed the drive deep into his pocket, donned his most confident walk and strolled along the entrance path.

He entered the building and stopped at the first resident, a teenage kid he'd never noticed in the building. "What's going on?" he whispered.

She gave him a surly look and shrugged.

An athletic-looking police officer asked for his ID. Christian held out his palm. A beep rang out from the officer's scanner, confirming Christian's ID.

The officer raised an eyebrow. "Christian Karlsson. Your neighbor called in a disturbance. That's why we're here."

Christian scanned the small crowd of residents, no more than six or seven in a building of fifty, and then turned back to the officer's indigo-blue eyes. "I need to get upstairs. How long will this take?"

"Christian Karlsson, there are rumors swirling about you being in the vicinity of Landström Estate the night of the fire."

He glanced at the huddled residents, acid churning his stomach. "They're full of shit. I was no where near the Estate when it burned down."

"You said you burned it down! We all saw you say it."

"It's called entertainment," Christian said between gritted teeth.

Another police officer stood in front of Christian. "The sooner we get information on your precise whereabouts, the sooner we can proceed with the next stage in this investigation of the case of arson."

This was all part of the game, had to be, Christian thought. But to involve the police? Unless, the Landström's network included the police. Christian held his feet firm to the floor. "I need to call a lawyer before I answer any questions."

The officer pressed a button on the front of his vest and a red light switched on. "I'll be recording this interview."

An elderly resident, in slippers, shuffled over to a police officer. He pointed his boney finger at Christian. "He's the one."

Christian eyed the old man. Him and his wife lived a floor down, and he rarely bumped into them in the lift, and certainly never on the staircase. "You're mistaken," Christian said, his voice firm.

"I saw you."

The old man turned to the officer.

Christian stepped forward. "He doesn't know what he's saying."

"Mr. Karlsson," the officer said, pulling Christian away from the old man, "everyone's feeling a bit confused today, but try to stay focused so I can record as many details as you can remember. It will really help the situation."

Christian's chest tightened. He needed to get these police officers, this old man, all these people who knew not a thing, off his back. "Look, officer. I was at Norrbro today. I need time."

His glasses fluttered against his chest. He glanced down and saw Owl flashing its red dot.

The officer dropped back, rested his hand on the baton and gave him a searching look.

Sweat peppered Christian's brow. "It's an emergency. I need to take this," he said, slowly pulling his glasses out of his pocket.

"Keep them in AR mode. I need to see your eyes," the officer said.

He put them on, keeping the glass translucent. Superimposed on the lobby's floor, he saw a photo of himself in the lobby, and he was talking to police officers. It was snapped just minutes ago, before the old man shoved his bony finger at him. "Call up the vital feeds," he said into the mic.

Sure enough, the photo was already plastered all over the boards.

Horror scenarios swirled in his mind. He glanced around the room, at every single police officer, at every resident, at every onlooker standing outside. Someone here snapped these shots, and it could be anyone, but the angle of the shot told him it was someone on the inside.

A ring chimed. A black screen appeared. He knew it was the caller.

"Christian Karlsson," the voice said, his tone deep.

He glanced around the room. "You again."

"The image is punishment for talking. If you don't want more out there, don't involve the police."

The line went dead.

Christian swayed. If he went along with the caller's request, it was no guarantee other photos, real or fake, would not appear online. "Connect with Kelly Blackwell," he said into the mic. "Message her to record everything she sees."

The officer faced him and switched on his body camera. "Please take off your glasses."

Christian removed the glasses, and held them, face out, on the crowd. "I was talking to my colleague Max," Christian said. "I need to get work to him."

The officer squinted. "Why don't you begin by telling me where you were this morning?"

Christian recalled the start of the day, recounting lunch, leaving Kelly out of the story, of course, and how the bomb suddenly went off. His memory of the American family of four was like an aftershock.

The officer whispered into another's ear. The second officer's face gradually tightened.

The caller's words echoed in Christian's mind. *No police*. And then, he realized, for all he knew, one of their police officers posted the image of him, which meant that the police were in the Landström network.

The second officer hooked his thumbs on his belt. "Karlsson, you need to come into the police station to give a statement."

"I just gave your colleague a lengthy statement."

"Let me lay it out for you, Karlsson. You were on national television confessing to all sorts of crimes earlier in the week, your apartment has been ransacked, and you happened to be at Norrbro today." The officer glanced at the residents huddled in the center of the lobby. The elderly resident, from the lower level, returned his glance and quickly looked away. "We have a witness who says you were here when your apartment was ransacked. From our point of view, you are a suspect."

Christian stared at the old man, the last person he thought would be involved in Q-scores, but Landström had their tendrils everywhere. "Looks like someone is out to destroy me," he said.

The two officers stood in front of Christian, their presence bearing down on him, designed, it seemed, to force compliance. "There have been arson developments at the Landström Estate as well. It would be best if you came in and answered further questions."

Anger bubbled in Christian, and he squashed it down with a deep inhale. "I'm calling my lawyer."

Christian dialed Schroeder, silently praying he was in the building.

On the fourth ring, Schroeder answered with a cough. "Hey."

"Schroeder, it's me Christian. I have a situation."

"Where are you?"

"Downstairs in the lobby. The police want me to go for more questioning having to do with the Landström Estate."

"Why? What happened?"

"That's just it! Nothing! Be my lawyer."

"I'll be right down."

Christian lowered his AR glasses. "My lawyer's on his way."

The officer wrinkled his lips.

Minutes later, an unshaven Schroeder shuffled into the lobby wearing baggy jeans and a white T-shirt. "I'm Schroeder, Christian Karlsson's lawyer." He flashed his palm at their scanner, and it confirmed his ID. "I understand you want to take Christian Karlsson in for questioning? Is that correct?"

"We think it's best."

"Unless charges are brought against him," Schroeder said in a definitive but neutral tone Christian hadn't before heard, "he is not obliged to go to the police station."

The officer looped his finger on his belt. "But charges are imminent," he said with a tangy look of defeat on his face. "I must advise you that all of your client's files at the Hall of

Records will be sealed as of midnight tonight. No one will be able to look into his records without our permission."

"As his lawyer, I can apply for whatever records I require to do my job," Schroeder said.

Christian stepped forward. "I need to go up to my apartment now."

The officers glanced at each other. "Go ahead, but make sure you stay in town. If new information arises, and it will, you'll have to answer for it."

Christian walked to the elevator, unsure what he was about to step into, wondering if he should've told the officer everything. But he also knew it wouldn't help. Someone in there had posted the image, and it could've been any one of them.

The only thing he did know was that his algorithms were in his pocket, and he'd do whatever it took to get them to Max. His reputation had taken enough blows, and it was his turn to hit Viktor.

CHRISTIAN INSERTED the key into his front door, half expecting the lock to be broken, part of the Landström's gift. Relieved, he crossed the living room and soft-pushed the hidden wall panel. It opened like a gateway to heaven. Viktor's photograph, the letter, the list of names secure, just as he had left them.

Feet shuffled down the living room hallway.

Quickly, he stuffed the contents inside the front of his jeans and shut the compartment door.

Schroeder's bushy hair poked through the arched entrance. "They left. What happened down there?"

"Thanks for your help."

Schroeder elbowed the door; it knocked against the wall. "I'll have to do some follow-up paperwork."

"I'll send you points. Now." Christian booted up his AR glasses. "C'mon, c'mon, c'mon," he muttered under his breath.

"It'll cover the admin fees," Schroeder said. "No rush."

A notice bounced in Christian's screen; his glasses read aloud:

"Christian, I found the info you need. Sent it through. Leaving for London tonight."

Hearing Kelly's voice filtered out the ugly mess all around him, and the breakthrough she delivered was the boon he needed. He wished he had met Kelly during a better time in his life.

Schroeder stepped into the room. "Was that Stormykitten I heard?"

Christian quietly slipped his glasses into his pocket. "She was thinking of coming to Stockholm."

Schroeder's face scrunched. "Bad timing."

"That's what I thought," Christian said, seizing clean under-garments from the pile of clothes on the floor. His back to Schroeder, he slipped the documents and clothes into a backpack. "Hey, man, let's catch up later."

Even if Schroeder was genuinely innocent—no one was ever genuinely innocent—Christian didn't want to bring him into his mess. "Thanks, but it's best if I find somewhere neutral for the night."

He loaded the backpack onto his shoulder. "I'll call you."

A sense of confidence ushered him down the stairwell, and he shoved open the building's fire escape door.

Landström had invaded his life, but soon it would all end. His algorithms in his pocket and the documents Max needed to launch O3 in his backpack, there was only one thing left to do. He looked at his palm. Kelly was right. This was a biotracker. He needed to get rid of it.

He trekked down Arbetargatan, and headed west. His destination: Max's place.

IN HER HOTEL ROOM, Kelly zipped her suitcase and carried it to the door. She glanced at the clock. Two hours to kill before her flight.

The trip was a bust, she thought. Christian's caginess, the bill that would soon hit the British government that she'd have to catch and redirect, him sneaking off to the opera after the bomb went off.

The bomb.

Sweden brought with it nothing but strife. The only thing that did go according to plan was retrieving Viktor Hansson's personal data, which she had already sent to Christian.

Her job was done.

She switched on the TV.

Every network reported on Norrbro and the bomb that rocked the city.

Agitation rumbled through her to get the hell out of Stockholm, but underneath the impatience and agitation lay a dissatisfaction with how it all went. Part of her wanted to leave this country behind. She had traveled to Stockholm to meet Christian in person and because finding foreign digital records was safer to do from within. She met both goals.

The dark-haired journalist from the bridge was being interviewed, his hair styled in the same manner as earlier that day. She pumped the volume.

"We were lucky to be alive," he said through the television speakers. "We arrived just minutes before it went off."

"Yeah, as if you were expecting something to happen," Kelly said to the TV. "All that destruction, what a scoop!"

Her mind drifted to her meeting with Christian. When they met, Christian said his father's death was from a heart attack. But there was a duplicate record saying he had drowned. Which of the two was it, exactly?

It bothered her. "Call up Christian Karlsson's history," she said.

Her brain-bot kicked into gear. Smooth as a high-speed Japanese train, his full file appeared in her mind's eye.

They went back to 2003. "That's strange."

She started with the latest record available, the death certificate, and planned to work her way backward.

She looked over the death record. It said the cause of death was a heart attack. She paused and recalled the first time she had seen the death certificate. Could there be another Lars Karlsson who died on the same day? Something's wrong with the record. "Call up Lars Karlsson's records."

Up popped the Lars Karlsson record, and she scrolled down until she came to his family. The heart attack and the drowning records both listed Christian Karlsson as his son.

It was the same man.

"Track the source of the records and give me the date and time both death certificates were posted."

Both records came from The Hall of Records. The heart attack was posted on 12 August 2028. The drowning was posted on 10 August 2028. Two days apart. This meant he died of drowning originally. Unless the doctor made a mistake the first time around. How would a doctor make such a mistake?

Christian was convinced his father had died of a heart attack.

"Who filed the heart attack death certificate?" Kelly asked.

A list of names appeared. She narrowed in on the name of the ME.

MEDICAL EXAMINAR: Dr. Öberg.

"Who was the on scene police officer who verified the record?"

OSO: Petty Officer Johan Seger I PID: 1005749832

"Locate Officer Seger, badge number ending 9832."

The location zeroed in on the residential neighborhood of Kungsholmen, the very same address she had been to earlier in the week. Christian's home.

A chill went through her. The officer who had falsified the death certificate was at Christian's place, and the caller had said something would be waiting for him at his place.

"Call Christian Karlsson," she said, her voice raised.

The line rang and rang.

She glanced at the clock. It was one hour before her flight departed. What compelled her to help this guy who wasn't willing to pick up the line? Was she really helping him, or was she helping herself?

She was the one who sent the message, or rather her bot had sent the "Stockholm is under attack" message, the message that started this whole thing.

The mystery was her own, and she needed answers for herself. Kelly shunted off the bed, opened her suitcase, and grabbed the truth serum pen.

"Call me a taxi. We're going to 55 Alströmergatan, Kung-sholmen."

KELLY ARRIVED at 55 Alströmergatan and buzzed the doorbell labeled Karlsson. No response. She stepped away from the building and looked up at the windows. Most of the lights in the building were eerily dark, as if most residents had vacated the quiet street.

She buzzed his door again.

Nothing.

"A message for Christian Karlsson," she ordered her bot.

She felt a presence behind her. Heat crawled up her back. From the corner of her eye, she made out a tall figure standing too close for her liking.

She pivoted.

A man in an overcoat reached out for her.

She dodged him and darted down the street.

"Stop!"

He ran after her, his heavy footsteps right behind. In what felt like seconds, he grabbed her arm, and she felt a prick pierce her skin. Within seconds, her muscles slackened, and she slumped to the ground.

"She won't be bothering us for a while," someone said.

A woozy unconsciousness swept over her.

CHAPTER 31

THE SUN'S RAYS BEAT THROUGH THE WINDOWS, INTO MAX'S living room. Christian woke in a pool of sweat, blood seeping through his bandaged hand. He shot up from the sofa.

"Relax, man," Max said, sitting at a desk in front of his laptop. "While you were sleeping, I checked your palm. It's all good. No infection. It'll bleed a little here and there until it heals up."

Christian wiped his sweat-soaked face with his T-shirt. "Thanks. At least that bio-whatever it was is out of me."

"But you still have your AR glasses. And they're traceable."

"I have a block on them."

"Naturally," Max said. "While you've been getting your beauty sleep, I got Octopus running like a dream. Most of your points are replenished. You're a Tier 2."

Christian groaned, but after everything he'd been through, he didn't have the energy to care. He eased down on the sofa.

"You were making noises all night," Max said. "Dreaming of someone special?"

Christian wished he could laugh, but the game weighed heavy

on him. "Did you get the photo of Viktor Hansson, his date of birth, place, and background?"

"It's loaded into O3 and ready to go."

Christian nodded. "I wouldn't put stock in his background, but his DOB should be accurate." He pulled up a chair next to Max and studied the preprogrammed directive. It was actually very simple. "All good. Viktor will get the strike he deserves."

"You're going to make him very mad."

Christian shrugged. "Yeah, Viktor doesn't like being exposed."

"When do you want to launch O3?"

"I need one more thing before we launch. Get a high res copy of the video of my SVT interview. We're going to make several different deep fakes of people also confessing to arson. Take the people from the audience and transpose them with me on the stage. I'll need it for when The Landström Society releases their deep fake of me, hoody removed, setting their Estate on fire."

"They're going to lay the arson on you?" Max swung himself around. "How do you know?"

Christian thought back to what Kelly had said when he fake-confessed to the arson on national television. "Because I would do the same."

"Rumors are one thing," Max said. "but manufacturing police evidence is illegal."

"And that's the point," Christian said. "Once the police find out someone at Landström Society doctored the arson video, they'll pay Viktor a visit. I need them to start asking questions."

"That could take a while."

"We'll use the time to turn the discussion into… the danger of doctored videos on society."

"And since your confession on SVT isn't admissible, the investigation will focus on Landström. Outstanding," Max said. "God I love working with you."

Christian dropped his hands. "Send me our audience deep fakes as soon as possible."

Max's smile subsided as though bitterness wedged itself between his teeth. "Did you actually burn down the Estate?"

The question jolted Christian like a stray bullet. "No, I didn't do it. Of course, I didn't."

Max focused on his laptop. "I had to ask."

"I'm glad you did." Christian sighed. "Be sure to protect yourself when you press the nuclear button on Viktor Hansson."

A timid lightness returned to Max's face. "Are you kidding? I wear titanium gloves when it comes to Landström."

"One day, Max, you won't have to," Christian said. "Be sure none of this can trace back to you."

Max rolled his chair away from the laptop and faced Christian. "So that takes care of the arson rumors. What about the manslaughter rumors? What really happened to Jacob?"

Christian closed his eyes, feeling an anguish charge through his hands. Had Jacob held on, they would've made a difference to society, and Jacob would've felt victory for once.

Christian opened his eyes and wiped away the sting. "Jacob was a genius with a sensitive soul, and he was born into a useless family." He cleared his throat. "They didn't understand him, thought he was dumb, and treated him that way. His braindead teachers didn't listen to him, his classmates ridiculed him. From day one, he was mistreated and misunderstood. Finally, one teacher recognized his brilliance and came to his rescue. She fought for him to get into the right school. That's when I met him."

He glanced at Max. "He was thirteen, and by then, all the bullying got stuck inside him." He stood up. "Viktor Hansson knew this, recruited him into the Landström Society, and Jacob was too soft for their initiation. They played on Jacob's vulnerabilities, and he started to fall apart. I went to the hotel. Karen, his wife, was there. I tried to talk him down. He confessed to burning down the Estate, but he didn't do it."

Christian shook his head. "For all the genius that Jacob was, no way was he a destructive soul. His last words to me were, 'Remember who you are, Christian.' Then, he jumped."

"Viktor and the Landström Society drove him to it," Max said, breaking the silence. "But why?"

"Because they can," Christian said. "They're heartless."

Max's forehead creased; he rubbed the back of his neck.

"Do you remember the Nationalbanken trial having to do with turning our currency into Q-score points?"

Max nodded. "Yeah, the Opposition Party's been pushing that currency agenda for a while. Didn't the trial get suspended?"

"Jacob was going to be the star witness. He was going to prove how Landström Society manipulated the Q-score leaderboard."

Max licked his lips. "Holy shit."

Christian nodded. "And now they're trying to do the same to me because they know that I know."

"They're accusing you of manslaughter and arson to bury you." Max slowly nodded as though the puzzle pieces were locking into place for him. "You said Karen was there in the hotel room when Jacob jumped. She's your witness."

"She's compromised." Christian pinched his chin. "So far, the manslaughter accusation is a rumor, and O3 is replenishing my points. I don't think they'll make any deep fake videos about Jacob because they'll have to explain why Karen and Jacob were in the hotel. It would all come out in court, and they don't like that amount of publicity. They'll just let that manslaughter rumor be a rumor."

"Is there any way we can prove they started the manslaughter rumor against you?"

"Perhaps." Christian stood up, resolute. "One way or another, I will expose them for who they are."

"The audience deep fakes should be ready in a couple of days," Max said. "Whenever you give me the go ahead, I'll launch."

Christian swallowed, his parched throat burned.

CHAPTER 32

KELLY WOKE UP ON A CONCRETE FLOOR ON HER SIDE. SHE ROLLED over. The low ceiling and bare walls echoed her breathing. She lifted herself up.

A single wooden chair sat in the corner of the room.

Looks like this is going to be an intelligence-gathering session, she thought. That meant she knew something that whoever brought her here needed to know.

She coughed.

A man entered the stark room, a beard covering most of his face. He smelled like the woods: scented pine and dead leaves.

Not saying a word, he brought the chair to the center of the room and sat down.

"Where am I?"

He didn't answer her.

"Who are you?"

"I'll be asking the questions," he said in a deep, mysterious accent.

"About what?"

"You need to stop talking now."

"Is this about Christian Karlsson?"

"They told me you would ask a lot of questions." He stared at her. "What were you doing with Christian Karlsson?"

"Who are they?" she said.

He pulled a scalpel from his inside breast pocket. "Kelly, we know who you are. You're a spy for the British Government."

She looked at the blade in his hand. "You won't need that."

Her heart beat faster. She took a deep breath and steadied her racing mind. She remembered her own scalpel, in the form of a truth serum, and it was nestled in her back pocket. She focused on the nuances of his accent, using the details to calm her mind.

He sounded German with French undertones thrown in. He must've been from the Alsace region or the border of France and Germany. Could he be from the German or the French secret police? Or maybe he was from Interpol.

He snickered. "So, you're going to tell me what I want to know?"

"I will."

He clutched the scalpel between his fingers. "So, tell me about Christian."

"Is there anything specific you want me to start with?"

The interrogator lowered the blade. "His father."

The only people who would be interested in Christian's father are those who lied about his manner of death, Kelly thought. This interrogator came from the Landström Society. She suppressed a laugh. "Yes, I can tell you something, but what do I get in return?"

"Your life."

"Did they tell you I have this awful habit of worrying about all sorts of things?" She laughed. "But today, my life is not one of those things."

She whipped out the truth serum pen out of her back pocket and shoved it into his thigh.

His eyes widened. Seconds later, his eyelids softened, and in no time he was putty in her hands.

CHAPTER 33

HARALD HOBBLED ONTO THE CHECKERBOARD FOYER OF THE
Landström meeting house and passed a police officer on the way
out. He paused. "Everything all right, officer?"

The officer nodded. "I came to see Viktor. How's the game
going?"

Harald grunted.

The swish of shuffling paper streamed out from the study. He
pulled a hardback off a shelf and shuffled down the hallway.

"Ah, Viktor." He entered the library. "I came to drop off a
book. It was one I borrowed a couple of months back and finally
got around to finishing it."

He dropped the book square on Viktor's desk, and it landed
with a thud.

Viktor laid his papers down. "I needed quiet time to read too."

"I saw an officer leave the building. Clearly, one of ours."

"Seems that Christian might've broken the rules of the game."
Viktor pushed away from the desk. "He's working with a spy."

"A spy? Is that what the police officer said?"

Viktor sniffed. "I'm going to call an emergency meeting to

discuss it with Gamemaster and the other members. I hope you'll join us."

"Of course."

The grandfather clock chimed.

"Time for the news," Viktor said, picking up the remote control.

A door on the shelf slid open, revealing a television screen. Good Morning, Sweden was on, and Lorelei Lindbergh was sitting on the familiar couch inside the SVT broadcast room.

Harald settled into his upholstered chair.

"We bring you an exclusive story," the TV blared.

The scene panned in on Lorelei Lindbergh. "You may recall the broadcast we aired two weeks ago of the Land-ström Estate."

The picture cut to Lorelei Lindbergh weeks earlier standing outside the gates of the Estate, smoke wafting into the air. Then, it cut to Christian confessing to arson days ago on that very same couch.

The scene reverted to Lorelei Lindbergh in present time. "Rumors and false confessions make good television entertainment, but when a trusted source provides hard evidence, we're obligated to broadcast it for the public's interest." She glanced at someone offstage. "Play the video."

The broadcast room dimmed.

A hooded figure traipsed across gravel, the sound of rocks

crunching underfoot. He carried a gas tank away from the Landström Estate, a fire gathering power behind him
The figure jounced, looking behind him, and the hood shifted from his face. The camera froze and zoomed in.

"Does he look familiar?" Lorelei Lindbergh said, her eyes grave. "This is proof that Christian Karlsson is the Landström Estate arsonist."

The audience gasped.

"Very dramatic," Harald said, turning to Viktor. "It will never hold."

Viktor lowered the volume. "It doesn't need to," Viktor said. "The police will do their cyber forensics, as they should. When they discover the video is a deep fake, our man in the police force will blame it on a couple of bored whiz kids playing a cyber prank. All I need is two weeks, and the game is mine."

CHAPTER 34

KELLY CIRCLED THE INTERROGATOR. HE WAS SLUMPED IN THE chair, dribble coming from his mouth, and he almost looked comatose. "How did Lars Karlsson die?"

"Killed by drowning."

"Why?" she asked.

"He wanted a different life. He made promises to keep quiet over the Q-score and the list of names."

"What list is that?"

"The list of people Viktor had targeted. But when Viktor saw the pages torn from the ledger, he knew it was Lars and went after him. Made it look like a heart attack with the help of one of the members."

She recalled the duplicated death certificate signed off by a doctor and witnessed by police officer Seger. "The doctor and the police officer who signed the fake certificate are both members?"

He slurred and nodded.

A wave of disgust went through her. "You knew Christian's father was murdered, and you covered it up; you all covered it up. And for what? A list of names? I can see why Christian is bent on exposing Landström Society."

"Lars is dead now," the interrogator said, his eyelids slow-closing and opening. "And they won't stop. When they win the game, Christian will be theirs."

She stared at him, and all the bitter coldness she felt seeped into her voice. "I won't let that happen."

BLACK-CLAD men blasted into the room.

Kelly's heart pounded, and she stepped back.

A woman in a navy-blue suit stepped out from behind them. Under the overhead light, her hair shined and her cheeks glowed pink, as though she had just come in from an afternoon jog. "We're running out of time, Kelly," she said in a British accent.

"How did you find me?"

The woman's ID tag dangled from her neck. "Your bot sent out the signals." She glanced at the interrogator. "What's wrong with him?"

"Truth serum is in his system," Kelly said.

The agent nodded. "One of SÄPO's case officers contacted us. We've confirmed that Sweden's security is at stake." She handed Kelly a translucent plastic card. "Your job is to get in touch with Stine Poulsen. Tell her Landström Society is seeking to take over the government of Sweden. Tell her SÄPO officer Bjorn sent you."

Kelly took the card. "What about Christian Karlsson?"

"He's none of our concern. Your priority is Stine Poulsen. Relay the information. Get her access to the Hall of Records."

"Why doesn't the SÄPO officer do it?"

"Communications are compromised here. Everything." The agent curled her lips. "Never thought I'd say this, but we could really use your bot's abilities. It's expedient. Then, you'll need to get back to England asap."

"You know," Kelly said, narrowing her eyes at the woman in front of her, "I didn't go through all this shit just to be told what to do. After Stine, I'm helping Christian. He's the key to everything. Eventually, you'll work that out."

The card vibrated in Kelly's hand. The word LEFT lit up on it.

She could hear the agent's sigh as she slipped out of the room, turned left, and treaded down a low-lit passage.

Through a door at the end of the passage, she stepped into a summer day that dazzled her face. She breathed it in. "Locate Stine Poulsen," she said.

CHAPTER 35

CHRISTIAN INSPECTED THE AUDIENCE'S OUTLINES ON THE DEEP fake video Max had sent him. The outlines were perfectly adhered to, no halo effects, the lighting was consistent, and, best of all, the transposed faces were real. Max's work was stellar. He closed the deep fake file, duplicated it, and opened a blank email.

To: Viktor
Cc: Harald, Gamemaster
From: Christian
Subject: Requesting a council meeting today to discuss.

He attached the videos and pressed send.

He took off his AR glasses, unbuttoned his shirt, and switched on the shower. Emptying his jeans pocket, he pulled out a ripped piece of paper.

Scribbled in blue ink was an IP address followed by the phrase:

IP address 555.032.669.017.

Stockholm is under attack. Repeat. Stockholm is under attack.

The handwriting looked rushed.

He thought back to when he had last worn these jeans. "Oh yes. The SVT interview." He laughed and shook his head. "Message for Kelly Blackwell," he yelled in the direction of his AR glasses.

Hey Kelly, it's Christian Karlsson, in case you've forgotten me.
Found a note from stuffed in my pocket. Must've been from that crazy protester. The one who jumped me at SVT.
Remember him?
Note says: IP address 555.032.669.017
Stockholm is under attack. Repeat. Stockholm is under attack.
Just thought I'd let you know.
Hope London is treating you well. Look forward to catching up at a better time when life isn't so crazy.
Over and out.

He hesitated at the send command because he felt a deep need within him to connect, deeper than he expected, deeper than he liked. "What the hell. Just send it," he mumbled.

The glasses dinged a confirmation bell.

He stepped into the shower and let the waterjet massage his tight muscles.

Minutes later, he laid down on his soft bed, but the anticipation of Viktor's call thwarted his much-needed rest.

CHRISTIAN WALKED into the library of the Landström meeting house where the four gentlemen waited, among them Gamemaster. "It was a good decision to meet. I hope you'll agree," he said.

"This better be good, Christian," the pudgy man said and dragged on his cigar. He exhaled a plume of smoke. "I don't like rushing through dinner to come here on short notice."

Viktor nodded in agreement.

"You and I know that video you put out on me burning down your Estate is fake."

"The only thing that matters is what the public thinks," Viktor said.

"This is true," Gamemaster said.

"Call this whole game off, stop this madness, and I won't release my own deep fakes."

An icy cold overtook Viktor's face. "I intend to win this game by the book."

Gamemaster cleared his throat. "We have one week to go. Do what you will, Christian."

"I wanted justice for Jacob, nothing more. You're hell-bent on power. I don't want to use my deep fakes, but I will if I must. Be warned, though, a national discussion will begin, and it will center on Landström Society. Is that what you want?"

"I wasn't going to mention this," Viktor said, "but it has come to my attention that my opponent has broken the rules."

"How?" Christian demanded.

"A woman spy. From SÄPO no less," Viktor said. "She knows everything about the Society." Viktor turned to Gamemaster. "Doesn't this automatically disqualify Christian from the game?"

The pudgy man sipped on his vodka tonic, and the ice cubes clanked in the silent room.

"I need to see evidence," Gamemaster said.

"Her name is Stine Poulsen." Viktor tossed a pack of black and white photographs on the desk. Images of Christian and Stine at the Hall of Records were sprawled before them.

Christian reeled back on his heel. "This evidence is nothing! These photos were taken before the Match began."

"You show us photos of two people chatting in the Hall of Records," Harald interjected. "People do this every day of the week. This is not proof that she knows anything."

Viktor pulled out a sound recorder, pressed play, and turned up the volume.

A woman's voice identified herself at Stine Poulsen, along with her agent status. At the end of the recording, she repeated how the Hall of Records archives were deliberately blocked and that the culprit could be someone at the Landström Society.

The room remained silent.

Christian stood dumbfounded. Stine was on the case. "I didn't hear anyone's name mentioned," he said.

"I agree," Harald said. "And, I would like to add something, if I may."

Gamemaster nodded.

"I spoke to the police officer who provided this... recording. That he'd been on Christian's tail the entire time, tracking him. Not a shred of evidence exists that he divulged the game. Quite the opposite, in fact. Christian has kept his word."

The members glanced at one another.

"We have one man's word against the other," Gamemaster said.

The pudgy member squeezed his cigar between his fingers and turned to Gamemaster. "This game is getting a bit unwieldy, I must admit. Lying to the public is one thing, but deep fake videos and getting government departments involved is a new level. I may have to side with Christian. Let's end this game before things get out of hand."

"There are no rules against lying," Gamemaster said. "Forging documents is also allowed. None of these actions contravene the playbook."

Harald rubbed his thumb and forefinger together. "And what about bombs?"

"I am aware."

The pudgy member coughed. "Viktor orchestrated the bomb?"

"Dummy bomb," Viktor corrected. "No one died. I brought in actors and so forth. I did have to use the code to get the journalists there, but they were very agreeable."

Christian's attention swirled. The bomb felt so real, sounded so real. The whole experience was a lie? He reached out and gripped the first thing his hand touched.

Gamemaster faced Viktor. "You are stretching the rules thin, I must say. We don't behave this way in this Society. For the bomb, I will be deducting 100,000 points."

"It was a good play."

"But too many people were involved, and it was too dangerous," Harald said. "People could have been killed."

"Well, then, gentlemen, the matter is settled," Gamemaster said. "The Arcadian Match continues, and we will conclude in one week."

Gamemaster walked out of the library.

Harald stepped up to Viktor. "This isn't like you, Viktor. You're usually more cunning than this. Are you afraid the boy will win?"

"I'll recover those points soon. I'm well ahead anyway."

Christian walked out of the library and into a nightmare he felt he would never escape. They would never see reason; they would tear the city apart if they had to, and they would do whatever it took to win.

Would he ever get Jacob the justice he deserved? Would he ever prove Viktor had pushed him to his death? Maybe the only way he could defeat Viktor was to defeat him here and now, in this Match. Be relentless. Be unforgiving. Be ruthless. He put on his AR glasses and selected Max from his call list.

"Release the audience deep fake videos to Lorelei Lindbergh. Give her code 0099. Tell her they're from Christian Karlsson and are to be played tonight."

CHAPTER 36

S<small>WEAT TRICKLED DOWN</small> S<small>TINE'S BACK AS SHE SAT UNDER THE</small> SVT stage lights. The camera operator's silent fingers gestured one, two, and the audience-packed broadcasting room quietened.

On three, the cameras went live.

"In recent weeks," Lorelei Lindbergh began, "the Hall of Records has been criticized for blocking members of the public from records meant to be available for all. Now, we have an issue with doctored videos. Today we are talking to Stine Poulsen, manager of the Hall of Records." She turned to Stine. "How do you answer the public's concerns that some official records might not be authentic?"

The pressure mounted. Stine knew this interview was being watched by people in government and SÄPO, and everything she said would be scrutinized. She cleared her throat.

"I apologize for the blocked records. During routine tech maintenance, we stumbled across a glitch in the system and chose to shut down certain records. We also allowed the public to make online requests for emergency cases, a service that wasn't available to the wider public prior the glitch."

"So what was the glitch?" Lorelei asked, glancing at the audience.

"We were working toward unlimited public access," Stine said. "It created a blockage in the system. Having a twenty-four-hour service available to the public is bound to have glitches. We were transparent about the challenges, and the Minister of Interior issued several public statements about it."

"Landström Estate seems to be at the center of the blocked records."

Stine nodded, feeling a setup in the question.

"Speaking of incorrect records," Lorelei said. "The Landström Society released a video of Christian Karlsson setting fire to their Estate. Didn't you date him?"

Sharp needles dug into Stine's back. What's-his-face brought nothing but trouble into her life and Lorelei was smearing her in a death-by-association tactic, once again. The deep fake rumor had nothing to do with her or her department. "I used to live with Christian Karlsson, yes, but I'm not sure —"

"When Karlsson's counter-deep fake videos emerged," Lorelei said, "the public questioned how the Hall of Records vetted the national archive. Are all the records authentic?"

"Do you mean, like the interview you had with Mr. Karlsson that was deep-faked and showed your audience members also confessing to arson?"

Lorelei's eyes flickered. "We've already addressed those deep fakes and the public agreed the demonstration was important. As you know, the nation is discussing the matter now, which is one of the reasons you're here." She adjusted her position in the chair. "So, what about the records at the Hall?"

"If records are tampered with once they hit the archive, that's an illegal act that falls within our domain to prosecute." Stine inhaled. "If files are missing —"

Lorelei Lindbergh gasped. "You mean to say the Hall of Records can be breached?"

"If you let me finish." Stine straightened her back. "If files are missing, we have a procedure in place which I'm happy to post on our website for the public to read."

"Let's go back to the blocked records." Lorelei's eyes swept her tablet. "When did you notice something wrong at the Hall of Records?"

"About five or six weeks back."

Lorelei leaned forward. "That long? And it's not yet been fixed?"

To this day, Stine hadn't received a credible explanation about why the records had been blocked, and why only Landström Society-related records seemed to be affected. Privately, she knew it was a power play for the Prime Minister's position, as Bjorn had said, and Landström Society was at the heart of this maneuver. Her issue was how to prove it.

Being a journalist, Stine thought, Lorelei must have heard there was a power play for the Prime Minister, and blocked records were a mere symptom. She wondered if the poodle would snap up an exposure angle. Stine clasped her hands on her lap. "Maybe the Hall of Records should open an investigation to the public and provide day-by-day updates on why and how the records are blocked. That would bring further transparency to our process and enable us to regain the public's trust."

The audience murmured what sounded like approval.

Lorelei's shoulders flinched with a nervous shrug. "Would the cyberpolice be happy to share their findings? It would be too tempting for cybercriminals to doctor even more data, don't you think?"

"There is a fine line between security and transparency, I agree," Stine said. "I'm not sure anyone has a comfortable answer for it. But my job is to shore up the public's confidence in the national archives."

"And my job is to play devil's advocate," Lorelei countered. "What you propose would require the Minister of Interior's approval, would it not?"

Stine ignored the question. "Maybe it's time we discuss the paperless policy that was rammed through Parliament," she said. "Did the opposition party consider the cybercriminals?" Stine leaned forward. "In an age where everything is digital, wouldn't it make sense to have paper as a backup?"

"Bold thinking," Lorelei said. "But paper records can be faked too."

"I recall that was one of the arguments for a paperless society, and Sweden must uphold its status as the world's first."

Lorelei gave Stine a curt smile. "Enlightening conversation. Thank you for coming in." She turned to the cameras. "And that concludes the frank and honest discussion with the head of the Hall of Records, Stine Poulsen."

Stine ripped off the mic and stepped offstage.

In the hour it took to field the questions, the public had deducted 10,000 Q-points from her, and more were falling by the second. Lorelei's disclosure of her past relationship with Christian took her to the bottom of Tier 2.

Outside SVT, she waited for a taxi. Why would Lorelei do that? Was she garnering Q-score points, or was it a deliberate smear tactic designed to marginalize Stine, the way Eriksson had tried? Lorelei might have asked the question, but who fed Lorelei the question?

And the way Lorelei reacted when Stine suggested putting the entire investigation online, you'd think she had a personal stake in it. Maybe she did.

A throng of taxis rumbled down the boulevard.

When it rains, it pours, Stine thought. "Take me to the Hall of Records," she said to the driver through the window.

"You're the head of the Hall, aren't you?"

Her hand froze on the door handle. "Yes," she said. "Does it matter?"

The driver sneered. "Figures. Another corrupt politician."

"Excuse me! I've dedicated my life to serving the people of this country."

The driver laughed. "Yeah, right. You're probably just lining your pockets with taxpayer money."

She whacked the door.

He flipped two fingers at her and drove off.

Fuming, she wretched her phone from her pocket. "Henrik, I'm having trouble getting a taxi. Could you pick me up outside SVT? I need to go to the Hall of Records. I have a sneaking suspicion Lorelei Lindbergh and Landström Society are connected. I'll need your expertise to get into the archives."

"More sleuth work? I'll be there in ten minutes."

All of this was political, but she couldn't figure out exactly how. The records might reveal something.

STINE AND HENRIK hunched at her desk in the Hall of Records, punching in Lorelei Lindbergh's history and her mysterious rise to broadcast fame.

"So, her father is none other than Viktor Hansson, the leader of the Landström Society," Henrik said, letting his chair trail away from the desk. "And she took her mother's maiden name when they divorced."

"Explains why she was so defensive during the broadcast," Stine said.

"Shouldn't she disclose her conflict of interest?" Henrik

asked. "I mean, she can't be objective when reporting on anything concerning Landström Estate."

"When you're protected by the most powerful Society in the country..."

Henrik's eyebrow arched.

He was catching on, Stine thought. "Look into the connection between Lorelei and the opposition party leader."

Henrik punched in the search. "She's interviewed him several times. Nothing unusual about that."

"Can you look up what Lorelei had been reporting on in the last three weeks, besides Landström Society?"

"That's a different archive, but yeah." Henrik rolled up his sleeves and entered a different database. "This one contains the news and video feeds." He typed in Lorelei Lindbergh and the date range.

From a sample of ten results, an overriding pattern emerged. The results showed an inordinate number of interviews with the leaders of the clubs, Ulrich Tokvej, being one of them.

"Looks like she's gathering information on the clubs," Stine said.

"And their leaders," Henrik added.

"This all reeks," Stine said. "The Prime Minister is fighting for his position, the opposition is pushing for the Q-scores to become our national currency, and Lorelei is investigating the clubs. And the Landström Society—the most obscure piece in the puzzle—is involved in all this somehow."

A bell rang from out front.

"Who the hell wants records at eleven at night?" Henrick said.

"You'd be surprised," Stine said. "I'll be right back."

Stine stepped into the Hall. A thirtysomething woman with a sharp bob stood at the desk, her eyes intense, hurried, and focused. She wasn't the usual Swedish patron; she had to be a foreigner.

"How can I help you," Stine said.

"I'm looking for Stine Poulsen."

Stine pegged her as a Brit. "And you are?"

"Kelly Blackwell. SÄPO officer Bjorn sent me."

"He mentioned you, but you're not what I pictured." Stine ran her eyes up and down Kelly. "Why are you here?"

"Landström Society is seeking to take over your government."

"They certainly have a reputation, but to say they're trying to take over the government is quite a claim," Stine said.

"I can unblock the records. Then you will see that they're attempting a coup."

"The head of IT has been working on the blockage for weeks now. What makes you think you can—"

"Let's just say I'm very well connected," Kelly said resolutely.

---

2 A.M.

Harald Seversson walked through the Hall of Records carrying a stack of papers. Low light beamed from the perma-tablets on the browser bar, softening the ornate ceiling.

The night duty officer stood up from behind the welcome desk.

Harald nodded in acknowledgment. A shadow obscured the details of the duty officer's face, but she was probably a student. "I'm dropping off papers for scanning."

She nodded and resumed reading whatever was on her tablet.

The brightly lit back room pained his eyes. He listened. It was even quieter back here than out in front.

Quickly, he walked over to Stine's desk and pulled open her drawer. Nothing but a key, her key to the storage room.

He woke up her computer screen, and the password window popped up.

The system offered to fill in the password. He pressed yes, and Stine's computer loaded right up.

He scrolled through her last search.

By the looks of it, she was making the connection between Landström and the opposition party.

His nerves rumbled. Viktor was turning Landström into a puppet master of the politicians. That was never meant to be. He closed down the screen, dropped the stack of papers inside the storage room, and exited the building.

Outside, he flipped open his phone and speed-dialed Bjorn. "Stine Poulsen is on the right track."

CHAPTER 37

THE TAXI'S LUMPY BACKREST DUG INTO CHRISTIAN'S BACK.
"Central Stockholm Police Station."

The driver's critical eye flashed through the rearview mirror.

"What?" Christian snapped.

When the police had called that morning, they requested his presence at the station. Said he needed to answer some questions, but they didn't say what about. They never gave much away in the calls, but it had to be about the slew of deep fake videos. Finally, they were asking questions. He'd point at Landström and brand them the prime developers of digital deception.

The cab came to a halt, and Christian jerked forward. He climbed out of the taxi.

Two police officers ambled out of the main entrance, chit-chatting with one another. Their stale sweat gave Christian the impression they had been in the station overnight.

A police officer manned the front desk, an electronic pen in her hand.

"I'm here at the request of Officer Lind," Christian said.

She rolled a gaze over him. "Your name?"

He straightened. "Christian Karlsson."

She picked up the phone and mumbled into the receiver. "Have a seat."

He remained standing in front of her, eager to get this interview underway, anxious to orient a crushing boulder in Viktor's direction.

A broad-shouldered officer shuffled through the security door. "Christian Karlsson, I'm Officer Madsson."

He held the security door ajar and gestured for Christian to follow him.

They walked down a brightly lit, narrow hall that smelled of sweet coffee. The officer escorted Christian into an interrogation room like ones he'd seen on TV cop shows hundreds of times. Still, the two-way mirror, taking up most of the wall, aroused a self-conscious edginess in him, reminding him that real life was a series of inescapable truths.

A second officer came into the room. This one looked brainy, with a thick chest. "I'm Officer Lind."

Christian nodded. "We spoke this morning."

The two officers sat across from Christian and looked at a shared tablet.

"Are those the deep fakes?" Christian asked. "Viktor Hansson—"

"No, they aren't the deep fakes," Lind said.

Christian's skin tightened. He studied both officers. "What are you looking at then?"

Lind pressed a button on a remote control, and the ceiling camera activated. "We will be recording the interview. Officer Lind and Officer Maddson are in room 406 with Christian Karlsson. The suspect has been informed this interview will be recorded." He looked at Christian. "I'm duty-bound to inform you that you are under investigation for the rape of Lisandra Nordin."

The words pounded Christian numb. "Who?"

Lind read him his rights.

"Those are your rights," Officer Madsson said. "It doesn't mean that we will keep you for six hours. We're merely reading out code 23:8 of the criminal procedures."

"Unless there are manifest reasons to hold you for more than six hours," Officer Lind continued, "we will notify you of your rights at that point."

"That only happens when a person becomes an official suspect," Madsson said. "I don't expect that to happen here with you today."

Disbelief darted up Christian's spine, his heart pounding in his chest. "But I'm here about the deep fake videos," he said, breathless. "Who the hell is Lisandra Nordin?"

Lind pointed at a camera attached to the ceiling. "Your answers are being recorded."

Heat fastened around Christian's throat, and the air in the room closed in. "You have it all wrong. I've done nothing." He hand-combed his hair. "I don't even know who that Lisandro person is!"

"She knows you."

"She's not a client, so who is she?"

"She says she met you at White's on the night of June 1st."

Christian's legs surged. Gingeraroma. That woman he went home with. He was setup from the start. All the way back then. He gripped the edge of the table. Viktor. Landström. The Match. "I'm not answering a single question without a lawyer."

———

CHRISTIAN PACED THE ROOM. "I don't care. Two calls. I need two calls."

"You don't have a lot of options here, Mr. Karlsson." Officer Madsson handed him a cell phone. "One call, and that's it."

"I'll use my own glasses," he snapped.

Officer Lind shook his head.

Christian couldn't tell if he was being judged or denied. "I need privacy," he said, pulling out his glasses.

Lind placed the phone on the table. "No glasses. This is an official interrogation. And remember, everything in this room is being recorded."

The officers left the room.

Christian dialed Schroeder and heard him pick up on the second ring. "I need your help."

"Christian, people are saying you're facing rape charges."

Anger rushed through him. "They're bogus charges. That woman...I barely know her."

"Your points, man. They're going into the negative."

"They're trying to ruin me."

"Who's they?"

Christian doubled over. The burn of such a charge should be scarring Viktor, not him, but he was feeling shame for having to make this call at all. "I need you to be my lawyer."

"I don't know," Schroeder said. "This isn't just a simple talk down. If I'm seen defending you, I'll be skewered."

"It's a game, Schroeder," Christian said, short of breath. "Just a game."

"A pretty serious game. The woman's name is Lisandra Nordin. It's all over the feeds."

Christian shot up, and his vision swirled in a haze. He rubbed his eyes. "I don't know anyone by that name."

"Her avatar is gingeraroma. Pretty blond. She says you went home with her after White's."

Snippets of that night flickered in Christian's mind like a broken projector.

"She said...," Schroeder cleared his throat. "You gave her Q-points for it. That's just sick, man."

Pain settled in Christian's bones. He faltered and lowered

himself on the chair. "It's a lie," he said in a voice so light he barely heard himself.

"No lie, man," Schroeder said. "You're in the police station, word is out, you're Tier 0. I might be a lawyer, but you know how it is."

The line went dead.

A helpless rage consumed him. He whacked his glasses against the wall, thrashing them until they were nothing but chunks of plastic covering the floor. All he wanted to do was escape.

CHAPTER 38

JUST PAST MIDNIGHT, CHRISTIAN SHUFFLED OUT OF THE POLICE station, a cloud of suspicion hanging over him. He surrendered to the night air.

A lone, self-driving street sweeper hummed in front of him, its bristles scratching the day's grime off the pavement.

A taxi came to a soft halt in front of him. He shuffled onto the backseat.

The driver passed judgement through the rearview mirror.

Christian's self-preservation kicked in. "Don't," he said. "Just take me to Alströmergatan."

The driver looked straight ahead and drove into the night.

From the passenger window he watched the unreachable world pass by. The victim had bruises, the police had said, and they showed him the photographs, DNA, and the doctor's conclusion. The Q-score points he sent her connected her to Christian — something he could not remember doing. It all looked so convincing that even he caught himself believing she had been raped and that Christian was the prime suspect.

Sickness swirled in his stomach. He rolled down the window and received the gentle air.

His thoughts drifted back to that night, that fateful night. They were drinking champagne non-stop, so most of it was a blur. He remembered the woman coming on to him. She did come onto him, didn't she? They stepped into a taxi together. Entered her apartment. They drank more alcohol. Both of them. After that, it was all instinct. He couldn't remember the details, but he felt it was consensual; that's what he thought.

Doubt crept in. He couldn't remember the clothes coming off, maybe he did— "No, no, that's not me," he declared.

Sleep had sobered him, that he did remember. He remembered the call from the office. When he left for work that morning, the woman had gone back to sleep. She seemed satisfied. She looked fine. Not a single complaint. His old AR glasses could prove that, but they no longer existed. His bio-tracker could have proven it too, but he'd gotten rid of that too. He rubbed his head. He had no evidence to convince anyone.

The case against him was fortified against him.

His jaw clenched, and tension seemed to soak up the air around him.

The one thing he possessed that might help him was that list of names. They meant something, though he didn't know what. With all that had happened, he hadn't had the time to search out who was who on that list. But that list terrified Landström Society. He kneaded his temples.

Doubt was growing inside him like a weed, not that he had raped her but that he would beat these allegations and prove his own innocence to the world. This had to be part of the game, right? He gripped the car door's rail.

The taxi stopped at his building. In the still night, he walked up the path and trudged into the lobby. Climbing the stairs one by one, his legs pumping, and he trailed the hall until he reached his front door.

The front door was ajar.

He stood back. The last time he was there, he locked the door. Or did he? He was in a rush to get to Max's; he might've left it open, unknowingly. He nudged the door.

It creaked.

He braced himself and stepped inside.

The darkness engulfed him, heavy as lead.

His hand fumbled along the wall for the light switch. He flipped it on.

The gaming chairs were toppled in the middle of the living room. A lamp lay on the floor, its lampshade dented, its bulb smashed. The sofa sat askew off the rug, its cushions cast helter-skelter against the wall. The coffee table glass had been hacked into wedges, covering the bruised hardwood floor.

Adrenaline raced through him, and his legs wobbled, threatening to descend into the anguish flooding his body. Christian leaned against a wall, but all he could feel were millions of tiny needles pushing back.

Raw will bolstered his withered resolve, and he darted to the master bedroom. The bedsheets lay crumpled on the floor. He dropped to his knees and stretched his fingers under the bed, his cheek brushing against the wooden floor. He scooted farther down the bed, deeper, frustration building inside the pit of his stomach. His ear burned against the floor as he glimpsed the whole underbed.

Empty.

His throat tightened. No junk box. His body sunk into the floor, and he watched a dull amber streetlight flicker against the walls.

"The list," he said.

Adrenaline surged into his veins, and his body kicked into action. He shoved the games cabinet away from the hidden panel. He soft pressed it, and the door swung open.

Empty.

Desperation sprinkled his forehead and heated his back. His wispy breath echoed off the arctic white walls. The list of names was nowhere to be found.

"What's going on in here!" A brusque voice reverberated through the apartment.

His elderly neighbor stood in the doorway, and his wife shielded herself behind him. Their eyes widened with fear. "Stop!" the man yelled.

"It's not what you think," he pleaded.

The man whispered into his wife's ear, and she scuttled off, giving Christian a quick glance back.

"We're calling the police," the old man said, defiant. "Don't come any closer."

"You have the wrong idea. It was like this when I got here."

The old man squinted his eyes. "We'll let the police decide."

A brown-haired woman stepped into the doorway. Her skin reflected the sickly blue of the overhead fluorescent hallway bulbs. "What's going on?"

"Did you see who broke into my flat?"

The girl cast a solemn gaze to the floor, her tangled hair swaying as she shook her head.

The old man's wife stood behind her husband again. "The police are on their way."

Empty hollowness built deep inside the pit of Christian's stomach. "None of you saw or heard anything? Useless!"

The old man elbowed the door as far open as it would go.

Christian slammed it shut. Behind the door lay a simple mobile phone, the kind someone would buy for a very specific purpose. He picked it up and pressed the power switch.

The old man's body slammed against the door. He wasn't as frail as he looked. "Open up! You can't hide for long. The police will be here any minute."

The door panel dug into Christian's back.

The mobile's screen lit up at last, and a logo twirled across the white screen.

Blood drained from Christian's face. The logo was the Landström twirling cube. His throat tightened in the unfolding nightmare.

They had it all. They had the whole thing planned. They played him from the start. They planted that woman on him. They had it sewn up.

His body numbed, and the pressure against the door loosened.

The old man surged through and pivoted around the door. He snatched the phone out of Christian's hand. "What's this? Who are you calling?"

He pried it out of the old man's arthritic fingers.

Surprisingly, the old man grabbed Christian by the elbow, shoving him toward the hall. "You're a thief and a hoodlum, but the police will deal with you now."

A dull yellow light flashed along the tiled walls of the hallway.

The old man stood behind Christian, nudging him forward.

Christian ran down the hall.

"Hey!" The old man called out.

Christian sprinted down the fire escape and headed to the one person who would believe him. Max.

MAX OPENED HIS APARTMENT DOOR, his face swollen and bruised.

Stunned, Christian could crumpled against the wall. "What have I done?"

Max pulled him to his feet. "Come inside."

Christian slammed onto the sofa and cupped his face, hiding the tears that rolled down his cheeks. "Landström did this. This should never have happened. I'm so sorry."

Max sat down on his swivel chair. "You gave me plenty of warning, Christian. I knew what I was doing. I just don't know how they knew I had your algorithms. I was testing the Viktor Hansson accounts, setting them up. Maybe it was that. But I doubt it."

"They probably tracked me here," Christian said, dejected.

Max hung his head. "I kept your biodevice. Thought you might want it back." He looked at Christian. "They probably tracked it and came here."

"And then they do this to you." Christian closed his eyes. That's why Viktor sent his thugs. They wanted the algorithms. That's what they wanted all along, just as Karen had mentioned in the park weeks ago. He opened his eyes. "Where are the algorithms now?"

Max licked his swollen lip. "I know how valuable the algorithms are to you, to everyone at Nyström, to our clients. And to me." He stood up and walked to the kitchen. Seconds later, he brought back the drive. "I denied having them."

Christian's eyes locked on the drive. "Thank God they didn't get their hands on them," he said, realizing how crass that sounded. "I mean—"

"I know what you mean, Christian. I'll heal up. But you. You might not have any bruises to show what they're putting you through, but I see it in your eyes. Your ordeal isn't over yet. Those rape allegations."

The Nationalbanken trial had been canceled. The list, his leverage, was gone. He was no closer to exposing Landström Society. Instead, he was the most hated man in Stockholm who was being propped up by O3. Far from winning the game, he was facing charges he couldn't see a way out of. Every wrong turn piled on top of him and pelted him in the gut.

"I need to be alone," he said.

"Stay here. They're not coming back."

Christian stood up.

"Don't leave like this. Stay here. Get some sleep. You'll feel fresher in the morning. Then, we'll talk about what to do."

Max handed him a blanket and pillow and closed the bedroom door.

His heart was grateful for the quiet safety of Max's living room, but his body shook and his mind raced through scenario after scenario, every one of them ending in catastrophe.

"They want the algorithms," he mumbled.

Agitation thundered through his limbs. He shot up from the sofa and dug out a bottle of schnaps from the freezer. After two shots, his thoughts sputtered.

Jacob. Landström. Viktor's. Facing charges. Ruin.

He swigged down three more shots.

No way out.

Maybe if he handed over the algorithms, they'd release him. But would they? They had him with rape charges. If he gave over the algorithms, his life would be destroyed. A fate worse than death.

He'd be beholden to them the rest of his life, a slave. They'd make him do all sorts, and he'd never live for himself ever again. Just like his father. He had become putty in Viktor's hands.

He crashed into the alcohol bottle, the stench of sticky booze wafting through the air. He kept his gaze glued on the rug and plodded, one foot in front of another and another. He staggered to the bathroom, turned on the bath tap, and stuck his head under the faucet.

Despair flowed down the drain.

The last thing he remembered was slipping under the warm water.

CHRISTIAN OPENED HIS EYES.

A saline IV drip was strapped to his hand. A heart rate machine beeped nearby.

The sound of feet pattered into the room, and a nurse pushed back the curtain. "Christian Karlsson, you're going to be just fine. Your friend Max said you've been under enormous stress lately. But don't worry; all the alcohol poisoning is out of your system. Rest up, and you'll be home tonight."

Her soft voice felt like balm on his tortured soul, but the last place he wanted to go was home.

CHAPTER 39

"CHRISTIAN KARLSSON DIDN'T DO IT," STINE DECLARED. "DID you bring his records?"

Henrik stood on her doorstep and waved a portable drive at her. "But he was taken in for questioning."

Stine gestured him inside. "I lived with the man for nearly two years. Whatever they're saying, it isn't true."

His eyes softened, and he wrapped his arm around her waist. Before she could say a word, he kissed her.

Stunned, all she could do was yield to his startling display of confidence.

He pulled back, and she took in his bright eyes. "When two people share a life-changing event, they're bonded for life, wouldn't you say?"

She wanted to collapse on the spot, instead, she stood motionless, wondering how long it would take her to recover from that kiss.

He closed the door and stepped inside. He stared at the chipboard on her wall sprawled with notes, maps, photographs, and drawings. "What's all this?"

She patted her lips dry with her fingertips, but the kiss

lingered. "Ever since the records were blocked, I've been piecing together who might be involved. When Kelly told us Landström was planning a government takeover, they went to the top of the board."

His eyes wandered to the left, and he took in the black and white picture of Christian pinned next to Landström Society. "Did you take this when you lived together?"

She held her breath, not knowing how he would take the truth. "It was hard to find. I had thrown most of his photos away."

He took it in and gently nodded. "So how does this collage work?"

Relieved that he had changed the subject, she threw her head back and laughed. "Collage? This isn't some art project. This is my evidence wall. I'm charting dates, IDs, people, and organizations as I come across them. The colored pins help me spot the patterns."

Henrik looked confused, probably because all he saw was a chaotic mess. He turned to her. "The fact is, Stine, we still don't fully understand what is happening and why, or what your old boyfriend has to do with it."

"The last time he was in the Hall of Records," she said, "he wanted to see Landström Estate blueprints. This was right after the fire. When the rumors about his burning it down happened, I began to wonder. But with this latest accusation, I know he didn't do it."

"From what I hear there's plenty of evidence against him. And as for Landström Society," Henrik said, glancing down as if he had said something he shouldn't have. "I'd leave them well alone."

"I can't. You know I can't." Stine pointed at the top of the evidence wall. "All roads lead to Landström." She turned to him. "And Kelly confirmed as much. I was right all along."

Henrik held out the drive. "Well, maybe something on here can shed light on things."

They inserted the drive into her laptop and up popped Christian's file. They scrolled through the places he'd lived, relationships, connections, and contacts.

"Looks clean to me," Henrik said.

Stine noticed a duplicate contact. "Back up. There's a dupe of that Karen Rasmussen contact."

Henrik opened both files and compared them side by side. "Identical. But that's odd because the system doesn't allow duplicate records." He looked at her. "Someone is tampering with the archive. We need to find all the duped records and report it."

"Get on it, Henrik. Make a record of every single duped record you find. But something's bothering me about this duplicated file. Who is Karen Rasmussen?"

"The wife of the guy who died a few of weeks back, Jacob Rasmussen."

The pit of Stine's stomach hollowed. "Christian was accused of foul play in his death. Remember?"

Color drained from Henrik's face as he looked at Stine, disbelief in his eyes. "That's not a coincidence, is it?"

Stine shook her head. "I need to get this over to Kelly Blackwell. She's trying to track Christian down."

He pushed away from the laptop. "If it's to do with Landström Society, let the police handle it. Don't get involved."

"I am involved." Stine stared at Henrik. "I suspect that Landström is infiltrating the government, and Christian is the key."

Stine positioned the laptop in front of her and punched in the IP address Bjorn had her memorize along with the passphrase: Stockholm is under attack.

Kelly, I'm sending you a name. Ask
Christian about it, or maybe your bot can
unravel it. It's a duped record in the
archive. Unusual. I don't have time to look
into it—have to be at a press conference.
Let me know what you find.

She attached Karen Rasmussen's file and pressed send. Within seconds, a notification popped up on the screen.

Stine clicked it open. "It's a message from Kelly," she said.

Received. Will look into it. Your
assignment is to protect the Prime
Minister. Good luck with the conference
tomorrow. If you need anything, ask. I'll
be in touch.

"God I love it when you get this way," Henrik said.

CHAPTER 40

CHRISTIAN SAT IN A GRAY ROOM UNDER A DULL HALOGEN BULB across from a social worker who looked as though life had zipped him up and thrown him away. Christian had already answered the same fundamental question—about ending things—five different ways.

The fact was that if he did have a thought about ending things at Max's, it was so fleeting that he barely remembered it. But he knew he would never have done it, not deliberately. If he wanted to end things, he'd have succeeded, and he wouldn't be sitting here having a conversation about it. Thinking of endings, he wondered when this meeting would terminate.

"It wasn't like that," he said for the sixth time.

The social worker swept his dreary looking eyes over his tablet as though the next question on his list. "Mr. Karlsson, thank you for taking the time to answer my questions." He laid the tablet on his lap. "Are there any comments you want to add?"

"My Q-score and my behavior have been erratic lately, I'll grant you that. I've been accused of all sorts of things, and some people believe it. I experienced a national tragedy firsthand, at the bridge, a tragedy that shocked the whole country. And then the charges against me…" He paused on the words as though they were hot chili on his tongue. "Nothing being said about me is true. After all that's happened, I think I'm allowed to get a little down, wouldn't you say?"

The social worker's worn face glanced down at his lap. "You can go home."

Christian rose from his seat. "I need to get a taxi home. As you know, my Q-points are a little low."

"The receptionist can make you a cash card direct from your Q-points."

"Is that something new?"

The worker shook his head. "It's part of the hospital care system so that patients can make quick payment for meds and such. When you deal with emergency situations, rarely do people have all their ID on them."

The social worker reached out to buzz the door open and his white coat drifted up his arm, exposing a tattoo. The tattoo was the Landström signature logo, the infamous 3D cube.

Christian's head swirled. The social worker was a Landström member. "Does Gamemaster approve?"

The social worker smiled.

Christian inhaled deeply. The Match, the Q-scores, the whole country, all of it was rigged. They had plants and moles everywhere. The country was lost, and Viktor could have it. He needed to get out of Sweden now. He signed for a cash card and scrambled out the door.

CHAPTER 41

CHRISTIAN ENTERED A SHOPPING CENTER. IN THE CENTRAL HUB, Lorelei Lindbergh's face filled a TV screen, behind her the setting of a press conference.

Pure noise, he thought, but shoppers paused in front to watch anyway.

A child tugged on her mother's arm and pointed at Christian. People started to gather around the screen, looking back at him, then at the screen, like catching a glimpse of a tiger in a cage.

The child's mother bent down. "Stop staring. It's not polite."

Christian skipped ahead and entered a clothing shop. Inside, he dug through the discount jackets on the clothes rack.

A pair of security guards lingered at the entrance of the clothing store, stealing glances.

Christian yanked a jacket off the rack and walked to the till, grabbing a pair of trousers, a hat, and a pair of boots along the way. He pulled out the cash card. It contained all the credit he had in the world, and he had drained his Q-scores to do it. Didn't matter since he wasn't planning on staying in Sweden anyway.

The cashier wrinkled her lips.

"Money's money," he muttered, snatching the shopping bag off the counter.

He walked past the security guards, head down.

People were now glued to the Hub's screens. Lorelei Lindbergh's not-so-dulcet tones blared from the speakers.

He squeezed his eyes, dreading what he'd see. There she was, Lisandra, the woman he'd slept with, sitting at a long conference table surrounded by the press. Beside her sat Schroeder, wearing a yellow bow tie.

Christian's knees weakened, and he gripped the nearest column. He tried to remember what Schroeder had said, but the betrayal dizzied him. He stared at the screen.

Of all the people in the world, Schroeder was one of them. He had been watching Christian the whole time, pretending to be a helpful neighbor.

"Christian Karlsson has been missing for over forty-eight hours," Schroeder said. "The public can't trust him, just as my client should never have trusted him. God knows what he's involved with this time. The police are hunting him as we speak. If you see him, please report him."

Christian knew that if he stayed, he would sink into the quicksand that Stockholm had become. He dashed out of the shopping center and ducked into the first cab. "Take me to the airport."

CHRISTIAN WALKED BRISKLY into the Stockholm airport, face hiding underneath the stiff hat, and made his way to the ticket counter.

"One-way ticket to London," he said.

"Can I have your ID, please?"

He pulled out his cash card.

"I'm going to need your passport," the ticket salesperson said.

His head dropped. His passport was at home. "Can I fill in my passport details later? I just need to purchase the ticket now."

She turned her rigid face to the screen. "The first flight out is tonight at eleven."

The clock read 3 p.m.—enough time to get his passport and get the hell away from here. "I'll take it."

The intercom crackled to life.

"Announcement for Mr. Karlsson."

He froze. They found him.

"Please come immediately to the information booth. Stormykitten has a message for you."

The message repeated.

He made his way down the escalator.

Two police officers spotted him on the other side.

They locked eyes.

In a split second, Christian ran up the steps. The police officers gave chase, running down on the other side, shoving people and their suitcase trolleys out of the way.

He jumped onto the stainless steel smooth slope, climbed up, and hit the floor running as fast as he could. He glanced behind, dashed through the automatic doors, hurried up to the information booth, and wedged himself between two travelers arguing at the counter.

"I'm Christian Karlsson," he said, breathless. "You messaged me. Please page Kelly Blackwell. It's urgent."

On the woman's face was a look of bewilderment. She narrowed in on her screen. "What message?"

"It was just announced," he said, trying to speak as calmly as he could. "Storymykitten?"

He glanced behind him.

The police were closing in.

"Oh, here it is. She says she's waiting for you in the worship room on the second level."

A tingling sensation shimmied up his spine. He climbed the steps to level two, each step robbing him of what little strength was left in his limbs. At last, he reached the worship room. He elongated his breath and slipped inside.

A woman sat alone in the front pew. She wore a wide yellow-rimmed hat, a blue metallic scarf elegantly draped around the base. She wasn't anything like he remembered when he first saw her in her grunge getup at SVT weeks ago.

"Kelly?"

"You have the right room." She rose from the chair, and her flowing, floral dress curled around her calves.

He sat, close enough but still somewhat at a distance.

She giggled. "I don't bite. You can come closer."

He parked a chair next to her. "I thought you went back to London."

She shook her head. "I had to find you. And I had a hell of a time tracking you down. Finally got your whereabouts when you paid with your cash card." She gestured air quotes around cash card. "I have something that will get you out of this mess." She opened her yellow handbag. "The last time we met, I told you about duplicated records of your father's death certificate. It nagged me. I looked into it, and I met Stine—"

"You met Stine?"

She nodded. "We investigated it. It seems that the same doctor and police officer signed off on both records. Now that just can't be, I said to myself. Turns out both the doctor and the police officer, a police officer Seger, are members of the Landström Society."

"It doesn't surprise me," Christian said. "The members are everywhere. Sweden is crawling with them. Precisely why I'm on the next flight out of this hell hole."

"Make that decision after I give you some information you

might find interesting. Stine sent me the name Karen Rasmussen. Another duped record."

He looked at her, and the thought of Jacob stabbed at him him once again. "She's Jacob Rasmussen's wife. Karen is one of them too. After Jacob took his life, I saw the Landström tattoo on her arm. None of this helps me, though."

"Listen to what I'm saying, Christian. It's a duped record. Someone inside the Hall of Records is duping records having to do with the members. The network is vast, and that's why the records got sealed. But Landström wasn't just hiding records. They were changing them for the benefit of their members, and it all happened in the last four or five weeks."

Awestruck, a glimmer of light sparkled in his mind. "That's when the game started. They set me up from the beginning, but I already know that. What shocks me is how well planned they had it this whole time. I underestimated them. Right from the start." He looked at her, taking in what he had just said. "Pretty much anyone I interacted with had to be a member."

"Highly likely," Kelly said. "What does the Landström Society want?"

"My algorithms. That's what Karen had said."

Kelly shook her head. "It's not your algorithms they want, Christian. They want something else."

He raked his hands through his hair. "The whole thing has—"

She lowered her chin and crossed her arms. "The game has blinded you so much you don't know what the real game is anymore. It's understandable, though. A lot of people were involved, a lot of hidden people. They were corralling you. They wanted you because you are the only one capable of developing future algorithms for them. They wanted your genius. Why would Landström Society want the milk when they can have the cow?"

He sat stunned, letting the truth of what she said seep into him like a call to arms.

"And I can tell you from experience," Kelly said, "records never get erased. There is always a backup. Somewhere. Stine and Henrik are tracing the duped records, and when they get the full web worked out, they'll be able to trace it all to Landström Society."

"Tampering with the national archive is an illegal offense," he said.

Kelly nodded. "They might just get what's coming to them." She glanced around the room and back at him. "But you know these people, and they don't care about the truth. They might find a way to squash the charges. Provided the Prime Minister stays in power, they will see justice."

She handed him sheets of paper. "With this proof, you can turn the game back on them, and simultaneously you give yourself options."

He took the thick, dependable papers and stared at the duped records of his father's death certificate. "You were talking about this when we last met, and I wasn't listening."

"You were absorbed by the game."

She brushed his cheek, and an electric shock ran through him.

"Will I see you again?" he asked.

"If you survive." She paused. "I'd love to show you around London. We've changed quite a lot over there."

"What brought you to Stockholm in the first place?"

"You did. I did. My bot did." Kelly sighed. "I stayed because I had to understand why I got a message from you a year ago saying that Stockholm was under attack. I thought it was a corrupted message at the time because it cut off and self-deleted. It was your voice, and it sounded like you knew me." She shifted her shoulders. "A few days ago, I got the same message, and it was duplicated. That's when I knew something deeper was going on at the Hall of Records. When I unblocked it, I saw a virus in the system. I got really worried for a while because I really hate viruses, but I looked into into anyway. Turns out it was code instructing the system to send certain files to Landström Society. Henrik is figuring out the rest. Personally, having lived with my bot for a while now, I think it discovered an anomaly in your system. The truth is, we can't lose Sweden. Too much work to recover this place."

"Who's we?"

"I like questions. Reminds me of me." She smiled. "This world is in a war. Not the traditional kind with guns and bombs. The war is for people's minds, and the bad guys are willing to do anything to win. Sweden is on the precipice, just like the UK was. You can't let it happen, Christian. You give up, and they own this country."

"They all said you were this untouchable, unreachable, mysterious woman."

She shrugged. "Having that kind of reputation sorta helps, don't you think?"

She giggled.

"I didn't tell you everything because I thought...I didn't want to bring danger into your life."

"I've been through hell and back myself. But if there's something I've learned it's that you can't run away from what scares you." Her brow wrinkled. "But I learned something more than that lately. I can play with my own masks. I can change my outfit, my hair, my shoes, my avatar, whatever." She flicked her hair. "And I'm still Kelly Blackwell, minus the anxiety, thank God. I'm still getting used to it, but life can be fun."

She stood up and rested her hand on the doorknob. "Viktor counted on you dismissing everything having to do with your father. He knew how much you disliked him."

"I should've looked in that junk box—"

"Doesn't matter now. You have all the keys you need now.

The game is much bigger than you realize. Now go and *play* the game."

A flame lit up inside Christian, and it burned away Landström's darkened dead-ends in his mind, blowtorching it all into nothing.

———

CHRISTIAN SHUTTLED down the airport elevator to the parking lot, planning the fastest route to his house. Tomorrow night was the last night of the Match, and it was now or never.

The airport doors opened to a throng of reporters. They swarmed around him, vultures on the attack.

A furry mic got shoved in his face. "What were you really doing at the opera house, Christian Karlsson?"

His cheeks heated and his face erupted with sweat; he pushed through, making his way to the taxi rank.

"When did you plant the bomb?"

Christian froze. A journalist and her crew crowded him and blocked his forward motion.

"Christian Karlsson, a suspected rapist, was caught trying to leave the country via Arlanda Airport. Police apprehended him."

Things couldn't get worse, he thought.

The journalist looked into the camera. "Christian Karlsson's anger issues stem from deep-seated childhood trauma, but selective memory has blocked him from remembering."

Another reporter yelled out, "Did you bomb the opera house?"

"Is it true you were kidnapped as a kid?"

A flaming rage stormed through him. He rammed into a reporter and broke the mic in two, "You've gone too far. The lies you spout make all of you a nasty piece of work. Tell Lorelei Lindberg I'm cashing in my last code, 0099, and the spotlight will be on her and her so-called survivor status."

A journalist froze.

He grabbed his mic and looked straight into a camera. "Viktor, I'm coming." He tossed the mic to the floor. "Now, get out of my way."

They stepped back all at once.

He hopped in front of a queue of jetlagged travelers and stole the first taxi that drove up. The queue roared a chorus of complaints.

"Emergency! Wife in labor," he yelled.

He pulled open the door and slid onto the back seat. "Take me to Alströmergatan, Kungsholmen."

CHAPTER 42

STINE RAN INTO THE ROSENBAD BUILDING, MINUTES LATE FOR THE start of the Prime Minister's press conference. She raced up the carpeted staircase, her muscles burning. She came to the first floor, finger-combed her hair, and walked past security personnel standing strategically along the walkway. Several security personnel were stationed at the sealed doors in the reception hall.

On the other side of the doors, she could hear Lorelei Lindbergh.

"No!" Stine threw up her hands. "I need to get in."

"Only preregistered press are allowed," the security guard said, stone-faced.

She pulled out her AR glasses and typed in Kelly's IP address.

"What's up?" Kelly said.

"I need to get to the Prime Minister's press conference, the one he's holding now. Can you get me in as a preregistered member of the press?"

"I'm going to control your glasses camera," Kelly said. "Point your eyesight to the guards at the press conference door, and I'll zoom into the badge numbers."

Stine faced the double doors, standing as still as her thumping heartbeat allowed.

"Your alias is now Karina Åström," Kelly said.

"Can you give me a rundown on Karina Åström?"

"She's a thirtysomething journalist whose mother was Danish and father Swedish, and she's worked for Stjärnnytt since 2029."

"That tabloid rag? Any chance you can get me onto a more reputable paper?"

"It's the best choice because no one from Stjärnnytt is there. They'll be obliged to let you in."

"They'll be shocked," Stine said.

"I'll load the info into your biodevice and feed your press pass to the security guard on your left. In five minutes, you'll be inside."

"Karina Åström from Stjärnnytt," Stine said to the security guard.

He scanned her palm and pulled on the door handle. "Standing room only."

Stine entered a crammed room.

Suited-up journalists sat uncomfortably close to one another while Lorelei Lindbergh, and her crew, had the whole second row of chairs to themselves. They all listened respectfully, it seemed, to the prime minister.

Stine flashed her palm at the usher. He pointed to the other side of the room, where video stands took up the entire back wall. The angle was too far away from the Prime Minister's podium. She nodded, walked toward the back wall, edged closer to the stage, and nestled between two photojournalists.

The Prime Minister's bright blue eyes set off his tanned skin and brown hair, parted on the side. He was a young, ambitious politician who started his political career in a rural town in northern Sweden. He tirelessly worked his way through the political arena all the way to Prime Minister. In office for a year and a half, his enemies were already calling for him to step down, citing the attack at Norrbro Bridge, the Hall of Records debacle, and his reluctance to consider converting the currency to Q-points.

Secret service personnel emerged from the door behind the podium, a signal that the prime minister was about to leave. The journalists snapped into action, and cameras were raised to eye level, pointing at the Prime Minister at the door.

Prime Minister Bergman finished his speech, justifying his neutral position on the background checks bill. Stine inched closer to the podium, hoping the new position would make her visible.

"The Prime Minister will take two more questions."

In the packed press room, Lorelei Lindbergh stood up and fired off a question.

"Cybercrime rates are climbing to levels we haven't seen for a decade. And yet you continue to believe that Sweden will weather the storm. Today marks the second showdown between the Prime Minister's government and Parliament, who are attempting to pass legislation over the question of security checks for members of the public who want access to public records. Public opinion has put incredible pressure on your office to pass the background checks law that would prevent the national archives from being tampered with, yet you vetoed the bill the first time around. Will you now uphold background security checks?"

"My office is considering the bill and all its ramifications. We cannot have knee-jerk reactions off the back of a single incident. We must be prudent unless we wish to erode the public's civil liberties and right to access the public record freely."

"In other words, you do not support this bill."

"I cannot confirm whether such legislation will pass into law. That is for the parliament to vote on, and I don't want to bias the outcome."

"It is rumored that members of parliament have threatened the extreme step of calling a vote of no confidence. What do you feel about that?"

"The parliament is entitled to do as it sees fit, of course. Now, last question."

Stine shot her arm up in the air.

The Prime Minister scanned the room, and his eyes landed on Lorelei Lindbergh. "You've had your time, Lorelei."

"We didn't get a definitive answer of the veto of the bill, Prime Minister. Do you affirm or deny the decision?"

Stine once again lifted her hand. The Prime Minister glanced down at the tablet on his podium and pointed directly at her. "Karina Åström from Stjärnnytt, please go ahead."

Journalists threw her their most hissing looks.

"Next, we'll have UFO News Weekly in here," someone said.

"All readers are equally important," the Prime Minister said. "Go ahead, Karina."

"There's been a lot of pressure for you to step down as Prime Minister over the currency question, but some in your cabinet worry that could cause a civil war. Are the rumors true?"

"I do not plan to step down over the currency matter. I'm confident we can weather the storm."

The Prime Minister looked at the roster again.

"One more, if I may." Stine bounced on her heels. "Some say you might have no choice. What would you say to your critics, who some say are connected to our intelligence agency, who are demanding that you step down?"

His eyebrows bunched, darkening his blue eyes. "Changing our currency cannot be done with an electronic point pen. However, the discussions will continue, and that is all."

The Prime Minister stepped away from the podium.

Lorelei stood in front of Stine. "Hey, Karina, or is it Stine Poulsen, manager of the Hall of Records. I interviewed you remember?"

"I moonlight as a journalist. Karina is my penname. It's not that hard. Anybody can do it," Stine said.

"Come by SVT sometime. Maybe we can talk more." Lorelei turned to her crew. "Let's go."

Stine opened her glasses and whispered, "Kelly."

CHAPTER 43

CHRISTIAN WOKE UP IN THE DARK, HIS BODY STIFF. 3:35 A.M. HE squeezed the aches between his shoulder blades. Today was the last day, the end of this game, and he wasn't sure if he'd survive it.

He fended off the arson and foul play accusations, but, when they accused him of rape, and used his alcohol-fueled evening against him it became personal.

He was in too deep, and the rape charges loomed over him. He needed evidence proving he didn't do what he was accused of, and it would take all his strength and know-how to squeeze the truth out of Schroeder. All of it.

The automatic timer clicked, and the talk radio buzzed on. He rubbed his head and sauntered to the kitchen.

A gentle knock at his door startled him. "Who is it!"

"Christian, it's me, Stine. Can we talk?"

Surprised at hearing Stine's voice, he opened the door.

"I know what you're involved in," she said, making her way to the kitchen. She pulled up a seat and showed him a picture on her tablet. "Look familiar?"

It was strange seeing himself in the center of the photo, especially with the woman from White's on top of him.

Christian scraped his hair back and exhaled. "Kelly said you worked to unblock the records at the Hall. Is all this from there?"

"Sort of."

He looked at the photo. Agitated discomfort settled on him. Then a new question entered his mind. He braced himself. "Was Jacob in on this too?"

"No. He was helping SÄPO and Viktor found out."

Christian let his head drop back. "I wish he had told me." So, Karen was working for Landström while Jacob was working with SÄPO. He looked at Stine. "How do you know?"

"I'm SÄPO," Stine said. "But Jacob wasn't in touch with me. He was in touch with my case officer, Bjorn."

He scrolled through photos of Norrbro Bridge on her tablet. "Reminds me of the Landström Estate," he said, his throat dry. "But that was a real fire."

Stine sat back into the kitchen chair. "Landström Estate seems so long ago."

"Only a few weeks..." Christian's voice trailed off, but he knew what she meant. The estate burning down. Jacob's death. Hell, even his introduction to the Match seemed a lifetime ago. He stopped scrolling through the photos.

"Some people perished in the Landström fire," Stine said.

Christian remembered the smell of flesh when he had visited the burned out Estate. He had dismissed it as forest animals caught in the blaze. "I didn't know. There wasn't any information about anyone dying."

"Of course not," she said, scooting up in the chair. "Two bodies were found at the site. They were SÄPO agents."

"Anyone you knew?" he asked.

She glanced at Christian and then back at the tablet. "No. But Jacob did. Unfortunately, sometimes procedures fail."

"So, their deaths freaked Jacob out. He must have thought was he next."

"Decided it was best to end his own life, otherwise he'd be forever running from Landström."

Christian's heart ached. "We can only do the best we can."

He examined the photo at Norrbro Bridge. Whoever had taken that photo was standing on the north end of the bridge. A crowd was gathered around an ambulance, and emergency workers were directing people away from the opera house. A bus blocked out a clean view. Smack in the middle of the photo was Christian, wide-eyed. A woman was pulling on his arm.

A woman he didn't recognize. But he very clearly remembered Kelly was with him, and she was pulling him away. This woman in the photo, this redhead, did not exist on that drive. "They've been doctored." He pushed it away. "Everything is being forged and doctored!"

"Makes you wonder what else gets doctored," Stine said. "I know you didn't do the rape, just like I know Jacob didn't set you up. I'm afraid I don't have evidence to give you, but I know it."

"So why are you here?"

"On behalf of SÄPO," Stine said. "You're the only one who's close enough to Landström Society and who hasn't caved to their pressure. And we need your help."

"My life is on the line right now, Stine."

"We think they're trying to take over the government, get rid of the Prime Minister, and install the opposition."

"Why?"

"Because they want to turn Q-score points into our national currency, and Prime Minister Bergman is standing in their way."

"What the hell can I do?"

"We need proof."

He laughed and shook his head. Nothing made sense. "SÄPO is coming to me for help? We really *are* in trouble."

"They're doctoring records, they're planting false flags, they killed two agents," she said. "And yet we can't pin them down."

Christian shifted in his seat.

"We are in unknown territory," she said. "Landström's new leader is ruthless and relentless. But this game you're in with them could yield something we can use."

"How do you know about the game?"

"We know a lot. We just can't act on it. That's where people like you come in."

"Are you telling me SÄPO will have my back if I help them?"

"Yes," Stine said with an earnest look in her eyes. "But you need to think it through. If you're going to defeat these men, you'll have to stop and think. They count on knee-jerk reactions to take you off your game."

Christian leaned back. "I've already planned it out."

"As I expected you would," Stine said.

But there was one thing he didn't have that would clear him immediately. His old AR glasses. He hated relying on anyone to do anything for him but this deal with SÄPO was one he could benefit from. "About the rape charges...," he said.

She handed him a legal document. "She's done it before."

He grabbed the document with fervor and hastily scanned it. The report was dated three years ago. He read how that woman had appeared before a court back in 2027, accusing a man by the name of Olaf Sanders.

A mix of horror and relief trickle down his spine, horror that some other man had lived this nightmare and relief that she was on SÄPO's radar. "We would have known this had the Hall of Records not been blocked."

"Exactly," Stine said. "We found bank records connecting one of its members to her. She gets a very comfortable pay out."

"Which member is that?"

"Someone by the name of Kolokov."

"And he's also forging records. I wonder what they have on him," Christian said, but he really didn't care. He turned his thoughts to Olaf Sanders, their victim.

"I'll do what I can, but I can't make any promises."

She placed a recording device, the size of a fingernail, on the counter. "When you talk to them, switch it on. It feeds and records directly into SÄPO." Stine sighed and nodded. "I can't imagine what you've been through. Get some rest, Christian. I'll show myself out."

CHAPTER 44

Christian Karlsson: Tier 0 | 2m points
vs
Viktor Hansson Tier 1 | 5.56m points

WITH TWENTY-FOUR HOURS TO GO UNTIL THE END OF THE Arcadian Match, Landström Society members gathered in the parlor of their meeting house.

Viktor filed to the front of the room and glanced at the Q-score leaderboard. Gamemaster and two Society newcomers came in behind him. The crown would soon be his, he thought.

Voices fell silent.

"Thank you, Gentlemen. I've taken the liberty of inviting the heads of two other Societies," Viktor said. "Ulrich Tokvej and Torn Vester."

The members clapped, a lackluster sort of clap. Merging Societies would come with its challenges, he thought, but he was prepared.

Gamemaster stepped forward. "Has everyone enjoyed the game so far?"

Members raised their wine glasses.

"It's been the most educational game. Bravo!" one said.

"We hope it was more than that," Viktor said.

"Your opponent has proved formidable, Viktor," the pudgy member said, cigar in hand. "The game isn't over until the fat lady sings."

Members chuckled.

"You're the only one who thinks the game isn't over because you're the only one who put down a bet on the loser!"

Members laughed and clinked their glasses together, saluting the observation.

"If Viktor lost," the cigar-smoker said, "that would be a turn-around unlike anything we've ever seen, and I will rake it in while all you will be cleaning my boots."

A member smacked his back. "It isn't over until it's over, right?"

"That's right!"

Agreement pattered the room.

"I expect my opponent to be in prison for a long time," Viktor said.

The crowd laughed.

"Let's say you're declared the winner," a young member shouted. "What will be your first act?"

Viktor could feel power pulse through his whole being. "We merge three Societies, and form a new social structure that Sweden, indeed the world, has never seen before. In a matter of months, the Prime Minister will be replaced, and Q-scores will be the national currency. Sweden will be fit for the future."

Gamemaster stepped into the center of the room. "Drink up, gentlemen. Enjoy the rest of the show."

CHAPTER 45

CHRISTIAN ENTERED WOODLAND CEMETERY UNDER A SKY OF gathering clouds. The weight of his father's death certificates hung heavy in his pocket as he made his way to the office of the on-site funeral director, his old client, Dan. He'd know the doctor who signed off on most death certificates.

Two grounds officers walked toward him.

Christian tightened his fist.

They walked past.

He exhaled, shook off the tension, and entered the administrative wing.

He mounted the dense carpet, came to Dan's office, and cracked open the door, like the breaking of a sacred seal.

Dan looked up from his dark wooden desk. "Christian," he said, a stunned daze in his eyes. "Come in."

Christian took up a seat in front of the aged desk. He pulled out the folded pages from his pocket.

Dan folded his hands over the faded leather plate. "Is that even legal?"

"I'm not here about what is right and what is wrong anymore, Dan. This is a matter of life and death, now."

"Well then, you're in the right place." Dan jerked open a side drawer, and something clinked and rolled against bare, dry wood. He pulled out a magnifying glass. "I take it you want me to look at something?"

"You know just about every doctor in this town who signs death certificates, don't you?"

"I do my job well."

Christian unfolded the pages and slipped them across the desk. "And this one?"

Dan hovered the magnifying glass over the pages.

"Take your time." Christian stood up. "I need the exact identity of the doctor who signed off the documents."

Christian turned his back to Dan and sauntered over to shelves that looked at though they carried the weight of gold on them. He pulled a book from the shelf.

Light in his hand, it was a plastic prop. One book after another, all vintage-looking props, all lightweight, all empty.

He opened the only book prop with Old Norse patterned on the spine. A coffee ring stained the cover.

A grassy aroma came off yellow-tinged newspaper clippings hiding inside. They were papers of historical political scandals from around 1972, and a metal insignia of a multi-dimensional cube.

He could hear Dan wheezing behind him, growing deeper and heavier.

He turned to Dan, who was now looking straight at him, face drained of color, his forehead lines deep.

A folded sheet of paper fell from Dan's hand and landed between them. "I don't know much of anything, Christian. I just did as I was told."

Christian placed the prop on the desk, lid open, and scooped the fallen page off the floor. "You were the last one I expected to be involved in the Match. What was your job exactly?"

Dan hugged his arms. "I was told to alert you to the Landström Estate fire. That's all."

Christian pulled a clipping from Dan's book prop and flagged the weathered sheet of paper in front of him. "Did the Landström have something to do with all these political scandals as well?"

Dan stumbled out of his chair. "I was going to make some tea. Would you like some?"

"You're such a fucking coward, Dan."

Dan hobbled over the kettle and popped it on. "They said they wanted to initiate you. That's what I was told."

"And you believed them?"

Dan's trembling hand placed a teabag in a mug. "They said you were made an initiate on your father's death anniversary." A glimmer of guilt whipped across his face. "It made sense to me."

"So you helped forge a death certificate for the records?"

Dan poured milk into a ceramic pitcher and set it on the table, his hands now shivering. "I put them in touch with the doctor who could."

Christian hoped that Dan was absorbing the cold in his eyes. "Is that the doctor's real name?"

He bowed, then shook his head. "The doctor's real name is Kolokov."

Christian's longstanding resentment against his father stirred inside him. He knew that name, had heard it before. Then he remembered. The name was the signature on the resignation letter to that science foundation. "How long has Kolokov been a member of Landström?"

Dan's eyes softened. "Longer than me. He's one of the older members." Steam evaporated from the water kettle. "He and Viktor are good friends."

"And who else? Who else knows about Kolokov?"

Dan's neck sank into his shoulders. "The girl's lawyer."

"Schroeder is—" Christian slammed his fist on Dan's desk,

and he held back the anger inside urging him to pummel the traitor in front of him. He needed his rage for someone else, and that someone else was Viktor. "Dan, I can guarantee that you will be a Tier less than zero by tomorrow," he said through clenched teeth. "Everyone will know what you've done. An accomplice to forging documents will be just the start of the charges against you."

Dan shook like a dead leaf along the ground. "I'll give you points, Christian. Anything. Name your price."

"The time for that is over," Christian said, picking up the book prop and walking out the door.

The fresh air tempered the fury raging through his body.

The sound of a gunshot thundered through the air; birds fluttered through the afternoon sky.

Christian halted.

Rather than facing the public's judgment, Dan took his own life. The Q-scores were not only powerful, they were deadly. But after the betrayal Christian endured, compassion was a luxury. "Maybe there is justice after all," he mumbled.

Schroeder, that traitor, was representing a bogus rape victim. Yes, Christian needed to hear what Schroeder had to say for himself, to hear Schroeder admit he too was in on the game to ruin him.

Schroeder was next.

"Do a search for Kolokov, a Landström Society member," Christian said to Max in his new AR glasses as he climbed the steps inside his building. "Grab any info you have on him. Link it to Viktor when you activate his account. Associate those two together, every dirty deed, every fine, every tiny mishap, and add it to the feed. Get their association linked so tight the public will think they're Siamese twins."

"When is this game over?" Max asked, still looking more than a little worse for wear.

"I'm on the hook for another twenty-two hours, and I will make every minute count."

"This is the moment I've been waiting for, Christian," Max said. "But if it all goes pear-shaped, I'll be on the next flight out with you, man."

"It's all going to work out just fine," Christian said.

He banged on Schroeder's door.

Silence.

The only thing standing between him and justice was Schroeder's wooden door. He rammed his whole body into it, again and again, and heavy thumps reverberated down the hall.

The solid oak door wouldn't budge.

He stalked down the hall, smashed through the safety glass, and grabbed the fire axe. Holding it by its neck, he carried it to Schroeder's front door. He laid the blade into the wood. The door splintered. Three more blows, and the door fell like timber.

Christian wiped his face and surveyed Schroeder's apartment for court documents, evidence, anything. Knowing Landström, who preferred paper, it wouldn't be hard to find.

He tore through every drawer, every box, every shelf, until a mound of junk piled onto the floor. There was nothing.

Huffing, he stood back and surveyed the damage. A yellow envelope stuck out from the pile. He pulled it out and turned it around. The Landström Society's broken red wax seal was still attached.

This was it. This was the envelope that had gone missing when his apartment was ransacked. The one containing Kolokov's letter, Viktor's photograph. The one containing the list. Schroeder had ransacked his apartment, and stolen everything.

A cold mist descended upon him.

Tick. Tock. Tick. Tock. Tick. Tock. Ice. Steel. Crack. Beat. Smear. Crush. Destroy.

Rage coursed through his veins, and it fueled him to smash everything in sight.

Christian grabbed a nearby vase and hurled it against the wall. Glass shattered, books flew across the room, furniture toppled over. This was what Schroeder deserved for betraying him. This was what Viktor deserved for destroying his life.

This was just the beginning.

He was going to find out what Schroeder knew and use it to destroy him and Viktor. And if that meant causing more destruction along the way, so be it. It was all worth it for the satisfaction of watching his enemies fall.

He had never felt more sublime.

Christian tasted blood dripping from his mouth, his hand solid like a gun. The cold hard steel of his blood warmed his heart, and his fury nourished his soul. He would rather die than let Viktor win.

And he was going for him. That man. That nobody. Was his.

"Christian?" Schroeder said, his voice sounding distant.

Christian rushed him and pinned him against the wall. "You stole from me."

"The last thing you need are charges against you for breaking and entering," Schroeder screamed.

Christian grabbed Schroeder by the collar, his face the picture of dread.

"I'm bound. You know that."

"You're a slave," Christian spat out. "The scare tactics used to make the Society appear more important than they truly are, are nothing but a heap of useless junk. They enslave you with all that distraction, and you're dumb enough to fall for it." He shoved Schroeder against the wall. "That woman you were on television with, doing that conference with, wearing their yellow bow tie. Who is she?"

"Client attorney privilege."

Christian slammed his hand against the wall. "I'm not going to ask again."

Schroeder's face went white. "She's a Landström contact." His voice trailed off, and fear filled his eyes. "I've seen a lot in my time as a state-appointed lawyer, some of the ugliest things. None of that is you, Christian. But the Match was part of the initiation."

Christian shoved his arm against Schroeder's throat.

Schroeder's face whitened.

"Now that the game is up, and I'm going to lose anyway, tell me who is controlling the girl. What do they have on her?"

Tears streamed from Schroeder's eyes. "I can't."

Christian punched him in the gut. "If you don't tell me, someone else will. Not only will you have Viktor breathing down your neck, you'll have me too."

Schroeder reached for a paper in the pile and scrambled for a pen. "Torn knows everything. Give him this when you see him."

He scribbled Kolokov down on a piece of paper, and the flimsy paper shook in Schroeder's outstretched hand.

Christian stuffed the envelope under his shirt and the paper in his pocket, "Don't bother calling Torn to warn him. A warning won't help him now."

"Are you going to kill him?"

"Of course not. It's against the rules," Christian said. "I intend to win this game."

CHAPTER 46

In front of Torn's residential building, Christian switched off his car's engine. Twilight blue streamed through the window as he prayed for the strength to do what he had to do.

He closed the car door and buzzed penthouse twelve.

No response.

He backed up and eyed the top of the building. "Torn, I can see the lights. Open up."

The intercom scratched to life.

"Open the door, Torn. We need to talk."

The door buzzed open. Inside the elevator, he switched on the recording device Stine had given him. The bell dinged when it reached the top.

Torn stood outside the door wearing a blue terrycloth bathrobe and slippers.

"You're not going to be at the festivities tonight?" Christian said, grinning, although feeling anything but happy.

He shook his head. "I was expecting you," Torn said, offering him a drink.

"I don't want to waste our time, Torn. Let's just get to it."

Vanilla white wallpaper clung to the wall, porcelain figurines dotted the shelves, and Christian could feel the loneliness of the room.

Torn tightened his robe's belt. "Please have a seat."

Christian pulled out the forged death certificates. "Who's Kolokov?" Christian demanded.

Torn lowered himself in the chair. "This is a situation I never wanted to be involved in."

Christian threw the papers on the coffee table. "Forging the death certificate of my father?"

"It wasn't me." Torn's voice trailed off.

"Did he really die of natural causes or did someone at Landström Society murder him?"

Torn cradled his head. "Viktor had to put a stop to your father snooping around, for the sake of the Society. That's what he said."

The truth stilled the turmoil inside Christian to a pinpoint. "So, the Landström Society knows what Viktor is capable of, and still you all let him run that place."

Christian's rage erupted; he grabbed a chair and threw it at the windows.

The glass splintered into a spider's web. He picked up the now-dented chair and weighed it in his arms. With all his strength, Christian heaved it back at the windows.

Torn could only stand and watch in horror as Christian picked up the chair a third time.

He threw it again and again, until the glass shattered into a million jagged pieces.

Torn buried his face in his hands. "It all went entirely too far." He looked at Christian, his cheeks and neck blotched red. "They needed the list your father had stolen from them."

"The list," Christian spat out. "I know my father stole it from the Society because he needed leverage against Viktor in case Viktor came after him. As it turns out, Viktor came after me," he said, smacking his chest.

"Had you joined the Society like your father did, none of this would've happened. So they set up the Arcadian Match, a game you could never win, as a trap to get you to become a member."

Hot tears streamed down Christian's cheeks. "They couldn't take no for an answer."

"Too much was at stake," Torn said, his hands pleading. "The Q-scores needed to prevail. Your algorithms kept blocking them. The Q-score system was the only way the Landström Society would—"

"Control the country," Christian said, and all the pieces fell into place. "So, my father knew Viktor's plans, took the list, and planned to out him. That's when Viktor ordered the hit on my father. Kolokov then forged the death on the certificate, and Dan fixed my father's body up so good he looked like a man who had lived a long and happy life."

"They wanted you in," Torn cried. "If you had just joined, all the power would be yours too."

"My freedom is my power," Christian said. "Landström is going down for forgery, murder, coercion, and corrupting the course of justice."

Torn wrung his hands. "They'll be merging with other Societies soon. All the members will be woven together, and it'll take years before they see justice."

Christian suddenly felt queasy. These sick people were everywhere, and they kept their secrets between them. "In all my years as a quant guy," he said, "I worked with the worst humanity offered. Knowing and seeing what lurks in the minds of men and women, and I've seen a lot, I didn't think I would ever encounter you."

Christian shook his head and looked up at the ceiling. "Right at the start of this whole game, when I was working with Jacob, you knew all along. You knew the Landström Society wanted to rope me in. Sure, you had some reservations, but that's because you wanted to look like you cared. I expect it from that bloodless snake, Viktor, but you? I'm surprised you can even face me."

"Viktor is ruthless," Torn pleaded. "You know that. I had no choice."

"You always have a choice," Christian said. "Isn't that what you said to me at SVT?"

Torn's pale face flushed red. "I followed instructions."

Christian stared at him.

"Viktor was behind the Landström Estate fire," Torn said. "He pinned it on Jacob, made Jacob believe that he had done it, but Jacob got plastered that night after White's, and didn't remember anything. The guy was innocent. He was nowhere near it, but Viktor convinced him. Viktor has so much dirt on everyone. If he merges societies, everyone's secrets will be his. Everything that people don't want others to know will be fair game. Everyone will be his pawn. The man knows no limit."

"I wonder what dirt he has on you, Torn."

Torn extended his arm as if reaching out for mercy. "I'll go away; I'll disappear."

"If what you're saying is true, Torn, Viktor is dead set on merging Societies in order to take over everyone's private lives, is that right? And he'll use the Q-score system to target the innocent and force them to comply."

Torn nodded. "He'll create a parallel society, one where everyone answers to the Society."

Christian cupped his hand across his stomach. Not. Gonna. Happen. He dropped his hands. A new focus tranquilized his rage, and birthed a new desire. "This will never happen again. If it's the last thing I do, I swear I will take you all down."

Torn sat hunched in his chair, a man resigned to his fate.

Christian stormed out the door and clicked off the recorder.

CHAPTER 47

TICK. TOCK. TICK. TOCK.

Christian strode down Alströmergatan, his face covered by a dark hat, his body robed in a gray trench coat, his feet engraved with the full reality of all that had happened.

In six hours, he'd be declared the winner or the damned.

He came to a stop at a red light and tapped the side of his new AR glasses. "Max, at seven p.m., make sure everything about Viktor Hansson is online. Everything. Wet the vultures' appetites."

"You got it," Max said.

Christian switched off AR mode, but his world was still black and white.

The traffic light turned green.

He scanned the road. Coast clear. He took a measured step onto the bridge.

The river's waves crashed against the bank. His trench coat flapped against his leg.

He turned the corner. The Landström Society meeting house loomed in the Square.

The lights inside glowed warm behind the windows, lively noise spilled onto the street.

Dreaded coziness, he thought. He checked his points. He was far down the cliff of doom, snug in Tier 0, he almost had no hope of ever recovering. He slowed, as if trying to slow fate itself.

The discussion he'd had with Kelly entered his mind: their talk of war, of games. Everyone used different words to describe what amounted to an unlawful takeover of the entire country. If he was a goner, so were they. The only choice left was to plunge headlong into the Arctic Sea and make the loudest splash the country had ever heard.

He tapped his mic. "Leave a message for Lorelei Lindbergh."

The text box popped up in his screen.

> I'm cashing in my last favor. Meet me at Norrbro Bridge in an hour. Bring your crew.

> I have a big announcement to make.

He strode forward as though riding on the back of a horse of the apocalypse.

He had arrived.

ON STRÖMGATEN, Stine walked passed four police cars stationed outside the Prime Minister's official residence, Sager House. Normally a quiet street, like most others, despite its close proximity to the parliament Rikstag, but not anymore. The bombing had changed everything.

She approached the security guards, posted at the front door.

They rested their hands on the machine guns and widened their stance.

"Stine Poulsen from SÄPO." She flashed her badge. "I have an appointment with Prime Minister Bergman."

A guard drew down the radio resting on his shoulder and spoke into it.

"Stine Poulsen, you're cleared," he said.

The front door shuttled open.

Inside, another guard patted her down. "I'll have to take your phone and your bag."

Instinctively, she clutched the strap. It carried recording equipment to document what side this Prime Minister was really on. Was he someone SÄPO would have to fight all the way, or would he cave under Landström pressure and their big-picture agenda? Or, would they get at him through the opposition party—Landström Society's proxy party.

"I'm on behalf of SÄPO," she said. "I need my equipment."

"We have a stenographer on site. You'll receive an electronic copy."

She huffed and reluctantly dropped her bag on the table. The guard showed her into the sitting room.

She sat on the soft lavender sofa dotted with mint green cushions. Her knees grazed the polished wood of the coffee table in front of her.

Within minutes, Prime Minister Bergman entered the room.

Close-up, the lines on his face told a story all their own. His blue eyes looked glassy and the bags under them said he hadn't slept in days, possibly weeks.

"Thank you for seeing me, Prime Minister," she said, rising to her full stature.

"You have ten minutes," he said briskly.

"SÄPO sent me."

"You wouldn't be here if they hadn't."

She glanced over his shoulder. "We have reason to believe a coup is underway."

"And?"

Surprise knocked her back, and she covered her shock with a quick scan of the room. The best course was the no-nonsense sort, the sort she was comfortable with. "How much are you willing to fight for this country? Or will you eventually cave to the opposition?"

"I don't intend to step down."

Besides the guards at the doors, she wondered how he protected himself, exactly. "Every politician has skeletons in his or her closet. How old are yours?"

He gave her a curious look, like he didn't quite know how to answer such a straightforward question.

"I only have ten minutes, Prime Minister," she reminded him.

"All skeletons are contained."

No skeleton is ever fully contained, she thought. Indeed, skeletons can be manufactured at a moment's notice. "How strong is the lock on the closet?"

"As strong as it needs to be."

That was as good an answer as any, but it didn't dislodge her unease. For the time being, she brushed her curiosity aside. "Do you know who you're really up against?"

"I know it's not the opposition party."

She nodded. "Unfortunately, they've also infiltrated the agency, but we're cleaning it up."

He squinted, looking as though he was probing his vulnerabilities, and whether his lock would hold. "This isn't the first time a coup has happened."

She remembered Olaf Palmer. "And it won't be the last time, either."

"The game never ends, but we get smarter with every decade," he said.

"And so do they," she said. "I suppose it will never end.

They've been lying low for the last ten years, but they will always worm their way through the loopholes."

He nodded. "Where was the breach this time?"

Stine wasn't sure what he meant by that question, for the answer was so broad. But if she had to narrow it down, the breach could only come from one place. "The Hall of Records," she said, a wave of shame washing over her. "On my watch."

The Prime Minister nodded. "If something happens to me, you'll need to find a way to shut that place down."

That's all she needed to hear. He was going to stand firm with every bit of strength inside him. "Nothing will happen to you, Prime Minister."

"Let's hope not."

"An asset will be on television tonight," she said. "You might find it an interesting watch."

Bergman nodded.

"If all goes according to plan, your position will be safe."

"For a year at least," he said. "Anything else?"

Satisfied that Bergman was a man of honor, and as strong as they came, she shook her head.

He picked up the phone. "Miss Poulsen is ready to leave."

A security guard entered.

"Take her through the passage," the Prime Minister said.

"But—"

"We can't have Miss Poulsen being followed."

"Of course, sir," the guard said.

Stine had her answer, but she still had no proof to hand to her SÄPO superiors. As hard as it was, she was just going to have to trust that Christian would pull through.

She followed the security toward the secret escape passage.

CHAPTER 48

Christian Karlsson: Tier 0 | .05m points
vs
Viktor Hansson Tier 2 | 1.6m points

CHRISTIAN STEPPED ONTO THE BLACK AND WHITE CHECKERBOARD tiled floor. His sweat soaked the grout, and he shivered as he knocked on the door. His points neared the bottom of Tier 0, a person non grata. He didn't even know that was possible.

He had to get a public hearing underway, encouraging them to score him—his last hope. He needed his plan to work, now or never.

The butler ushered him in. "Right on time, Mr. Karlsson."

The murmur of male voices filled the room, and the chandelier lit their faces with a warm amber hue.

The butler stood close to the door, arms crossed in front of him, standing at ease, as if guarding it.

Gamemaster, Harald, and their counsel sat at a long table on the side of the room. Viktor was bent over, chatting to the man with the cigar, who had placed his money on Christian as a fun bet.

Christian wondered what kind of deal they were making.

"Good to see you here, Christian," the cigar man said. "You should be proud of yourself."

Viktor slowly turned. The look on his face was smug satisfaction, his hand casually hanging from of his trousers' pocket.

A large screen displayed the scores of the game. Viktor stood at 1.6million while Christian languished far behind at 500,000 and dropping.

He scanned the faces of the men before him, solemn and stiff, their champagne flutes frozen in heir hands.

His stomach lurched. He expected such a look from Gamemaster, possibly even Harald, but not the weight of judgement from the entire room. He wasn't on trial, he thought, but he felt guilty of crimes he hadn't committed all the same. The game wasn't over, he reminded himself.

"Though it appears I will soon be the loser in this game, I would ask you, gentlemen, to please indulge me one last time."

Viktor faced him full-on. "I'm not sure what you're planning, young Christian, but you can't possibly win the game at this late stage. May I suggest you do the gentlemanly thing and step aside."

"I still have time," Christian spat back and quickly recomposed himself. "I would respectfully ask that you indulge me in these final minutes."

"What did you have in mind?" a voice shouted.

"Let's take a stroll to Norrbro Bridge."

Excitement clambered in the room, glass screeched on marble.

"Well, let's do this!"

"We're game. Show us the way, Christian."

"Is this really necessary?" Viktor said. "In less than three hours, I will be declared the winner of the game, and I will resume leadership of the Society."

"Think of this as your opponent's last hurrah," Gamemaster said.

Viktor all but grabbed his coat. "Very well."

CHRISTIAN STOOD on the south side of Norrbro Bridge under a lamp light, the gentlemen of the Society surrounding him. He stared out, mesmerized by the swirls of the dark blue Norrström River water forming whirlpools and then transforming into form-less shapes crashing into the bridge's stone pillars.

He rubbed his eyes and glanced toward the north. In the distance, he could see the damaged bridge, the Opera House, and on the south side of the bridge, Old Town, Gamla Stan.

A ruckus crashed through the night air. He followed the sound, pivoting toward the old town. Lorelei Lindbergh pranced up the cobblestone street, passing a sleepy cafe usually teeming with shoppers and tourists. He couldn't see the details of her face but knew she could see him.

A camera flashed a white light, readying for the big announce-ment. In earlier days, in better circumstances, he would have smiled knowing he had an opportunity to deliver a client's message, but everything had changed.

A seagull flew overhead, squawking at Christian, it seemed, for a breadcrumb. He attempted to fuse with the peace of Gamla Stan, but his nerves buzzed with what was about to happen. He forced himself to stop thinking about everything that could go wrong and turned his attention to the stone bridge he stood on.

Lorelei sidled up to him. "This better be good, Christian," she snarled. "After that prank you pulled at the airport, I have a mind to—"

"But you can't because you're their slave."

She glared at him. "We're ready. Like I said, this better be good!"

His taut nerves eased because he knew he was as ready as he would ever be.

"Twenty minutes, Christian. We're waiting," a Landström member said.

Christian rubbed his hands against his trench coat. He nodded at Lorelei. "I'm ready."

Two single lights blasted his face.

Christian felt steeped in boiling water. From head to toe, his body tensed, and he wanted nothing more than to run.

"It's been fun, gentlemen," he began. " I learned far more about this game than I intended. To the people at home, watching, I first want to apologize for putting you through so much." He gestured to the bridge. "The city has been damaged, the national heritage site of the Landström Estate, a three-hundred-year-old building that houses the history of our nation, burned to the ground. I know the man who did it, and I said nothing. I covered it up."

The Society members on the bridge stirred.

"What is he saying?" a member said.

The only member to bet on Christian sucked on his cigar and leaned against the bridge. He glanced sideways at Christian.

"Quiet!" Gamemaster yelled back. "The rules are not being broken. Let the man speak."

"Yes, I want to hear what he has to say."

"Keep rolling, Lorelei," Christian ordered.

A crowd of people started to gather along the bridge, watching, whispering.

"I am guilty of covering things up. I've had affairs with married women, I've slept with journalists to get a story out, I've saved guilty people with bad reputations online. I covered up for gangsters and criminals."

"Your points are dropping faster than the Titanic," someone yelled.

"I suggest you get on with your life," another voice said.

"Get on with my life?" Christian answered. "My life is in ruins. I'm on God knows how many most wanted lists. My family is a mess." He shook his head. "I always looked the other way because I had to do my job. If people could pay, I manipulated the Q-scores in their favor." He stared into the night sky. He had no choice but to confess, take off his mask, and tell the public what he did, and why. "I made those decisions because I lied for a living. I was chasing points, chasing popularity. I thought that if I did that, I'd get to keep my life going as it was. I had to get the points. Tier 1 status," Christian yelled into the night air.

"Pathetic," Viktor blurted. "How much longer do we have to listen to this sob story?"

AR glasses began to buzz all around him.

"I threatened an old client. Told him he'd face the public's ire once they, *you*," he said, pointing at the crowd, "found out the truth of his business. I ransacked a neighbor's apartment to get information. That's what I did. I chose to do those things over points, over reputation."

"He's falling off the cliff," someone shouted. "Less than zero."

The crowd hushed.

Christian's hands trembled, and his mouth went dry. Words abandoned him. He looked at the faces around him, some laughing, some drinking in his shame, some turned away.

"You can stop now, Christian," Gamemaster proposed. "Join us, and we will review your case, fairly."

Christian yearned for the prettiest choice he could make right now: to stop. Stop the madness and join them. What was the big deal anyway? He'd have their power, their backing, their network, their protection. This whole sordid game would come to a stop if he just said yes. He beheld the light night sky.

A flock of birds flew above him as though Jacob was looking down at him, reminding him: *Remember who you are, Christian. Never a pawn.*

His eyes watered, and he swallowed back the tears. "I thought I was untouchable," he said. "That nothing would change. I knew the system was rigged." He patted his heart. "I knew it was rigged, and I kept propping it up. But," He raised a finger. "I did none of the things I've been publicly accused of. Not arson, not foul play, not rape."

Viktor motioned for Lorelei Lindbergh. Her heels clicked on the tarmac until she stood in front of him. "I found the girl he raped wandering the streets," Viktor said in the furry mic. "I immediately called the police and reported it."

The public applauded him, and a throng of dings rang out from AR glasses all around.

Christian stared at Viktor in disbelief. "Lies!"

"Viktor's points are skyrocketing," a member said.

A woman stepped out from the crowd. "The victim said you did it." She pointed at Christian. "She even posted her doctor's confirmation," she said, waving her glasses in the air.

"Did it happen to be a Doctor Kolokov?" Christian demanded.

"That's right," someone shouted back, holding a palm-sized screen in the air. "The record confirms."

"Kolokov has been forging documents in the national archive," Christian shouted back. "The woman who accused me of rape has also accused another innocent man of rape!"

The crowd gasped.

The camera focused on Lorelei Lindbergh. "This is a momentous night. One man's word against another. Allegations are buzzing around the Hall of Records and its faulty system. But right now, the story is Christian Karlsson and his less than zero points."

The cameras returned to Christian.

Christian pointed at Viktor. "You see that man over there? That's Viktor Hansson."

Viktor shielded his face with his hand.

"He ordered the national records to be forged," Christian said. "He and Kolokov have known each other for years."

"I will sue you for salacious rumors!" Viktor yelled.

Christian threw the black and white photo of Viktor, Kolokov, and his father at him, and it floated toward the crowd.

The crowd passed the photo around one to the other, looking at Viktor then at the photo.

The buzz of AR glasses grew louder.

"That photo is online too! Viktor Hansson, born 19 September 1964, member of the Landstrom Society."

Viktor grabbed Lorelei's mic. "Where did you get that information?"

"It's all online. And there's more."

Christian's shoulders eased. Max had unleashed O3.

"Did you see Christian's score?" a man from the crowd said. "He's up a million points."

The cigar-smoking member smiled. "Before long, those two will be neck and neck."

Viktor stepped forward. "The Landström Society runs on an honor system that I have vowed to uphold. I offered to help Christian through all the troubles he faced, especially after his father died."

"You killed Jacob," Christian said through steeled teeth.

The crowd gasped.

"Nothing but rumors," Viktor snarled.

"The scores are going crazy," someone yelled.

An air of excitement hung over the bridge. Someone in the

crowd began shouting out the scores, adding and subtracting from Christian to Viktor and back again in a flurry, faster than a spinning top.

"The leaderboard is freaking out."

Christian nodded at the people on the bridge, then nodded at the cameras, feeding the the fickle, hapless audience who would eventually forget tonight's spectacle. In a week, a new story would capture their attention, but right now the stage was his, and it was only eleven o'clock.

He knew how the Q-scores worked. He was the expert. But this time was different. If he was going to get what he wanted, bust the Q-system, take away Landström's power, he had to display his heart of hearts, and that's what scared him the most. He took the gamble anyway because it was his last card.

"I used to be a Tier 1, and now I really don't care," he said, feeling the truth of the words fortify his spine, rejuvenate his soul. "I really don't fucking care," he shouted.

The crowd was subdued. For the first time that he could recall, peace comforted him.

"You're climbing back," someone yelled out. "Soon you'll be Tier 3."

"I don't care," Christian exclaimed, a sense of freedom boosting his voice.

"Five to three, Christian wins," a member shouted.

"The system is overloaded with people scoring," someone else said.

"Five minutes to go, gentlemen," Gamemaster interjected.

"All you had to do was play the game, Christian!" Viktor yelled.

"And then what?"

"If you had bowed out, I would have taken care of you. Your father was my best friend."

"You killed my father, kept it hidden from the Society, from justice."

"More lies and rumors," Viktor said.

Plumes of cigar smoke whisked past Christian.

"This is the best show I've seen in ages," someone said.

In the distance, the somber tone of the clock struck. The lightness of midnight was approaching.

"I can't send any points," someone said.

"The website's down."

"Holy shit! The system got shut down!"

"No!"

"Can't be," the crowd cried.

"The leaderboard has been shut down!"

"It is now midnight, gentlemen," Gamemaster said, raising his voice above the restless crowd. "Silence! The points are in. Everyone meet at the House in one hour. There, the winner will be announced, bets honored."

An air of frustration rocketed through the crowd.

"What winner? Is this a game? Old man, what are you talking about?"

"He's part of the Landström Society," someone said.

"So? Was this a game?"

"What was this all about?" an onlooker said.

Christian's body seemed to harmonize all the tension he'd been carrying all at once, and his feet bolted to the ground. At last, the public was asking questions.

Lorelei Lindberg gazed into the camera, her mic frozen in her hand, as though she knew she was next. "I think it's all over now," she said.

She dropped the mic on the tarmac, and a piercing noise blared into the night air.

CHAPTER 49

AT HALF PAST MIDNIGHT, CHRISTIAN KARLSSON SAT ON THE street curb outside Riddarholmen Church. He recalled his father's funeral, remembering the eulogy he had spent all night polishing to perfection.

As his father's only child, he had to be the one to stand up and deliver words of admiration, painting the man as a loving, devoted husband and father, when all he felt was relief that never again would he wonder why his father had devoted every waking hour to that Society. Woven through that memory was a feeling that he could never shake, and it stabbed in his heart one last time. He rubbed his chest.

Everyone watched the old man's coffin be lowered into the moist earth while the hole in his heart froze over. When he tossed his handful of dirt onto his father's casket, he thought he was tossing all the pain and hurt away. But all he managed to do, he realized now, was bury those feelings, not quite dormant. Sitting alone here on the step, his caged hurt begged to be encased in a tear.

Footsteps drew near.

Instinctively, he straightened his back.

"I'm too old to bend down and sit on the curb." Harald pulled a key from his pocket. "You'll have to come inside and sit with me in a pew."

Together they walked inside the dark, airless church. Harald flipped a switch.

Christian gazed at the ceiling.

"The names of the men who built this place aren't recorded anywhere. They erected layers of scaffolding to help them climb, brick by brick. No safety nets in those days. Their sweat is on these stones." Harald touched the wall delicately, respectfully. "They risked their lives, shouldered the burden, the rough edges of stone digging into their flesh. All to build a place that you and I are able to walk inside of."

"Every time I've been in this church I feel the same way about this place."

Harald glanced at him. "Which is?"

"Heavy."

"History can do that to a person." Harald shuffled over to a pew and sat down.

Christian slid in next to him, fatigue heavy in his legs.

"We can't erase the past, no matter how hard we try," Harald said. "Forged documents, rewriting history, retelling the story it's all useless. We know in our hearts and places like this exist to help us remember. We honor our history, all the sacrifice, the sweat, blood, and day after day pain because we have to honor how we have evolved."

Christian's heart stirred.

"I know what happened to your father, but I couldn't do anything about it," Harald said. "I hoped you would play this game, to prove what happened, and get Viktor out of the Society. He counted on you hating your father so much that you'd not bother looking in his box. But that box contained everything you needed to fuel you."

"I almost did ignore it."

"And thank God you didn't. It gave you choices."

"I will hand over my father's list of names to SÄPO and it will prove Viktor's interference with the Q-scores. Landström Society will go down."

Harald shrugged. "If it's that rotten, it should sink."

"I'm surprised to hear that from you, Harald."

Harald grabbed his cane. "The Society was never meant to control government and the country," he grumbled. "We are meant to serve as a reminder of our nation's traditions and our past. Not because Sweden had some glorious past." Harald waved his hand. "The point of the past is to show us how far we've come."

He paused and turned. "You have the key to my office, don't you Christian?"

"No."

"It was in the vase for the longest time, I recall," Harald said, looking at his watch. "That key is customized to unlock the door to my office, as well as a filing cabinet underneath my desk. Inside are some files that will bury Viktor for good. Be careful how you handle them."

The church door creaked open.

"Ah, Viktor. Right on time."

FIRE LIT in Christian's belly, the heat surged as he stared at Viktor.

"What's the meaning of this?" Viktor said.

Christian shot up from the pew. "You burned down the Estate for your own benefit, Viktor. You blamed Jacob because you knew he couldn't withstand the pressure you put on him. And you knew it would get to me. And it did."

"You fabricated evidence against him, got his wife, Karen to lie too. You concocted a deadly game to cover up your agenda to take over the Q-scores," Christian continued. "Jacob Rasmussen had proof that you created algorithms that have been manipulating the Q-scores all along, and you used those algorithms to attack and ruin the lives of innocent people who declined any of your requests, just like you tried to do to me."

"You had to be contained!" Viktor yelled. "The Q-scores were creating a utopia. The first on earth. Think of it. No crime. First country ever to achieve such a feat. No paper. First country ever to be ecologically steadfast. Sweden is the most law-abiding country in the history of the world. You were getting in the way of all that with your own algorithms blocking us at every turn. Christian, you had to be contained!"

"You wanted to contain me and you made me an initiate without my consent."

Viktor walked to the front of the church. "Your father should never have had that list. He stole it from us."

"And you killed him because of it. The records will prove that."

"What records."

"A journalist has unblocked the records and they will be all over the social feeds."

"The young man has you cornered," Harald said. "I suggest you step down from the leadership of the Society."

Viktor wrung his hands.

"And the list that will prove your manipulation of the Q-scores will soon be in SÄPO's hands."

Blue lights flashed through the church.

The police had arrived.

THE NIGHT BREEZE sponged the sweat from Christian's face.

Christian stepped into the meeting house; some men argued over what just happened, others debated what it meant for the game.

Gamemaster stood paces away, allowing the tension and confusion to reign. The moment he saw Christian and Harald, he raised a dainty brass bell and swung it.

A high-pitched ding rang out and broke through the warlike noise, dispelling the thunderous men until they stood quiet as lambs.

"Harald has arrived, and I think he has a few words to say on this momentous evening that none of us will ever forget."

Harald stood in the middle of the room.

"When the Landström Society embarked upon this Match, we entered new territory. Some of us thought it would be a straight-forward blow-by-blow, win-or-lose affair. It turned out to be anything but. We learned a lot in the course of this month, the lengths some people go." He gripped his cane. "Despite the pressure, Christian withstood every obstacle Viktor put in his way. A Landström man does not cave in.

"We abide by the rules because the rules guide us. But they are not meant to hinder us or hold us back or make us feel like we have no choice. Unfortunately, Viktor showed us just how far he was willing to go to win." He threw a scalding glare at the crowd. "Some of you were in on this. And you will be dealt with."

Gamemaster stepped forward. "No matter who is declared the winner tonight, we all benefited from the event," he said, his cool words tapping down heat in the room. "And may we never have to live through this again."

The members lifted their glasses.

Harald nodded to Gamemaster.

Time seemed to slow.

Christian thought back to the start of the game, and he couldn't believe he had dreamed of winning it.

"The tally is in," Gamemaster announced.

Christian didn't care.

"The moment everyone has been waiting for so eagerly has arrived." Gamemaster lifted his chin and read from the card in his hand. "Christian 2.7m points. Viktor 2.71m points. The winner of the Arcadian Match is Viktor Hansson."

Voices stilled, and the men stole mice-like glances at Christian.

Christian lowered his head. "First time I lost anything in my life."

The men clapped. "Good man."

"Best game ever, Christian."

Several men came up to shake his hand and pat him on the back.

A member whispered in Gamemaster's ear. He clinked his champagne glass with a silver spoon.

The noise softened.

"In the hour since the display on the bridge, we did some research into the allegations made." Gamemaster searched the eyes in the room. "Member Kolokov has confirmed that Viktor did indeed force him to forge Lars Karlsson's death certificate."

Hushed confusion swept through the room.

"Viktor has attempted to cover up the murder of a fellow member, Christian's father. A death that Viktor ordered. And for that, Viktor will see swift justice from the Society."

"Where is Viktor?"

"He's been arrested," Christian said.

Voices grumbled in the crowd. With the Society's vast network, Christian knew Viktor would escape justice easily.

"Harald, did you allow the national record to be changed?" A member shouted. "After all, you are the Minister of Interior."

"I had a suspicion Viktor was behind the forged documents, but I believe that an agent of SÄPO made the connection. It's being investigated."

Christian tensed. Stine would be in Viktor's crosshairs.

"What now?" one man shouted, his voice laced with fear.

"I must say, this is an unprecedented situation," Gamemaster said.

He leafed through the Landström Membership Handbook running his eyes down each page, shaking his head each time. He looked into the crowd and shut the book. "The choice is yours, Christian."

Christian glanced at Harald. Viktor had to be taken care of, properly. He knew all the ways to get into the Society, activate its network, and that was something Christian could never let happen. "I'll stand in as the leader of the Landström Society, but only for a short time. After that, I intend to disband it so thoroughly it will be but a distant memory in the nation's psyche."

The cigar-smoking member threw his head back and howled with laughter. "Not before I get my money!"

CHAPTER 50

A WEEK AFTER THE ARCADIAN MATCH ENDED, CHRISTIAN entered his apartment and dropped his luggage in the hallway.

A bright yellow paper note was glued to his coffee table.

He tensed.It was from Viktor, reminding him of their pact. He ripped the note from the table and tossed it in the trash.

His glasses vibrated against his chest. "Hey, Stine."

"Thanks for the list and the recordings of Torn confessing all."

"Hold on," he said, and he pulled the list of names out of the manila envelope and scrolled through it. Olaf Sanders was a name on the list, and he'd never forget how he could have been Sanders. "If you research the list, you'll see many innocent lives who've been ruined."

"We're making our way through the list now." Stine licked her lips. "We're building a watertight case now. How are you doing?"

"Trying to relax."

"Thanks for handing us Viktor. So glad to see the back of him. I got a promotion over it. And, I'm hiring Henrik to help me out."

Christian smiled. "You deserve it."

"Viktor is going down for everything," she said. "We have a lot on him. In fact, with the recording from Torn, we had everything we needed." She inhaled. "Your confession on the bridge wasn't necessary. Not really. Why did you do it?"

His looked down at his hands. He lived that moment, that desperate night on Norrbro Bridge, spilling out his less than heroic deeds for the world to hear and withstood the pang in his gut. He let the memory play all the way to the end, and as it did, the feeling lessened. It didn't break him. A sigh escaped his lips. "I had nothing left to lose except my soul," he said.

"We'll stay in touch," Stine said.

"Hey, before you go, I found a note on my coffee table today. Must have been from one of Viktor's men."

"Bag it. We could use evidence as we hunt down his network," Stine said.

As sure as Christian was standing in his living room, he knew Viktor would slip off SÄPO's handcuffs, and Christian would never have peace. What then? There were no easy choices.

When it came down to it, it was either him or Viktor, and there were many ways to skin a cat.

Christian walked to the kitchen and grabbed Harald's office key from the key cabinet. "Let's talk later, Stine."

"I know it's hard to trust the justice process, Christian, especially after everything you've been through. My own confidence in the system was knocked too." Stine sighed. "Sometimes it's better to trust yourself."

"Not sometimes," he said. "All the time."

"I won't stand in your way. Do what you have to do."

HALF AN HOUR LATER, Christian stood in front of Harald's office.

He switched on his AR glasses. If there was one thing Viktor hated above all else, it was being exposed, and Christian knew the person to help him do it. "Text to Kelly Blackwell."

I'm going to send you some documents
that will need to go public, worldwide. Get
them into every inbox, every newswire,
every PR feed.

Please call me when you receive them.

Christian inserted Harald's key and unlocked the office of the Minister of Interior.

It creaked open.

He felt along the bare wall until he came to a switch, and he turned on the light.

The Journal

2 AUGUST 2032

Q-SCORES AS NATIONAL CURRENCY HAS BEEN PUT ON HOLD, INDEFINATELY, OFFICE OF PRIME MINISTER REPORTS

15C

12 SEPTEMBER 2032

SVERIGE DAGLIGEN

LANDSTRÖM SOCIETY MEMBERS LEAVE IN DROVES

"The oldest society won't survive," anonymous sources say.

SVERIGE DAGLIGEN

12C

SUSANNE NYSTRÖM: IT'S ABOUT TIME WE HAVE RELIABLE RECORDS

HALL OF RECORDS

Paper records returned to citizens of Sweden under Christine Poulsen

---

NYHETER EXTRA

9C

4 OCTOBER 2032

VETEREN JOURNALIST LORELEI LINDBERGH STEPS DOWN FROM ILLUSTRIOUS CAREER

"I look forward to starting a family, a new life," she said.

ACKNOWLEDGMENTS

This story was a challenging project that spanned a few years. As any writer knows, the work in progress stays with you until it is done, and this one hung on for a while.

I wish to thank my sister and husband for their day-to-day support throughout the writing of this challenging project. I pulled on their energy and resources, and ears, while I rejigged the plot. Several plot twists later, I got there. Thank you for your patience!

I started this project in 2019, and acknowledgements go to editor and coach Savannah Gilbo—the first person who read through this story as I wrote it. I don't envy anyone reading Draft 0 of any manuscript, but Savannah is a dedicated professional.

I put the draft down for a time, and I picked it back up in late 2021. The revision presented me with a massive challenge, and I would like to thank Kristen Simmons, Joey, and several beta readers for their feedback that helped push this manuscript to the next level. Thanks to Anne Victory for catching those pesky typos. And finally, to Robert, for encouraging me to use a particular version of the prologue. It worked a dream.

Cover design credit goes to Nick Castle, (great job again, Nick!), and the fantastic illustration designs credit goes to BMR Williams.

ABOUT THE AUTHOR

Anne Mortensen has been writing in one form or another most of her life. In between it all, she held various full-time positions including typesetter, PR executive, cafe owner, photographer, and journalist. In 2021, she completed her debut, *The Truth Effect*. She carries the theme forward in *The Arcadian Match,* exploring how people and AI might coexist in a challenged world.

Originally from El Paso, Texas, Anne now lives in London with her husband and gentle tabby, Meli.

Other Works

FICTION
The Truth Effect

NONFICTION
Writers in Black & White (photographer)
60 Minute Briefings Series (2018)
Several articles covering Press Issues

For book updates, go to www.annemortensenwriter.com

Milton Keynes UK
Ingram Content Group UK Ltd.
UKHW040910171123
432750UK00005B/436